Inherit the Throne
Peacekeepers X-Alpha #1

A Thriller

by Steve DeWinter

Summary

Some lines should never be crossed.

A shadow organization is ready to replace the President of the United States with someone they control. There is someone who can stop them. If they want to succeed, she must be the first to die.

But staying alive, is her number one skill. Her second best skill? Returning the favor.

INHERIT THE THRONE is a heart-stopping action-thriller that takes you from the gritty back streets of Washington D.C. to the fog shrouded forests of the Pacific Northwest.

This book is also available serialized under the following titles:
The Alternative Gambit
The Alternative Paradigm
The Alternative Ploy
The Alternative World

This book is a work of fiction. References to real people, events, establishments, organization, or locales are intended only to provide a sense of authenticity, and are used fictitiously. All other characters, and all incidents and dialogue, are drawn from the author's imagination and are not to be construed as real.

Ramblin' Prose Publishing
Copyright © 2015 Steve DeWinter
All rights reserved. Used under authorization.
www.stevedw.com

eBook Edition
ISBN-10: 1-61978-096-8
ISBN-13: 978-1-61978-096-5

Paperback Edition
ISBN-10: 1-61978-101-8
ISBN-13: 978-1-61978-101-6

Chapter 1

Melissa Stone sat down on the empty crate from the morning's egg delivery to rest for only a moment. Her shift was over in fifteen minutes, and she planned to go home and soak her feet for at least an hour or more. Working the job of a small motel restaurant and lounge server at the base of Mt. Hood in Government Camp, Oregon, did not help.

She was only thirty years old, but she had been living her third life for nearly three years now. Three lifetimes worth of stress seemed to age her more quickly than she would have liked. Outwardly, she looked as young as her chronological age, but during these long weekday shifts, she felt every past injury her body had endured.

The neon sign outside the motel laid claim to a restaurant on site, but in all honesty, it was nothing more than a glorified lounge with tables set up on the old dance floor that had seen better days. They provided a good view of the tiny stage that hosted Karaoke on Friday and Saturday nights.

Tonight was a typically quiet Thursday night that only brought motel residents in who were tired from their hike around Mt. Hood. Every night they dragged themselves into the restaurant section of the lounge, exhausted and chatty about what they had accomplished during the day. She never received a complaint about the grease-stained menus. The hikers were always too hungry to notice and happily ordered food that was both good tasting and bad for them at the same time.

Tonight there were only two occupied tables, and she was glad to have the hiking family at her table. The single man at the other table sat alone, and had only ordered coffee. He held the menu up in front of him the entire time, but had continued to wave Julie, the other server on duty, off for the past twenty minutes. She would not have wanted to stay late because "Mr. Undecided" could not make a simple decision.

If Julie's table did not order anything besides coffee, she would offer to split her tips from the family. She did not need the money but took the server job to stay busy and keep her mind off what brought her to the middle of nowhere in the first place.

If certain people knew where she was, the rest of the world would view her death as just another statistic of seemingly random violence and move on with their lives. Since she made sure she could not be found, her family was put in as much, if not more, danger. Their lives could become leverage to force her out of hiding. It had taken considerable resources to hide her family, but the very requirement of staying hidden meant certain freedoms, normally taken for granted, must be stripped away.

Even the harmless freedom of using the telephone just to say "hi."

Someone, somewhere, was always listening.

Despite the dangers and risks of discovery, she and her son had developed a system to stay in touch via online anonymous chat rooms.

Her Blackberry chimed and she pulled it out of the pocket of her uniform. The screen displayed three simple letters that made her smile.

"RUT," which stood for aRe yoU There?

It was Billy, her son. She had chatted with him every week in the three years since she sent him, his father, and his new stepmother into hiding under assumed identities. She looked through the swinging kitchen door. Her family was still working on their meals as they chatted about the day's adventures.

She had time.

She mouthed the letters as she typed her response on the tiny keyboard using only her thumbs.

"SOT" Short On Time "im on break"

"WYWH" Wish You Were Here

She lived her life with a strict code of no regrets. But she did have one regret that always brought a tear to her eye. She wiped that tiny tear away as she thumbed her response.

"me 2 what are U doing up at this hour"

"cant sleep"

The time difference between them put him still up in the early hours of the morning. She knew what he wanted. Her eyes misted again as she knew that what he wanted would not be possible.

She gripped the Blackberry and typed again.

"RUOK" Are you OK

She waited as no response came immediately to her screen. Next week was his thirteenth birthday, and he would officially become a teenager. She wanted to be there, but the risks were too high. If she let her guard down even once – she didn't even want to think what might happen to all of them.

"when can we meet IRL" In Real Life

She started to type the same speech all over again, but paused halfway through. She held down the delete button with one thumb and wiped her eyes with the other. It was time to give him something more than letters on a screen.

"ANFSCD" And Now For Something Completely Different "will call you soon"

The reply came quickly.

"cant wait"

"me 2"

"when WYCM" Will You Call Me

"bday" birthday

She looked through the swinging kitchen door again and saw the family pushing empty plates into the center of the table. This signaled they finished with dinner, and she hoped the food left on some of the plates meant they would not be ordering dessert.

"gotta go break over"

"i luv U mom"

"RBAY" Right Back At You

She pocketed the Blackberry and stood up. She smoothed her uniform and wiped at her eyes. Her nose had started to run slightly, and she sniffed in the wetness. She straightened the nametag that stated in bold black letters against a faded pink background that her name was Karen. She strode through the door into the restaurant and pasted a convincing smile on her face for the remainder of her shift.

Chapter 2

On the other side of the continent, William Hartford sat motionless in his red leather wing chair. The single green banker's light perched on the corner of his antique leather-topped desk provided the only illumination in his twelve thousand square foot Washington, DC apartment.

The glass of Blair Athol Whisky sat untouched on the end table by the side of the leather wing chair. He had poured and ignored it. The ice was gone leaving only a thin layer of clear water to reflect the banker's lamp as it floated on top of the amber liquid. A twelve-year-old single malt whisky should never be treated with such disdain.

He let the cool September wind rustle the papers on the desk behind him. As the wind picked up and papers began to shift across the desk, he leaned forward and pushed the window to just within an inch of closed. This would permit the night sounds to drift in without interfering with the arrangement of the files on his desk.

In stark contrast to the antique Georgian mahogany wood and the dark green tooled leather top of the hundred-year-old partner's desk, a small LED clock burned bright blue on the far right corner. The time showed as 11:32 p.m., and he used these last few moments of each day to reflect as he glanced at the clear liquid floating on top of the whisky. He'd been sober now for twelve years, three months and five days, and during that time had managed to become a respected politician. He was so well-trusted that he had been voted almost unanimously to preside over Congress for the last two years. But with the change in leadership expected in the upcoming election, his time in a position of power was ending.

The phone on the leather-topped desk rang.

He was used to late-night calls from all around the world, even on a politically uneventful Thursday night, and answered after only the second ring. The caller ID showed up as blocked, but the soft melodic voice he recognized instantly.

"In one week you will be President of the United States."

"Hannah!?" He sat up in shock and absently reached for the glass of whisky before stopping himself short. Twelve years, three months and five days was not that long, after all.

"Are you ready for what I have spent over a decade preparing you for?" The soft voice betrayed the sinister nature of her statement.

"Without you, I would never have gotten this far, but how can you be so sure you can actually make me the President?"

"The Presidential Succession Act will make you President. I'm only clearing the way."

A small-town city councilman, who spent every weekend in a drunken stupor, was the last person that should have been selected to become the leader of the most powerful nation in the world. But she had told him that if he sobered up and promised to stay away from the devil's nectar, she would make that happen for him.

For the last twelve years, three months and five days, he had kept his side of the bargain, and, as he was maneuvered up the ranks of the political ladder, it was obvious that she was keeping hers.

Not bad for someone he had never met face-to-face. They always spoke over the phone, or, in recent months, he met with her second in command.

He glanced at the glass of whisky.

This dependency.

This crutch.

She had proven to him that he was better off without it, that success was more achievable when it was left out of his life.

He had been silent for too long, and she said exactly what he needed to hear. "Play it my way, and we both get what we want."

"Why now?"

"Because the window of opportunity is fast closing."

The call ended with a click that sounded more final than anything he had ever heard in his life. Dealing with her was like talking to a bad doctor. You never understood what they meant until it was too late.

Like an avalanche on a snow-packed mountain, now that it had started, not even William Hartford, The Speaker of the House of Representatives himself, could stop it.

As soon as he became Speaker of the House, he was just two heartbeats away from the throne of the most powerful country in the world.

And to make matters worse, he was not in control. Even if he wanted to change his mind, it was already too late. It was too late twelve years ago when he put aside his own personal issues and went along with the most ludicrous scheme he had ever heard in his life.

He grabbed the glass of amber liquid, spilling a little of the watered-down whisky onto the leather-topped desk. He gulped down the entire contents of the glass in a single swallow and let the warm liquid burn his throat and sear the inside of his nostrils. He would not be the first United States President who had overcome a drinking problem in his past.

Chapter 3

Special Agent in Charge Carlos Jimenez pushed on the door leading to the employee restroom. The hinges squealed in protest, their cries of pain echoing off the alternating black and white tiles that covered the walls and the floor of the restroom. He marveled that no how matter how posh or swank the hotel was, the employee restroom always looked like a restroom you'd expect to find in the middle of a deserted highway. He considered himself a professional on the subject of the greater metropolitan DC area employee restrooms, a connoisseur, if you will, as he had seen more than his fair share during his fifteen years on Secret Service detail.

Those fifteen years had brought him through many dark and dingy lower worlds, the Hades of Washington, DC whose every entrance was guarded by the modern-day version of Cerberus, the three-headed dog.

A simple plastic plaque that stated its warning in no uncertain terms.

"Employees Only – No Admittance."

He had little doubt he entered the very bowels of hell every time he crossed that plaque. And tonight was no different. He let the door swing fully open before absentmindedly wiping his fingertips on the side of his slacks. His time in the Secret Service brought him to more of these places than he cared to admit, and being promoted to Special Agent in Charge only ensured that he was the first through every door.

His highly trained senses took in the room all at once, and he wished that just once he would open that door and find an employee restroom that was as pristine and polished as the restrooms in the lobby. But then again, he thought, that is the true mark of insanity. Doing the same thing repeatedly and expecting a different result.

He walked into the dimly lit, and fortunately unoccupied, bathroom. He hated having to kick people out, but then again, that was his job. There was no higher calling than keeping the world safe for democracy, but tonight, his job was to keep the bathroom safe for the Vice President of the United States.

He paced out to the center of the room, careful not to slip on the thin film of oily residue that was the unfortunate result of sharing a ventilation shaft with the kitchen. Tonight his job would be easier than usual. The management had posted a sign on the door stating that the restroom was going to be for the personal use of the Vice President of the United States and requested employees to take care of their needs elsewhere. Despite the sign, he still did his duty and entered the room ahead of anyone else.

The two urinals stood empty. In stark contrast to the coloring of the walls and the floor, they gleamed in brilliant porcelain white, the pungent odor of chlorine the only telltale sign to the cause of their cleanliness. Two of the stall doors stood open with the middle stall closed and a crude handwritten sign stating "out of order" in blocky red letters taped to the door.

As the special agent walked past the broken stall, he nearly did a double-take as he thought he saw a shadow move underneath. He paused for only a moment and stared hard under the locked door. Just then, a voice broke his concentration. He looked up to see the eager face of the youngest recruit ever to get Vice Presidential detail. An honor that, until this kid had come along, had been his.

"He said to let you know that he's had quite a bit to drink, and he doesn't know how much longer he can hold it."

He held up his hand, silencing the recruit. He drew his automatic pistol and pointed silently at the locked bathroom stall. The recruit understood and drew his own service weapon and pointed it at the stall door.

He kicked hard at the door, and the lock gave way with a shriek. The door slammed against the back wall of the empty stall.

He holstered his weapon and looked at the kid who had stolen his record.

"Let him know it's all clear."

Just as he finished his sentence, a large well-groomed man of six foot two pushed his way into the restroom. "God dammit, Carlos. I swear, you seem to take longer every single time."

"Just doing my job to keep you safe, sir."

The Vice President rushed past, unzipping his pants before he even made it to the urinal against the wall. "Now that I'm safe, how about a little privacy?"

He reached the door and pulled it closed behind him, "Of course, sir. I'll be outside if you need anything."

As soon as he heard the door close, Andrew quietly lowered himself down from the sling that had held him hidden under the wide imitation marble sinks along the wall opposite the urinals. The Fentanyl had finally kicked in, and the pain had subsided enough that he was able to concentrate on sneaking up behind the Vice President without alerting him that he was even there.

Five years ago if someone had told the highly decorated United States Army Special Forces Captain that, on an otherwise ordinary Thursday night, he would be hiding from the Secret Service in a filthy bathroom waiting to make a move against the second most powerful man in the United States, he would've told them to go do something unnatural with themselves. But cancer has a way of changing a man, making him willing to do things he wouldn't normally consider.

The Vice President finished, zipped up his pants and turned around. Andrew understood the reason for the sudden look of confusion on the Vice President's face. He was staring into the face of someone who looked exactly like him.

"What the…" was all the Vice President could utter before he swiftly stabbed the needle into the arm of the career politician and plunged the entire contents of the syringe deep into the muscle tissue. The Vice President stared down at the needle sticking out of his arm and then back up to look him squarely in the eyes. The chemical worked quickly, and as the Vice President realized he was losing all muscle control, his eyes sought out the doorway that led to an entire squadron of heavily armed and highly trained men whose job it was to protect him.

He opened his mouth to scream for help, but the only noise he made was a low moan accompanied by a gurgling sound right before he collapsed into Andrew's waiting arms.

Chapter 4

Melissa twisted the key in the ignition, and the Super Duty 455 V8 roared to life. Denny's love for her meant that she, his girlfriend of ten months, was the only one allowed to drive his beloved muscle car. But it was his love for a mid-seventies television show that meant she was gripping the steering wheel of a gold-colored 1974 Pontiac Firebird Esprit 400, made famous as the car of choice for Los Angeles-based private investigator, Jim Rockford. He even had a Polaroid picture hanging in the living room of his apartment, yes, a Polaroid picture, showing him and a much older James Garner both leaning on the hood of this very car.

She depressed the clutch, shifted the manual transmission into the first of four gears, and smiled. He had no idea how she would have treated a baby like this if it were her own. Her own 1986 Dodge Aries K was a four-cylinder wimp and could never respond like the powerhouse sitting under her right foot waiting for her to make the first move.

She wanted to tear the pavement up and put this monster through its paces but knew that if she were pulled over, her hastily sketched identity would never withstand the examination of a police database query. She could feel the 170 horsepower beast tremble under her grip as it begged to be set free. Instead, she slowly released her weight on the clutch and gradually depressed the accelerator to ease the Firebird out onto the highway in the direction of home.

The next corner came up far too quickly, and she jerked the wheel as the tires squealed in delight all the way through the power slide around the tight bend. She glanced down to see she was doing nearly seventy miles an hour without even realizing it.

She eased up on the accelerator and turned the Firebird off the main road and onto a smaller paved road. For several minutes, she passed a few homes that were set back and hidden behind the trees. The only hint that someone lived there was the occasional mailbox next to a rutted dirt road leading away from the paved road. Once she reached the eighth mailbox, she turned right onto a dirt road classified more as a widened deer trail and not listed on any map.

She guided the Firebird down the narrow dirt road. It led her back to the house that was in a small clearing of trees. The house was far enough from the main road that, unless you knew it was there, you wouldn't find it.

She pulled the Firebird next to her Dodge, its hood raised up with engine parts lying all around it. When she shut off the Firebird's engine, the stillness of the woods moved in ever so slightly. She sat quietly and listened to the engine tick as it cooled unevenly. She slipped the Blackberry from her pocket and started dialing a number. She paused before hitting the send button. She wanted to call him and tell him that she would always be there for him. To hear his voice after so long. She wondered if it had started to change yet. Would she even recognize the voice of her own son if she did call him?

But it was a risk she wasn't willing to take. One call, and

they would find her.

She stared at the phone number on the lit screen of her Blackberry for so long that the engine now ticked only occasionally. A phone number that had the power to bring the voice of her son to her in seconds. With a practiced move made many times before, she turned off the phone and slipped it back into the pocket of her polyester uniform.

As she stared out into the darkness of the forest, she reminded herself that she had made a promise that was too dangerous to keep.

She had promised to call him on his birthday.

She consoled herself in the belief that she was not alone in practicing the ancient traditions of parenthood, a tradition practiced by countless generations before her, and most assuredly would be practiced by countless generations after. The time-honored tradition of parents everywhere, the tradition of breaking promises.

She wiped away the dampness forming at the base of her eyes and climbed out of the car.

Dressed all in black and wearing a bulletproof vest, the man crouched in the bushes watched Melissa exit the Firebird and go into the dark house. At first, he thought she had spotted him as she had sat in the car for the longest time practically staring straight at him.

He paid close attention as the interior lights revealed her journey throughout the inside of the house. They stopped with the flicker of the bathroom light. She was settling in. But more important was that she was alone. He would give her a few more minutes to become completely relaxed before moving in.

The Heckler & Koch MP5SD with intergraded sound-suppressor scraped against the bushes as the watcher slid past them. The neighbors weren't very close, but in the woods late at night, gunshots carried much greater distances than they ever did in the city. The silencer would ensure that the threat to the lone occupant of the house would not be heard by anyone else.

He shifted the weight of the bulletproof vest on his shoulders and crept out of the forest.

Melissa went from room to room but couldn't find Denny. She had his car, and the Dodge was half in pieces. Where could he have gone? He never talked about his time in the service, but being ex-military herself, she understood the demons he had rattling around inside of his head. He would often just hike out into the woods for a little quiet time.

He would be back soon.

But while she waited, it was the perfect time for that one luxury she still allowed herself. No amount of Special Forces training ever fully eliminated the need for a strawberry-scented bubble bath.

Still in her uniform, she poured the entire contents of the bottle of red liquid stenciled with the words LOVE in gold on the side into the filling tub. She watched the liquid spread through the tub and dilute to a faint shade of pink. Bubbles began forming around the base of the flowing water.

Her stomach growled slightly, reminding her that she hadn't eaten dinner and was starving. Maybe she could find a snack, or at least something to drink, before settling in for a good long soak.

She left the kitchen light off as she entered. She pulled on the handle, and the light from the fridge spread across the kitchen floor like a rising sun.

The watcher approached the side of the house and saw the light increase through the large windows over the sink in the kitchen. The occupant of the house held the fridge door open, the light from the fridge illuminating her profile.

He smiled and moved around to the side of the house. He looked through the sliding glass door straight into the kitchen and at the back of his objective as she stared into the fridge. The first shot would go wild as it broke the glass on the sliding door. The remaining shots would be under better control as they entered the kitchen unobstructed.

With a direct line of sight, he knelt into a crouched shooting position and switched on the laser dot. He moved his laser dot onto his target and waited for the right moment.

As he changed the angle of the MP5SD, the red dot shifted slightly.

She held the fridge door open, not sure what she wanted to pull from its contents. Single men never had a well-stocked fridge, and Denny was no exception. As soon as he got home, she would give him a list of items that should be in the fridge if he expected her to spend the night ever again.

A flash of bright red light glinted to her left. She froze for a moment. A second glint made her glance at the source. The toaster was polished to a mirror finish, reflecting the source of a laser sight from outside the house.

She dove down behind the center kitchen island just before the sliding glass door exploded and the contents of the fridge erupted. She didn't hear anything except the impact of the bullets as they ricocheted across the kitchen, searching for her. She guessed the weapon of choice was a silenced machine pistol. If so, in another moment, the magazine would be empty, and she would be ready.

The watcher swept the barrel back and forth while he held the trigger and left the kitchen a complete wasteland. The MP5SD chamber clicked loudly to signal the last bullet had exited the chamber.

As soon as she heard the loud click of the magazine release, she darted back into the house and away from the open kitchen. Her blood churned through her body, and her adrenaline surged. She hadn't felt this much fear since that day in the jungle when she was pursued by an entire U.S. Army Delta Force. She hit the light switches as she moved from room to room and plunged the house back into complete darkness.

This was a complete reversal of how she had entered the house less than fifteen minutes before. Only this time she avoided the living room with its floor-to-ceiling windows.

Those windows gave a spectacular view of the surrounding forested mountains during a cold winter sunset, but right now, they gave the best view into the house from the outside. If there were others surrounding the house, she would be exposed while she approached the light switch.

And exposure meant death. Those lights would just have to stay on.

She moved on to hit the lights in the den and stopped. Her warrior spirit, suppressed for so long, fought its way to the surface long enough to tickle her memory. She turned the den lights back on again and stared at the gun safe in the far corner. Denny had urged her to go hunting with him on several occasions. She always told him she was afraid of guns and refused. She never touched a gun in his presence, but had watched him access the safe enough times to memorize the combination. Along with a couple of rifles, she had seen the small black case on the top shelf that would contain a pistol. Rifles weren't much use in close-quarters fighting, but the pistol would improve her situation dramatically.

She spun the dial several times to reset it. It had been awhile, and she worried that Denny changed the combination on a regular basis. She concentrated her memory on the first number and spun the dial.

Chapter 5

The watcher circled around to the front of the house and noticed the lights going out one by one. One room suddenly lit back up. He smiled. This was what he was waiting for. She finally noticed the gun safe and was ready to fight back.

He had visited the house earlier. Her boyfriend was tough, but like all the others, he soon gave him what he wanted. With the code to the gun safe in hand, he replaced the bullets in the pistol on the shelf with blanks. Even though he knew he was the superior fighter, it never hurt to swing the odds in his favor. The first bullet of the magazine was real in case she checked, so he had to be sure he didn't get hit by that first bullet. Even if he did, the bulletproof vest would protect him, but he would feel it in the morning.

It was not the thrill of the kill that got his blood pumping, it was the thrill of the chase. The targets that fought back always provided a more invigorating experience. He never felt more alive than when the fear crescendoed to a fever pitch in his victims. And why not have a little fun with your job? Even if your job was killing people for a living.

From the provided dossier, she would be his most challenging assignment to date, and it just wouldn't be any fun to kill her too quickly.

He selected the magazine with rubber bullets and slammed it into the MP5SD.

Melissa twisted the dial to the last number and jerked up on the handle. The safe opened with a clunk to reveal the lethality inside. She reached up to the top shelf and removed the small zippered case. She pulled the cold metal zipper all the way around the fabric case to reveal the GLOCK 17 pistol inside.

She grabbed the contour grip and hefted the mighty pistol. She closed her eyes briefly as she felt every groove. Holding a gun for the first time in three years felt like the first drink of a recovered alcoholic. She felt euphoric and powerful. And these feelings were dangerous. She opened her eyes and forced her old self back down. Despite the numerous promises she had broken, and would continue to break, there was still one promise she vowed to keep. She would use the GLOCK 17 to lay down suppressing fire so she could escape.

Nothing more than that.

She fingered the magazine release and saw that it was fully loaded with ammunition. She snapped the magazine back in place and was ready to make a run for the Firebird.

She paused as her former self rose briefly to prod at her memory again.

The MP5SD carried thirty rounds, and her GLOCK held only 10. She needed to even those odds even if just a little. She turned back to the gun safe and reached up to the top shelf to pull down a box of 9mm ammunition and a second magazine for the GLOCK. She loaded the second magazine and stuffed it into the pocket of the waitress uniform that she unfortunately wasn't going to have time to change out of.

The watcher circled around and waited by the front door. The only logical avenue of escape was the Firebird. His prey would make a move for the car soon. He heard the sound of crunching glass as it carried from around the back of the house. She had left through the shattered sliding glass door and was going to circle around to the front of the house. He moved back twenty feet into the surrounding forest and settled in. He trained his MP5SD onto the side of the house nearest the Firebird.

The moon burst from behind a cloud and lit up the house like a spotlight. Shadows formed on the ground, and he would see when his prey was right behind the corner of the house. He sighted just past the corner of the house and waited.

Melissa exited the back of the house without resistance. That meant there might be only one adversary, and he had moved around to another side of the house. She moved her lips in a silent prayer that he would not be anywhere near the Firebird. The clouds slid away from the moon, and the forest lit up. She made her way to the corner of the house nearest to the Firebird. This was her chance to get away and still keep her promise. She surveyed the surrounding forest. She held her breath and listened. Nobody approached from deep in the forest. Her jungle training would have immediately alerted her to anyone within a hundred yards. She peeked around the corner to check around the front.

A hail of bullets kicked the dirt up all around her. She ducked back and pressed herself against the corner of the house. She shoved the GLOCK around the corner and fired five rounds in the general direction of the faint muzzle flash she saw before being forced back around the corner. The Firebird was too far away for her to make a run for it. She would be cut down before she even made it half way. She had to draw her attacker back into the house if she was going to make it to the gold Firebird. It was the only way.

His contemporaries used sniper rifles from a distance. One shot, one kill. That was far too impersonal for his liking. Death was the ultimate in intimacy. All pretext was erased, and the true nature of the human experience was always present at someone's final breath. The watcher made sure he was with his victims when they took their last breath.

He sat back up. Her first shot went very wild and now her GLOCK was loaded only with blanks. It was safe to step up the pressure and move into the house. She would feel that she had the home field advantage and would take greater risks. The neighbors must have heard those first five shots, but they happened so fast nobody would have called the police just yet. The neighbors would be awake for the next round of shooting and would definitely call the police then. But he would be long gone before the police arrived.

He entered through the destroyed sliding glass kitchen doors. His footfalls ground the glass under him into the wood flooring. The sound carried into the house and announced his presence to his prey. He could almost hear her heart beat faster. He could almost taste the salty perspiration that was forming on her skin as she ran.

And he intended to let her run.

But she would not escape.

Melissa heard the crunch of glass as her attacker walked through the kitchen. She moved to the edge of the living room and sighted down the hallway with her GLOCK. She focused on the sound coming from the kitchen doorway at the other end of the hallway and waited.

The barrel of the MP5SD swept around the corner, but she waited until the attacker was in full view. The GLOCK safety released under the trigger pressure, and she fired three rounds down the hallway. She didn't notice that the bullets failed to hit her attacker or puncture the wall where her GLOCK was aimed. She was too focused on moving while her attacker dove back into the kitchen. Her opponent poked the MP5SD around the corner to let loose another volley of death.

She wasn't anywhere near where she had fired from. Her training made her fire and move before the return fire came. The enemy always returned fire to where she was moments ago.

Only a few rounds remained in the MP5SD and she needed to get him to use them. If she could bring the fight into hand-to-hand territory, she could even the odds a lot better in her favor. She fired another round into the kitchen opening. The MP5SD poked around again and emptied the remaining rounds in its magazine. She fired her last shot and let him hear the unmistakable click of her empty gun as she pulled the trigger once more.

Everything was going according to his carefully laid plans. He stood up and moved into the hallway.

His prey was standing at the other end of the hallway. The living room light provided a stark silhouette. She pointed her gun right at him with her right hand. She must have felt confident because her left hand sat relaxed in the pocket of her uniform. He decided to break a personal rule and talk to this one.

The watcher smiled. "You're out of bullets."

He raised his MP5SD and pulled the trigger, only to be rewarded with a soft click.

"So are you," she responded.

She hadn't even flinched when he pulled the trigger. Her training was much better than he gave her credit for. He was going to enjoy getting to know the real her when she took her last breath.

He tossed the Heckler & Koch machine pistol down and pulled a serrated combat knife out of the sheath clipped to his belt and approached slowly. He was going to be close enough to smell the fear emanating from her. That was worth more than the price of admission.

He stopped short when his prey smiled back.

He stood motionless as she thumbed the magazine release on the GLOCK. At the same moment that the spent magazine clattered to the ground, she pulled another magazine from her pocket with her left hand and smacked it into the bottom of the GLOCK. He didn't even have time to turn around before three rounds slammed into his chest and sprawled him backwards into the kitchen.

Chapter 6

Melissa pointed the GLOCK at the still form lying at the end of the hallway as she approached. As she got closer, she noticed that he was still breathing. Then she saw the bulky jacket around his chest. The bastard was wearing a bulletproof vest.

Her attacker coughed himself awake.

She reached down and tugged the hood off. Staring at his face, she recognized him as "Mr. Undecided" from the restaurant. He had been surveilling her, and she hadn't even realized it. She had let her guard down and almost paid the ultimate price for her lack of vigilance.

She stood over him and kept her pistol at the ready. She tilted her head as he looked at her defiantly.

"Who are you?" she hissed.

The man shifted slightly on the ground and tried to look away. She kicked him to keep his attention on her.

"Who sent you?"

He coughed and blood dribbled out of his mouth as he said only two words. "Thank you."

"What?" She wasn't certain she had heard him correctly.

The man only smiled as he let a large cylindrical object roll out of his hand and land with a clunk on the floor. It was much larger than a hand grenade, and the blinking LED light on one end was getting faster.

She sprinted out the front door and was halfway to the Firebird when the shockwave knocked her to her feet. If the neighbors hadn't heard anything else that had taken place here tonight, they most certainly heard that.

She rolled onto her side and slowly stood back up. As she stumbled against the Dodge for support, she jumped back from the sudden thumping coming from inside the trunk. She fumbled with her keys and finally unlocked the trunk. Denny spilled out and gasped for air, his face bruised and swollen.

She hefted him into the passenger seat of the Firebird and leaped into the driver's seat. As the Firebird's engine roared to life, the remaining half of the house that had not blown apart collapsed inward and was immediately engulfed in flames.

She took off into the night with no clear destination.

Chapter 7

The explosion of Denny's house in the woods outside of a small tourist town should not have warranted the heavily manned roadblocks that had forced Melissa to turn around on two occasions in the last four hours. She was trapped in Oregon, and there was no way she would be able to drive anywhere. Even if she tried to cross the roadblocks, they would quickly notice her passenger's condition. And that would lead to too many questions that she couldn't answer about what had happened, who she was, and why someone had sent a professional hit man to kill her.

The moon retreated again behind a cloud as he groaned in the seat next to her.

There was only one person she could call for help with this kind of trouble. She reached in her pocket and pulled out half of her Blackberry. She stared at the shattered piece of plastic. In the age of a mobile phone in every pocket or purse, she had to find a pay phone.

It was another twenty minutes before she pulled next to the lit phone booth at the darkened gas station. A sign by the road stated, "GAS 24 HOURS." There was a button next to the garage hand-labeled, "ring for service any hour." Times were tough everywhere, and this owner did not want to miss a single sale because he was closed. She dug a quarter out of the Firebird's ashtray. Denny didn't smoke and used his ashtray for his spare change.

She slipped the quarter in the slot and dialed the number she had committed to memory many years ago. She hoped that not only did the number work, but also would connect her to someone who could help.

When the number rang, her shoulders dropped in instant relief. It had been so long since she was given this number that it might have been disconnected.

When the voicemail answered, she punched in a series of numbers and the pre-recorded voice was instantly replaced with several clicks and then another ringing tone. The clicks meant that her call was being traced and her location pinpointed long before the ringing had even started.

The voice that picked up was familiar and foreign all at the same time.

"Hello?"

"It's me. I need your help."

"Of course, what do you need?"

No introduction. No, "how come you haven't called in so long." Just an immediate response to her plea for help.

"How fast can you get a plane to me?"

"Let's see, you're in Oregon."

She unconsciously flinched that he knew so quickly where she was. But this was all part of why he was the only one who could help her.

"How soon can you get to the Municipal Airport in Madras?"

"I can be there in half an hour."

"I'll have a private jet waiting for you."

"That fast?"

"It's why you called me instead of somebody else, isn't it?"

She felt all her problems melt away. He would take care

of her.

"Thanks, Nick."

"It's my pleasure, Melissa, I owe you. Where do you want me to tell the pilot to take you?"

While looking for a pay phone, she had thought long and hard about how she would answer this question when he asked.

And she knew her answer.

"Just bring me home."

Chapter 8

Melissa spotted the strip mall on the outskirts of Madras and turned the Firebird into the parking lot. She pulled around and saw the drug store on the corner. A few lights were left on to keep anyone from doing what she came here to do. She looked up and saw the apartments built on top of the strip mall. This was the small town's response to what cities had known all along. Not only do they get the benefit of commercial properties on the land, but people can also live above the shops, restaurants and coffee houses. It was almost like getting double taxes for every square foot of dirt.

She shut down the motor to the Firebird and looked over at Denny. He had his arm wrapped around his chest and grimaced slightly with each slow breath. He hadn't asked where they were going, and hadn't questioned each time she turned around. She knew that she would have to tell him something soon.

"Stay here. I'm going to get you something for the pain."

He rolled his head across the back of the seat and looked across the parking lot. His head rolled back to look at her.

"They're closed."

"I know." She tugged at the handle of her door and stepped into the chilly night. She wrapped her bare arms around her. The wind cut right through the polyester waitress uniform. There were a couple of lights on in the apartments above. She scanned the apartments for any movement. When she saw nothing, she stepped away from the Firebird and walked briskly across the parking lot. The

GLOCK weighed heavily in the front pocket of her uniform. She hoped she wouldn't need to use it.

She noticed the thin silver strip around the edges of the drug store windows. She couldn't break them without setting off an alarm. She walked around to the back of the store and saw a late model Mustang sitting by the rear delivery door. She checked the hood. It was still warm.

She walked up to the door and pulled on the handle. The door swung open silently. Someone was definitely here. It could be the night manager closing up or even the owner double-checking his employees' untrustworthy work. Whatever the reason, she couldn't risk any type of confrontation now.

She turned to leave and then heard people talking as they approached the door from the inside. She slipped into the door and ducked down into the shadows behind boxes in the storage room. She was now inside and could do what she came for once they left.

"That's stealing."

"I do the inventory. Mr. Wiles will never know there's a package missing."

"I don't know…"

"Come on, it's perfect. You're perfect."

She smiled at the obvious line. These kids must still be in high school. That meant the line just might work.

"Okay, but just one."

"Hey, I just had a thought."

"Not here."

"Oh, come on, it'll be hot."

"Dammit Jason, this is supposed to be special."

"You're right, you're always right."

She heard the shuffle of feet as they approached closer. She ducked further into the shadows as the two teenagers came into view. The boy had his arm around the girl.

"How about Hunter's Point?"

The girl smiled, and they left out the back door with a slam. She waited until she heard the Mustang start up and drive away. When the sound of the engine faded, she stood up.

She wandered into the drug store. She had learned the finer points of theft while training in the jungle. It had surprised her how quickly she had overcome her childhood upbringing that taught her stealing was wrong.

She was thankful that stores in America insisted on leaving lights on twenty-four hours a day. This made her task much easier. She headed straight for the pharmacy section and abruptly stopped. On a rack at the end of an aisle hung goose down jackets. She looked down at her thin uniform and tugged a large overstuffed split-hood down jacket with faux fur collar off the rack. This would help against the cold outside, and she needed the extra large side zippered pockets to carry the medication. They were all the same black color, and she didn't care what size she grabbed. She shrugged the down jacket on and continued to the pharmacy.

She found the Vicodin on an upper rack in less than a minute. She cleared the entire shelf into the side zippered pockets. She looked around and saw the ACE bandages. She grabbed several of those and stuffed them down the front of the down jacket.

"Where did you leave it?" The voice broke the silence.

She dropped into a crouch.

"I don't remember."

Dammit! The kids were back.

"Try over by the – you know, the things."

She looked to her right and stared at boxes of condoms.

"I don't know why you have to have it now."

"It has my cell phone in it. If my dad calls and I don't answer, he'll come looking for me."

The boy stepped through the doorway into the pharmacy. She looked around and saw the purse on the shelf.

"I don't see it."

"Are you by the..."

"I'm almost there."

She slid the purse into the middle of the aisle. The boy stopped at the other end of the aisle.

"Found it." He walked over and bent to pick it up.

She held her breath. If he turned his head more to the left, he would see her. He lifted the purse, turned to leave, and then stopped walking.

"One more box," he said to himself.

He swiveled his whole body and looked right at her.

She sprang into action. She grabbed the boy and spun him around, clamping a hand over his mouth.

"If your girlfriend finds out I'm here, you both die."

She smelled the faint odor of warm urine.

Good.

The boy understood her perfectly.

"Tell her to wait in the car." She quickly removed her

hand from his mouth and gripped his lower jaw. "Now!"

"Hey…hey, Rebecca?"

"Did you find it?"

"Yeah. Go wait in the car."

"Bring my purse."

She gripped his jaw harder.

"Just wait in the fuckin' car!"

"Fuck you too!" And with that, the girl stormed out the back door.

She leaned in close to the boy's ear.

"Good. Now I'm going to help you out. Take as many boxes of condoms as you want."

The boy didn't move. She grabbed a box of condoms off the shelf and shoved them into his coat pocket. She pushed the boy to the ground.

"Be a good little boy and count to a hundred before getting up."

She walked calmly away from the pharmacy counter and stepped out the back delivery door into the crisp night. She walked past the Mustang and made eye contact with the girl sitting in the passenger seat. She rounded the corner. As soon as she was out of sight of the girl, she broke into a full run.

She jumped into the Firebird and shoved the key into the ignition. She kept the car lights off until they were back on the highway and out of view of the strip mall.

In less than ten minutes, she followed the exit sign for the Madras Municipal Airport. She pulled into the deserted airport and headed to the only hanger lit up at this hour. The throaty grumble of the V8 engine announced her arrival as she pulled next to the Bombardier Global Express XRS private jet that waited patiently on the edge of the runway.

The pilot stepped down the built-in steps of the open door and walked over to her. "We have clearance to leave any time."

"Thank you. Help me with my friend."

The pilot didn't even react when he saw Denny's swollen face. He just took the other arm and together, he and Melissa carried her injured partner up into the jet. He helped place Denny carefully on the bed in the private stateroom at the back of the jet.

As soon as Denny looked comfortable, she looked at the pilot. "We'd like to leave now."

"Of course."

The pilot closed the door to the stateroom, and in less than a minute, he had taxied onto the runway and received the final clearance.

She leaned in to Denny and held him so that he wouldn't fall out of bed as the jet throttled up for takeoff.

"As soon as we're airborne, I'm going to take a look at your injuries."

He moaned in response.

Chapter 9

Back in Washington, D.C., Andrew carefully laid the Vice President down on the gritty bathroom floor. It took him only a few moments to change shoes with the Vice President. He was already dressed in exactly the same suit and tie so that the switch could be made in as little time as possible. The only thing that he couldn't replicate was the transponder built into the heel of the Vice President's left shoe, and so a quick swap ensured that both visually and electronically he was now the Vice President of the United States.

He stood up and looked at himself in the grimy mirror. Multiple several-hour surgeries had made him look exactly like the man lying unconscious on the floor, and for the past six weeks, a vocal coach taught him how to speak and sound just like him.

He practiced flashing the world renowned smile in the mirror, and then suddenly doubled over the sink. The breakthrough pain was getting more severe each time. With one hand gripping the side of the rust-stained sink, he reached into his pocket and pulled out the bottle of Fentanyl tablets. He stared at the large red warning letters on the bottle in his trembling hand. He actually laughed out loud as he read that, amongst the dangers of overdose, was a high probability of death. This warning label did not apply to him. He would be dead in less than half an hour anyway.

He popped the top of the bottle with his thumb and let go of the sink long enough to pour the remaining four tablets into his waiting palm. One by one, he nestled the tablets into his cheeks just behind each molar. They dissolved quickly, and he glanced at the sleeping body on the floor. A wave of emotion flooded over him, and he instantly snapped to attention. With a fluid practiced motion, his hand jerked to his brow in salute.

"United States Army – 5th Special Forces Group. Captain Andrew Stovall at your complete disposal. It is my distinct pleasure to die in your place, Mr. Vice President."

The sleeping man never stirred, never even reacted to what he had just said. He released his salute and let his hand drop to his side. The shaking was subsiding, and that meant it was time to fulfill his duty. The public would never know of the sacrifice he'd made for his country. But then again, the cancer would have taken him in less than six months anyway, and he didn't do this for a medal.

He did this because it had to be done.

He did this because he believed in the oath he had taken to protect the leaders of this great nation.

He pulled open the bathroom door just enough to slip out into the hallway. It wouldn't be a good idea to have anyone outside this door look in and see his doppelganger lying prone on the alternating black and white discolored tiles.

The concerned face of Carlos Jimenez, Special Agent in Charge, was the first thing he encountered in the hallway.

"Are you alright, sir? You were in there quite a while."

He immediately employed his six weeks of vocal training. "Like I said before, Carlos, I just had a little too much to drink. I'll be all right. I think I'm ready to leave now."

"Of course, sir. The motorcade's right this way."

Jimenez pointed down the hallway with an outstretched open palm. Just like Moses raising his staff over the Red Sea, as soon as the Special Agent in Charge raised his arm to point the way, a sea of Secret Service agents parted to either side of the hallway.

He scanned the hallway in front of them and then turned to look back in the opposite direction, searching the faces of every hotel employee.

Jimenez touched him briefly on the elbow. "This way, sir."

A sudden wave of terror enveloped him as he searched the faces of the hotel employees in both directions of the hallway. His frantic actions must have alarmed the Secret Service agents closest to him as their gun hands instinctively started moving for their holsters.

"Is there anything wrong, sir?"

He glanced at Jimenez, hoping that his fear was not reflected in his eyes. "I, uhh…"

Someone coughed down the hallway and made several of the agents jump reflexively. He looked at the banquet server who had just coughed, and instantly all anxiety flowed out of every muscle as, when their eyes met, the banquet server gave an almost imperceptible nod. The Vice President would be safe.

He quickly turned to the lead Secret Service agent and flashed the Vice President's award-winning smile. "I am so sorry, Carlos. I think I had more to drink than I planned. I was disoriented for a moment there. You know how it is, too many employee bathrooms in too many hotels."

Jimenez searched his eyes looking for the answer to a question he didn't even know he was asking.

"Take me home."

The Special Agent in Charge visibly relaxed, and finally let go of his arm.

"Right this way, sir."

Chapter 10

Jonathan Wilkes snapped shut the sleek black Motorola RAZR V3 and dropped it into the nearest trash can on the street. He had received confirmation from Hannah to proceed and wouldn't need to use that phone ever again. When it was time to contact her again, he would purchase a disposable phone using cash.

He checked the pace of traffic and crossed the street to join the growing crowd of protesters.

The former United States Marine Corps Force Reconnaissance warrior gripped the nylon backpack that was slung over the shoulder of his Port Authority black leather bomber jacket. He generally preferred to wear the durable and ready-for-action Battle Dress Uniform, but despite coming in a variety of camouflage patterns and solid colors, he decided he would blend in better if he wore civilian clothes.

Good call. As soon as he stepped into the crowd of protesters, he noted that there were at least fifteen other men in black leather jackets and blue jeans and not a single person in BDUs. He quickly scanned the crowd looking for potential accomplices and found them huddled together in front of the window of a shoe store closed for the night. They cast furtive glances around as they passed something small between them, each taking a turn putting it to their lips.

They were perfect.

He strode over and stopped a couple feet outside the

circle. He quickly evaluated the small group of boys and noted that the oldest couldn't have been more than seventeen. They obviously thought that forming a circle would magically keep anyone from smelling what it was they were really up to. A sudden exchange of whispers caused the entire group to simultaneously turn their heads and look at him.

"We ain't got nothin' for sale." The 17-year-old was obviously the leader. Probably because he was their supplier.

"I just wanted to know if you boys can help me and my friends out," he nodded his head towards the crowd of protesters. "You see, the Vice President's motorcade is gonna come by in about fifteen minutes, and I've got a few cartons of eggs in my bag. You interested?"

"What are you protesting?"

He smiled. "Does it really matter? You wanna throw eggs at the VPs limo or not?"

Heads pivoted back and forth amongst the circle of boys as they looked at each other trying to determine if this was a trap or not. All eyes finally settled on the leader who looked back at him and flashed a big grin exposing several gaps were teeth should have been. "You only live once, right?"

He slid the backpack off his shoulder and bent down to unzip the bag. He lifted the first carton of eggs out of the backpack and held it out to the leader.

"Take the eggs out of the cartons here and spend the next few minutes working your way into the crowd. Try not to stick together. Remember, the key word here is to blend in. The Vice President's car will be the second limousine six cars back from the front of the motorcade. Now, don't any of you get too excited and start throwing eggs early. Wait for the Vice President."

One of the boys, who couldn't have been more than fifteen, took a carton of eggs and held it up to show the others.

"Hey – organic free range, nice."

He handed out the rest of the egg cartons. "Only the very best for the leaders of our country."

Eggs were quickly dispersed amongst the small group when the leader paused and looked at him. "What about you, man, you gonna take an egg?"

"Already got one," he replied, as he slipped an egg out of the pocket of his black leather bomber jacket. "Remember – wait for the Vice President's car."

"We got it, man."

Chapter 11

Wilkes cradled the egg in the palm of his hand while he made his way through the protesters. He glanced around to see that all the pothead kids had done exactly as he asked. They all stood waiting amongst the crowd.

The man with the megaphone hadn't stopped shouting his political diatribe since he first arrived, and he wondered how the man could sustain saying the same thing repeatedly without tiring or getting bored of himself.

I guess he likes hearing himself talk, he thought. But that still didn't explain how the rest of the people in the crowd put up with it. It's true what they say, some are born leaders while the rest are born followers.

He had been a leader of men, strong men, not like the sheep that surrounded him now. He commanded one of the most active Force Recon units within the Marine Corps Special Operations Command, designated as Detachment One. Detachment One was the pilot program that brought Marine Force Recon units and the United States Special Operations Command together to work side-by-side.

He led his unit through numerous successes in multiple theaters. That is until the United States Marine Corps Forces Special Operations Command was officially activated on February 24th of 2006. With the formation of this new layer of political significance, the United States Marine Corps had become directly involved with SOCOM and no longer required the pilot program.

The first action of MARSOC was the disbanding of

Detachment One, leaving Master Gunnery Sergeant Jonathan Wilkes without a unit to command, and a promotion to the Marine Corps Mountain Warfare Training Center that took him out of harm's way.

He had always envisioned that he would die during a combat operation, and running simulated exercises up and down a snowy mountain along the California-Nevada border was not his idea of combat operations.

So he left and became a mercenary for hire. He quickly made a name for himself as the one who could get the job done. He wondered why he had not left the service sooner. The pay was much better, and the danger was far more consistent. He could work back-to-back contracts without waiting for someone higher up in the chain of command to decide to deploy him or not. This was the life he was meant for; this was the life that gave him meaning.

The sound of distant sirens pierced through the thick night. They were still far enough away that he could only hear them when mister megaphone paused to take a breath. A cell phone rang, and mister megaphone instantly stopped shouting as he reached into his jacket pocket to answer the phone. He listened for a moment and then shoved the phone back in his pocket. "Ladies and gentlemen, I just received word that the Vice President is headed this way."

The crowd immediately reacted as a single organism, and everyone in the front of the crowd seemed to grow three feet taller as they lifted signs and banners into the air, each one hand-lettered and all detailing their discourse with the decisions of the current administration.

"Aw, shit!" he muttered as he looked at the wall of signs

and banners along the edge of the street. There was no way they would hit the limo with those in the way. He made his way to the closest pothead.

"Hey, buddy, tell your friends to get in front of those signs. And hurry. He'll be here any second."

"You got it, man." The kid dashed into the crowd being a little more obvious than he should have. "Hey, guys, get to the curb. He's coming."

He breathed a sigh of relief as the kids all recognized their friend's voice and made their way to the street, eggs in hand. He also moved forward. He hadn't wanted to expose himself this much, but it was more important that his special egg made contact with the Vice President's limousine.

He moved to the front of the line to stand right next to mister megaphone and hoped that if questions were asked, he would be remembered as just another one of the protesters in a black leather jacket and blue jeans.

He looked down the street and noted all the signal lights turning green, marking the path that the Vice President was about to take. The volume of the sirens exploded into a monstrous wale as two police motorcycles rounded the nearby corner, followed closely by the long procession of vehicles in the motorcade. He counted out the vehicles and prayed that the potheads had enough brain cells left to remember his instructions.

The Vice President's limousine rounded the corner, and he knew it was now or never. He glanced down the street, caught the eye of one of the kids, and nodded. He then turned his full attention to the speeding limousine, pulled his arm back and hurled the egg to where he knew the limousine was going to be in half a second.

His egg made direct contact with the roof, the small magnetized object hidden inside sticking instantly to the reinforced bulletproof limousine. As if on cue, a hail of eggs sailed from within the crowd. Most of them splattered all over the Vice President's limousine while others missed and smeared the pavement with their slimy residue.

The Metropolitan police, dispatched to monitor the protesters, sprang into action and barked orders at the young kids who were now dashing in all directions.

He spotted the lead officer making his way over to mister megaphone.

And him.

He stepped backwards and let the crowd envelope him as he stripped off his black leather jacket and quickly handed it to someone as he stepped past. "Here, hold this."

Just like a sheep, the man took the jacket that was thrust into his stomach.

Out of the corner of his eye, he watched the man look around confused for who had just shoved a jacket into his hands, but he had already disappeared into the crowd, and the man had barely seen him.

Chapter 12

Jacob Jordan hunched over the ruggedized clamshell of his Panasonic Toughbook. At only seventeen, he didn't feel the effects of such poor posture over an extended period of time, but the cold September wind whistled through every crack and crevice in the un-insulated downtown warehouse and bit into his fingertips as he typed furiously on the keyboard. He paused for a brief moment to flex his fingers and rub his hands together.

His peripheral vision was suddenly blotted out by a massive shape. "What's fuckin' taking so long?"

He glanced up at Henderson, whose six foot five, 260 pounds of pure muscle took up his entire view.

"I thought you said you were ready."

Through a series of well-placed bruises, Henderson had taught him that having an IQ of over 140 didn't mean you were smart. He quickly looked back at the monitor of his Toughbook and didn't make eye contact for his response. "The city upgraded the firmware on some of their traffic cameras last weekend. ARGUS can handle the reduced input, but I thought, while I had time, I could update the adaptive module and see if we can't talk to all the visual devices."

"What the fuck did you just say!?"

"I really wish you wouldn't use that kind of language around me."

"What!? What language? English? You want me speak in Russian? Vay nemnogaya derymo!"

"You're the little shit," he muttered under his breath.

Henderson responded with such fluid speed that, during a single blink of his eyes, he went from sitting with the Panasonic Toughbook on his lap to listening as the hardened magnesium alloy case clattered on the gray concrete floor of the warehouse, his feet dangling just below Henderson's knees.

"You wanna run that by me again, Sunshine?"

"Were supposed to be working together, Henderson."

"We are working together. My job is to keep you in line."

He could smell the tinge of alcohol on Henderson's breath and readied himself for another lesson. Just then, his micro receiver ear bud hissed to life.

"White Wolf to Red Wolf and Blue Wolf, come in."

He wondered if Wilkes understood the significance of naming him Blue Wolf and Henderson Red Wolf since, in military exercises, the red and blue teams were always adversaries.

"This is Red Wolf. Go ahead, White Wolf."

"Is Blue Wolf ready?"

He didn't answer right away, so Henderson, who still had him suspended by the lapels of his jacket, shook him a little giving him the look of, "you'd better respond."

"Uhh, yeah, I'm ready."

"Good. Everything is in place, and you should start getting a strong signal in about ten minutes."

"As soon as the signal is confirmed, I'll boot up the Blitzkrieg simulator and send out the mobile unit."

"Roger that. White Wolf out." With a final crack of static, the communication was severed.

"Hear that, you little turd, you need to be ready."

"I was good and ready before you picked me up with your Sasquatch hands."

And with that remark, Henderson let go. He landed clumsily, almost collapsing to his knees, but didn't want to give Henderson the satisfaction. Instead, he used the momentum to lean forward and collect the Panasonic Toughbook.

"You better not have broken this, or we're all screwed."

"I didn't break nothin'."

He flipped the Panasonic Toughbook over and was relieved to see the screen was still displaying the running program. As he ran the final diagnostic, he looked around the freezing cold warehouse, and his eyes settled on the back of his partner, the psychopathic killer, who was fiddling with something in a wooden crate.

Good.

Let him fiddle with whatever he wants to.

As long as he doesn't bother me.

This certainly wasn't the life he expected when he graduated in the top of his class from Tel Aviv University at age twelve. When the Interdisciplinary Center for Technological Analysis and Forecasting, the Israeli government's multidisciplinary think-tank, offered him a fully-funded scholarship to work for the Defense Advanced Research Projects Agency, known as DARPA, in the United States, he knew that Ha-Shem had finally shown favor on him, and all those hours spent in prayer at the shul had not been wasted.

A sharp sound brought him back to the present just as

Henderson swung around from the wooden crate and pulled back on the charging handle of his Heckler & Koch XM8 Compact Carbine. The loud snap of the charging handle returning to its original position echoed in the hollow metal corrugated warehouse. He only had a moment to notice that the 100-round drum magazine was already loaded when Henderson pointed the XM8 right at him and pulled the trigger.

Chapter 13

"Jesus!" Jacob was on his feet in an instant, and the Panasonic Toughbook once again clattered onto the concrete floor of the warehouse.

"Never heard a Jew pray to Jesus before." Henderson lowered the empty XM8 Compact Carbine and laughed. He stopped laughing and cocked his head a little as he looked at him. "Oh my god, did you just piss your pants?"

He didn't need to look down as he could feel the warmth running down his legs. "Fuck you, Henderson!"

Henderson laughed even harder.

"Fuck you!"

The Panasonic Toughbook lying face down on the floor emitted a sharp beep. Henderson immediately stopped laughing. The Toughbook beeped again.

"Pick it up, tough guy, or I'll use bullets next time."

For the second time in two minutes, he scooped up the Toughbook from the floor and was again relieved to see that it still functioned. Panasonic wasn't kidding when they said that these laptops were built to handle just about anything you could throw at them – or throw them at.

Henderson was instantly at his side as if nothing had just happened. "Is that the signal?"

He didn't look up but instead focused his full attention on the display. He thought about not answering, but knew that would only provoke the already overly violent Henderson. "Signals coming in strong. Open the rollup door."

"Are you ready to release the R/C car?"

"It's not a remote-controlled car. It's a fully autonomous ground mobile combat system with real-time adaptive decision-making."

"You control it with your computer, right?"

"I program in the parameters of its mission orders, yes."

"Then it's an R/C car."

"It's a six million dollar modern marvel in autonomous robotics."

"Then it's a fuckin' expensive R/C car."

"Just open the door."

"Are you giving me orders now, squirt?"

"I just want to get this over with and get away from you as quickly as possible."

"Finally, something we can agree on."

Henderson strolled over to the chain dangling in a loop next to the corrugated steel door. He grasped the chain in both hands and started working it hand over hand, slowly raising the rollup door like an ancient medieval castle gate being raised to release a dragon from the depths of the dungeon. That wasn't too far from the truth. He looked over at the quiet Audi Q7. It had been painted a jet-black color, aptly named Phantom Black Pearl, by the manufacturer.

A couple of swift keystrokes initiated the Linux command window enabling him to type the command strings that would be encrypted and transmitted to their dragon. He paused for a moment reviewing the dynamic dispatch cascading messages before softly depressing the enter key. Moments later, the twelve-cylinder diesel engine in the Audi Q7 roared to life.

He watched as the Deep Green computer system that filled the entire two front seats of the passenger compartment communicated in response with the protocols and commands being sent by his Panasonic Toughbook. He watched silently as one by one, Deep Green booted up the software agents it would employ during tonight's mission.

He watched as the Urban Reasoning and Geospatial Exploitation Technology (URGENT) program confirmed it was communicating with the Autonomous Real-Time Ground Ubiquitous Surveillance – Imaging System (ARGUS-IS). He was most proud of the add-on he had worked into the ARGUS that enabled it to connect directly to the District Department of Transportation traffic camera system. Independently, URGENT and ARGUS were scary smart computer programs, if smart was the word for it, but together, under the command of Deep Green, they gave the Audi Q7 something not available in any dealership. The factory-provided GPS told the Audi where it was, ARGUS told it where everything else was, and URGENT made it smart enough to get where it wanted to go without hitting anything that it didn't want to hit.

The final program booted up. This was the belle of the ball. The Real-Time Adversarial Intelligence and Decision-Making (RAID) software made the Audi intelligent. Without this program, none of the other programs, even in combination, could turn an SUV into a lethal targetable weapon. RAID made sure that they would be able to hit a moving target with precision accuracy.

He listened to the soft rumble coming from the SUV. It

was a much quieter sound than he expected from a six-liter V12 turbocharged direct injection diesel engine. He had already disabled the electronically-capped top speed of 155 mph, and with an engine producing 500 horsepower in such a large vehicle, this was something that no manufacturer of limousine armor had intended to come up against. To make matters worse, the remaining interior space of the Audi was filled with C-4 plastic explosives formed into shaped charges that would direct all their explosive force straight at whatever the Audi collided with.

The Audi Q7 V12 model was not available for sale in the United States, and it was sobering for him to think that the only one to travel the streets of Washington, DC would have such a limited run. He stared at the screen as Deep Green ran its final diagnostic checks.

A rattling thunk made him look up. Henderson was walking back from the open loading door. "Hurry up and release the beast." Henderson was enjoying this far too much. "We've got more to do tonight."

He hated being put in these situations; being forced to work with people like Henderson. But then again, somebody with his past had relatively few options.

The launch command waited in a separate window. Using the built-in Panasonic Toughbook's touchpad, he switched window controls. "Stand back." With his eyes closed, he pressed the enter key. The all-wheel drive of the Audi Q7 propelled its dragon out into the world to unleash its fiery destruction on an unsuspecting town.

Chapter 14

Andrew perched on the edge of the back seat and watched as the dimly lit buildings of Washington, DC at night blurred past the limousine window. He felt like he was standing still while the rest of the world was streaming by. When that first egg hit the top of the car, he almost jumped out of his skin. It had sounded so loud, like a gunshot. Then more followed, hitting the sides and the top. He was immediately pressed backwards into the soft leather seat by the sudden acceleration as the motorcade sped away from the scene.

Well, they got that part right. This meant that the rest, no matter how incredible it sounded, was most likely true. It was probably the most overused plot in low-budget sci-fi movies, but he knew that somewhere, out there in the night, there was an intelligent robotic killing machine looking for him. There was nothing left for him to do but sit back and wait.

Knowing that the end was drawing near, he naturally reflected on his life. But all he could focus on was the whirlwind year he was about to complete. Ten months ago, after the surgery, he learned the informal medical term "new lease on life." He set out to make his bucket list, the list of things he always wanted to do but never took the time. And now he finally had the time.

But when a sharp stabbing pain forced an emergency evacuation by helicopter from the peak of Half Dome in Yosemite, he learned a new medical term only six months into his "new life." Metastatic cancer. Not only had the cancer returned, it had returned with a vengeance.

And now, four months later, here he was.

Sitting in a limousine posing as the Vice President of the United States.

Waiting to die.

He reflexively winced through every intersection as the convoy of vehicles screamed through at high speed. At this hour, there was almost no traffic, and every cross street provided ample opportunity for a high-speed side-impact collision.

This was taking way too damn long.

He suddenly glanced up at the roof of the limousine. An overpowering desire to live washed over him. He knew why that first egg sounded so loud. Maybe he could reach it. Pull it off and throw it out into the street? There were other treatments he could try. He didn't have to die right now, did he?

He shook his head as his vision blurred slightly. He knew that this euphoric thinking was a direct result of the opiates in his system caused by the breakthrough pain medication.

Still, he had a lot to live for, didn't he?

Of course he did.

That settled it.

He leaned to his left and fingered the controls to roll down the back window. A strong wind immediately blew around inside the cabin of the limousine. They must've been traveling at least seventy miles an hour.

With the window rolled down all the way, he sat with his back to the window and reached up behind him to grip the door frame where it met the roof. With a single motion, he lifted himself up and out and sat down on the edge of the closed door. The wind threatened to pull him the rest of the way out of the limousine, and he splayed his legs on opposite sides of the door's interior to create an anchor for himself.

The wind buffeted him fiercely.

He squinted against the harsh conditions and scanned the roof of the limousine for what he knew must be there. And then he saw it. The tiny magnetic transponder sat just this side of dead center on the roof.

If he could just reach it, he could alter his fate.

Clamping his legs to the frame of the car, he pushed a little higher to give himself a longer reach. Flashing lights from his right drew his attention away from the tiny device. He glanced over at the Chevy Suburban filled with Secret Service agents. They were frantically flashing their headlights at him.

What did they think that would achieve?

Did they think he didn't know what he was doing?

He returned his full attention back to the device that sat, mockingly, just out of reach. Losing leverage but gaining more reach, he pushed up ever so slightly with his legs.

Just a little further.

He almost toppled out of the limousine when a motorcycle officer appeared on the opposite side, right into his field of view. The loud roar of the wind rushing past at over seventy miles an hour made it almost impossible to hear the officer, but not quite. "Get back in the car!"

With his left arm splayed forward on the roof to provide

additional stability, he made one final push and gripped the tiny object with his fingertips. A second motorcycle officer joined the first, and they took turns hollering questions and commands at him. He tugged at the device. It resisted slightly before releasing its magnetic grip and came free into his fingers.

He had done it!

He waved the device in front of him showing it to the two motorcycle officers with a big smile on his face. "I got it!"

And then his face fell as he looked past the two motorcycle officers to see the blurred grill of an SUV heading straight for them at impossible speed.

As soon as the Audi Q7's bumper made contact with the second motorcycle, the collision detectors triggered the shaped C-4 charges, which focused all of their explosive power directly at the limousine right in front of it.

It happened so quickly that he never even felt the end of his life.

Chapter 15

The wrought iron gates started to close immediately after Representative Hartford's armored limousine sped through them. His driver guided the stretch Cadillac DeVille Touring Sedan down the empty streets of Washington, DC.

As soon as he had received the call from Hannah, not just any call but "the" call, he knew he couldn't be the man she wanted him to be. He immediately called his chauffeur and demanded to be driven to his estate in Pennsylvania. He had always paid his staff very well. He also insisted that everyone who worked for him live in the lower floors of his apartment building.

Half an hour after the call, he was speeding through the empty streets of the nation's capital, the bottle of whisky he took with him now nearly empty. The combination of light traffic along with the red and blue flashing emergency lights built into the grill of the modified limousine meant the driver would complete the hundred and fifteen mile trip in just a little over an hour.

Ten miles from his apartment, however, the driver slowed the limousine and lowered the tinted partition. "Someone's blocking the road, sir."

Sitting in the driver's seat of the street legal variant of the robotic Audi Q7, Henderson slipped the tactical sling of his Heckler & Koch XM8 Compact Carbine over his head. "Unlock his doors, Jake."

"It's Jacob, never Jake."

"Whatever, piss ant, just do it."

And with that, Henderson slid out of the Audi Q7 Quattro SUV.

When microprocessors were first produced in the early 1970s, a short-range wireless system was integrated into the low level design during original conception. Since the technology was unknown to all but a select few, it was widely accepted by the engineers as part of the fundamental requirements of a microprocessor. And now thirty years later, anything that used a microprocessor, which was practically everything, had a dormant wireless back door just waiting for the proper activation code.

And Hannah had provided that code to Jacob.

During the armored limousine's customization process, everything about the Cadillac DTS was enhanced, modified or replaced, including the electronics. But it didn't matter. The original car manufacturer's embedded electronics would have granted him access.

His hands flew over the keyboard of his Panasonic Toughbook as he remotely accessed the computer in the limousine that supplied virtual processors for the cruise control, the air-conditioning and the door locks.

Hartford watched through the windshield as someone approached the limousine before the figure disappeared along the tinted side windows. What could only be described as an assault rifle was in the hands of the man who walked towards him at the back of the limo.

But he was not worried. Nothing short of a rocket-propelled grenade would be able to open the door he was sitting next to.

Suddenly the door locks popped up, the door immediately swung open, and the assault rifle pointed right at him.

"Hello, Mr. Speaker."

"What do you want?"

"I already have everything I want." The man holding the assault rifle leaned down to look into the limousine and smiled. "Hannah has seen to that."

He lowered the assault rifle, sat down next to him and closed the door. "But we would like to borrow your house for a while."

"What do you need my house for?"

"I have a very special houseguest, but I don't have a house." The man turned and looked him directly in the eyes. "Hannah said we could borrow yours."

And with that, the man swiftly exited the limousine and strode back to his own car. He watched as the SUV backed up off of the road to let them pass. He shivered with the dreadful knowledge that he could never hide from her.

After the call, his first thought was to escape to his Pennsylvania estate and give himself time to figure out how to sever all ties to her. Politics was a game played much like chess, and he had always considered himself to be a skillful player, when he was sober. But as the headlights from the SUV shown through the back window of the limousine as they drove north towards his estate, he realized he was not a player but just a piece on the board. And not one of the good pieces like the king or bishop or even a rook, he realized he was nothing but a lowly pawn.

And with Hannah as the grandmaster, he had no free will.

And with her playing such a strong game, who was she playing against?

And who were the other players on the board?

Chapter 16

Robert Brubaker sat at the massive mahogany desk in the Presidential Emergency Operations Center buried deep underground below the East Wing of the White House. It had been almost an hour since the attack on the Vice President's limo, and everyone of importance in Washington, DC had been awakened by the Secret Service and shuffled, in various states of undress, into massive underground bunkers all up and down the East Coast.

Even the President himself had been whisked swiftly away from Camp David and flown six miles northeast to the Raven Rock Mountain Complex known simply as Site R. With the President safely secured at another underground facility over a hundred miles away, he took full advantage of the situation and sat at the President's desk.

He had no desire to become the next President of the United States because he already held the most coveted position in the world.

He was the voice of the President of the United States.

Known by everyone as The Scribe, he had written six of the last eight speeches given by the President. Through his careful wordsmithing, and his uncanny ability to craft a speech that always pulled on the heartstrings of the American heartland, he single-handedly had done more to bolster public confidence in the current administration than anyone else in the last fifty years.

And now he had less than six hours to craft what would most likely be the most important speech of the President's term in office. He had to write the words that would not only tell the world that the Vice President was the latest victim of a brutal terrorist attack, but he also had to make it sound like the President and his administration were still in control.

Despite the tragic loss of the Vice President, it was his job – no, his mission to put the precise words into the mouth of the President that would make the people of the United States feel both safe in their own homes and confident that those responsible would quickly be brought to justice.

His finger pressed and held down the backspace key as he realized it was time to take this speech in a different direction, yet again. Without even remembering whose desk he was sitting at, he snatched up the phone after the first ring.

"Brubaker."

"It's a good thing I know the President is currently at Site R, or I would've thought I'd dialed a wrong number."

Every hair on his body simultaneously stood at attention as he immediately recognized who the caller was, or at least what she represented, and reached over to push the trace button built into the side of the phone.

"You and I both know I can never be traced."

He glanced left and right quickly. *She couldn't possibly see me.*

"I know what you're thinking. And despite your security team's assurances to the contrary, I can see you."

"What do you want, Hannah?" he replied through gritted teeth. If the country knew, hell, if anyone knew about the influence the soft melodic voice on the other side of this phone had with the President of the United States, the entire world would collapse into anarchy.

He had accidentally discovered the President's best-kept secret only three years ago. He had been putting the final touches on a speech the President had scheduled for the United Nations Counter-Terrorism Conference when he answered the President's private line in the small private study adjacent to the Oval Office. What he had witnessed over the next several months was permanently etched into his memory.

Hannah was someone you never forgot.

"I'm pleased to see you remember me."

Even though the voice on the phone sounded female, he knew the name of the caller was not one selected by chance. Being the President's speech writer, it was his job to know the right word to say at any given moment. But he also prided himself on knowing the history of words. It's what made him the best wordsmith this country had ever seen, even though they didn't know it. And it gave him a unique perspective when he first came in contact with the person who went by the name of Hannah. He didn't know why, but he had instantly remembered that the word "Hannah" was also the second part of the Latin name for the King Cobra, Ophiophagus Hannah.

The first word, Ophiophagus, literally meant "snake-eater". A fitting name since the King Cobra's diet primarily consisted of other snakes.

And he had watched men, men who felt that they were at the top of their game, both personally and politically, be completely consumed and destroyed by the resources at the disposal of the voice that only referred to herself as Hannah. She truly was an eater of snakes.

He would never forget her.

"What do you want?"

"I wanted to let you know that the speech you're writing is not entirely accurate. If you'll allow me…"

The computer emitted a single beep, and he watched as new text filled the screen.

"My fellow Americans."

"I've always wanted to see the great Alan Sparks say that, but feel free to edit to fit his style."

"Last night terrorists took bold action against one of the most powerful nations in the world. I sincerely believe that it was their intent to plunge this nation into chaos by killing the Vice President of the United States. Let me assure you that despite everything you've heard on every news channel worldwide, the terrorists did not succeed."

He stared at the screen not fully understanding what he was reading. The initial shock of her ability to control his computer gave way as he continued to read the text as it filled the screen.

"Let me remind you that the war on terror is still a war and, as such, certain decisions, hard decisions, have to be made. Last night's attempt on the Vice President did not happen because we did not know about it.

"I am hesitant to admit that not only did I know about the impending attack, but I was willing to let it happen. I want to assure the American people that while we had the resources and the time to prevent this brutal attack in the nation's capital, it was necessary to allow the terrorists to think that they had succeeded long enough for us to root them out.

"And root them out we did.

"While they thought we were scrambling to deal with the death of one of our own, they let their guard down, and we were able to successfully eliminate four terrorist cells that had been deeply embedded within the borders of the forty-eight contiguous states before the sun even came up this morning."

He stared at the screen. What game was she playing by typing out all these lies?

"None of this is true."

"Would you like it to be?"

"Even you can't turn back the hands of time."

"I don't have to. The sun doesn't come up for another five hours. More than enough time to pick up the Vice President —"

"The world will not be fooled by someone who looks like the Vice President."

"Please don't interrupt me, Robert. Not only do I have the Vice President, the real Vice President, safe and sound, but I also have Hartford, the Speaker of the House of Representatives. You will also receive the locations of four terrorist cells operating within the borders of the United States, and, as an added bonus, I will provide you the name of the man in your own government who paid for the assassination attempt."

"Now I know you're lying."

"Don't be so naïve, Robert, I would never make such a

claim without proof."

His mind churned at the speed of thought as he contemplated everything that she was telling him. She now had control of almost the entire top tier of the presidential line of succession. And if everything else she was telling him was true, then tonight's attack was not a terrorist act. Her involvement meant that it was something more.

He had seen how she operated in the past and knew that nothing was ever offered for free.

"So how much do you want for the safe return of the Vice President and the Speaker?"

She chuckled softly. "How well you know me and how little you know me all at the same time. Your precious line of succession and the four terrorist cells I give to you for free. It's the identity of the traitor within your midst that comes with a price tag."

"And how much is that going to cost?"

"All I want is a signature."

He was almost afraid to ask. "Whose signature?"

He knew the answer before she had even uttered it. "Why, the President's, of course."

Chapter 17

Samuel Clarke, the Assistant to the President for National Security Affairs, glanced again at the single-page security briefs. They were scattered around in front of him at the massive conference table in the White House Situation Room located in the basement of the West Wing. Unfortunately, they held no information as to who was behind the attack on the Vice President.

He looked around at the other members of the Executive Office of the President seated around the conference table before looking back at the large LCD wall monitor that held the image of the President.

Samuel continued his briefing to the President.

"The NSA is reviewing everything again, but let me reiterate that there was no increase in chatter leading up to the attack tonight from any of the monitoring stations."

President Alan Sparks' image on the monitor could have been his picture with how little he moved or blinked. His brow crinkled right before he spoke. "Has anyone claimed responsibility for this, yet?"

"No sir."

"Maybe they haven't heard about it."

"They've heard about it. Within fifteen minutes of the attack, every single group we monitor worldwide started spreading the word. It's like they were all competing to be the first ones to tell the others. I don't think any of them knew this was going to happen."

"And still no one is taking responsibility?"

"I think it goes beyond that. It's almost as if they are afraid to take responsibility for this one."

"What do you mean by that, Sam?"

"Immediately after any major attack, several of the usual suspects scramble to be the first to claim responsibility. And almost just as quickly we start getting chatter from several other groups trying to put together subsequent copycat strikes. But not this time, sir. As far as I can tell, they are all burrowing into their little holes and waiting this one out."

The President's brow creased even further. "What is your hypothesis, Sam?"

"If you'll excuse my comparison, sir, but I recently went to that Walking with Dinosaurs show with my son, and something they said seems to fit this scenario very well."

"Oh, my god…" Bruce Cutler, Director of the Homeland Security Council, slammed his fist down on the conference table to add an exclamation point to his outburst. "I am not going to sit here and listen to him talk about some show he went to with his son while our nation is under attack."

"Bruce," the President interrupted. "You will be given a chance to speak."

"With all due respect, Mr. President."

"Shut up, Bruce! If Sam thinks it's important to say, then by god I want to hear it."

Sam pushed his horn-rimmed glasses that had slid slightly down his nose back into position. "Thank you, Mr. President. As I was saying, during that show they brought out predators that had existed during the Jurassic era, but mentioned that when the granddaddy of all predators, the

Tyrannosaurus Rex, showed up, all the other predators would disappear. No one challenged the Tyrannosaurus Rex."

The Director of Homeland Security shuffled noisily in his seat. "Is there a point to all this?"

The President also shifted nervously on the screen. "If you could please just say what you need to say, Sam."

Sam slowly glanced around at all the faces in the room before settling back to the video display of the President staring back at him from the wall.

"I think what we're dealing with here is a super predator."

Bruce Cutler stood up. "This is ridiculous! We should be figuring out exactly who did this and not waste the President's time talking about dinosaurs."

"Every terrorist organization we know about is dropping off the radar. All chatter has come to a standstill. These are people who fear nothing, not even death itself, and they are terrified. If we can all admit that in the world of international politics they are the predators, then what are they hiding from?"

If it weren't for the silence that responded to the NSA's question, the faint knock at the door behind the President would have been missed. The door opened immediately without waiting for an answer.

The President of the United States swiveled slightly in his chair to face the petite blonde girl who had just opened the door. "I gave explicit instructions that this meeting was not to be disturbed."

The mousy intern cringed slightly at the admonishment

before she responded. "I'm sorry, sir."

She hesitated and gripped the edge of the door, unwilling to speak further.

"What is it, Allison?"

"Robert Brubaker is on line two."

"I don't care who it is. I want all my calls held until I tell you otherwise."

"I told him that, sir, but…"

She stood there, her neatly manicured nails practically digging into the wood of the door.

"Out with it, Allison!"

"Hannah called him."

The President swung back to face the group of his most trusted advisers. "I believe we have located your super predator, Sam. Meeting adjourned."

And with that, the screen went black before being immediately replaced by the Seal of the President of the United States.

Chapter 18

Within milliseconds of the send button being pressed on the pre-paid disposable cell phone, a brilliant neon blue LED flickered to life on one of the stacked row of servers located at the National Security Analysis Center in Fort Meade, Maryland. The solid blue light was the only indication that the FBI's Digital Collection System Network surveillance software program, code-named Digital Storm, started recording before the secure and encrypted landline even started ringing.

The call was answered after only one ring, and Digital Storm was ready to capture every word and every syllable with crystal clarity.

A female voice was logged as coming from an encrypted landline. The call was instantly flagged for priority review for taking place on an unregistered landline. "Excellent work."

A male voice responded from a disposable cell phone that showed its last known registered owner as a store in Washington, DC that sold the phone over the counter for cash. "My team is ready for the next target."

"Disband the team. You will handle the next target alone."

"I need my team to get the President."

The $75 million voice recognition software flagged this file for immediate review at the mention of the word "President."

"He will be taken care of another way. What I am

concerned about is the resolve of our President-to-be. Keep this phone with you. I will contact you again with further instructions."

And with that, the line was disconnected.

Right before the line went completely dead, the secure landline transmitted a set of high-pitched tones in rapid succession. Digital Storm interpreted the tones as programming instructions. Immediately, the recorded file was erased, and that sector of the hard drive was set to accept the next recording of any call, thus obliterating any recoverable data from the call.

There would be no evidence that the conversation ever took place.

Chapter 19

In the brilliant afternoon sun, the Global Express jet's wheels hit the ground at LaGuardia Airport with a squeal. The plane bounced once and settled firmly back down onto the pavement. The engines reversed their thrust and forced the occupants forward into their seat belts as the jet slowed on the runway.

Melissa glanced over her shoulder at Denny. He wasn't wincing as much from the cracked rib. He had downed dangerous amounts of painkillers she had taken from the drug store to ease the pain. He would be fine as long as he didn't get into any barroom brawls for the next six weeks. He looked in her direction, and their eyes met. He smiled. She smiled back and turned to look out the window at the New York skyline.

They hadn't spoken much since the attack at his place. He had slept most of the night away anyway. She didn't know how much longer she had before the questions started. His current silence gave her a little more time to figure out how much of the truth she was willing to include in her answers.

The jet slowed to a full stop, and the lights went back on in the cabin. The door slid open, and the stairs lowered into place. The doorway darkened slightly and then Nick stepped through the threshold and back into her life.

She followed Nick and Denny down the stairs and into Nick's waiting car.

It took them nearly forty-five minutes to fight through

the oppressive New York traffic before Nick turned into what looked like a back alley bordered on both sides by graffiti-covered and dilapidated warehouses all huddled together uncomfortably under the imposing presence of the Manhattan Bridge. With the engine running, Nick hopped out and fiddled with a massive padlock that clung to the side of a metal sliding door before it rattled upward to disappear into the building.

He hopped back into the car and smiled at her. "Home, sweet home."

She looked into the dark opening of the warehouse. There were no lights on inside, and with the sun almost completely set, she couldn't see more than ten feet into the void of the warehouse. He pulled the car over the bump of the threshold and stopped a few feet inside. She heard the metal doors rattle behind her as they dropped back to the ground and plunged them into complete darkness.

Chapter 20

Overhead lights flickered into existence, and Melissa blinked at the sudden brightness. She looked outside the car at the plastic and metal cases stacked throughout the warehouse. She saw electronic equipment set up along a table. Nick had definitely been planning something for a long time.

He walked over to the car from the large switch next to the rolling doors he had just closed.

"Welcome to the bat cave." His voice echoed against the steel wall construction.

Denny climbed out of the car with a grunt. He would need another handful of painkillers soon. She stepped out of the car and looked around. The bat cave was certainly an appropriate description. There were computer stations all around one side of the warehouse. Behind a locked cage on the other side were weapons of all shapes and sizes and pallets of ammunition stacked six feet high.

Nick came around the car and stood next to her.

"Every weapon in my arsenal is chambered for either the standard 9mm or the 5.56mm NATO round," he said. "I needed to be sure I was never caught with my pants down."

"Is there a restroom in here somewhere?" Denny asked.

He pointed to a small door along the back wall. "Right through there."

"Thanks."

Denny limped away.

He turned to her and a smile spread across his face. "I

have something for you. Come with me."

He led her over to the locked cage area and extracted a key from his pocket. He twisted the key in the lock and slid the gate open along its runners.

He disappeared amongst the crates stacked to the ceiling of the ten-foot cage. He quickly returned with a small wooden box slightly larger than a cigar box but just as ornately designed.

"You asked me to dispose of this, but I couldn't bring myself to do it."

He smiled as he lifted the lid and showed her the contents.

Inside was her SIG-Sauer P226 X-Five. This was the second most accurate pistol ever designed by the Schweizerische Industrie Gesellschaft, the Swiss Industrial Council. The exceptional accuracy of the X-Five combined with her training and the 19-round 9mm magazine made her one powerful force. Back when she practiced daily, she could hit her intended target with a sub-1 inch 5-shot grouping from 25 meters.

Her eyes misted over as she looked up at him.

"Go ahead, she's all yours," he said.

She lifted the P226 out of the velvet pillow that held it in place. The X-Five settled into her grip like an old friend. She inspected every centimeter of the pistol like a lover reacquainting herself with a long lost partner. She ejected the magazine and popped the final round in a fluid motion. She sighted down the barrel. Something was different.

"I threaded it to accept a silencer," he remarked. "I didn't think you would mind."

She smiled. He handed her the sound-suppressor, and she twisted it onto the end of the SIG-Sauer P226. It made the already menacing gun even more threatening. Despite the reduction in muzzle velocity and the potential for hindering the accuracy, the silencer created a psychological effect on the enemy that far outweighed any performance limitations.

A sudden realization dawned and her smile faded. "You were expecting me back?"

He smiled. "I always expected you to come back. Just not this way."

She held the pistol backwards out to him. "I can't accept it."

He didn't even try to reach for it. "There's nothing to accept. It was yours to begin with. Keep it, you might need it."

"For what?"

"For whatever caused you to call me in the middle of the night after three years of silence."

She didn't know how to respond, but it was Denny who limped over and finally broke the awkward silence.

"The medication is wearing off, and I can think a little more clearly now. It's time we talk about what happened back at my house."

She held her hands up.

"I don't really have an answer for you."

"Let's start with the guy who did this to me." Denny motioned to the cuts on his face and the light bruising.

"I don't know."

"He tortured me, and all he wanted was the combination

to the gun safe. His MP5 was worth ten times anything in my safe. Why is that all he wanted from me?"

"I don't know."

"Then what do you know?!"

She started to say something, then her shoulders dropped. "I don't know."

Nick moved in closer and produced another warm smile.

"I think I can help here."

Chapter 21

Melissa nodded to Nick and lowered her head. He turned to Denny.

"Three years ago, Melissa and I…"

"Who's Melissa?"

She looked at Denny. "I am."

He cocked his head to the side. "You told me your name was Karen."

She started to speak when Nick cut her off.

"Let me. We both upset some very powerful people a few years ago who, if they found either of us, we would be dead. Melissa changed her name and moved to the West Coast while I made preparations for the inevitable 'final battle', if you will."

She turned to Denny. "I couldn't tell you the truth, even after we started dating. It would have put you in danger."

He laughed, then cringed from the pain. "That didn't work out too well, did it?"

Her shoulders dropped again. "Not quite."

"So you know who did this?"

She responded. "I have an idea, but no way of knowing where they are or when they'll strike next."

"We're a thousand miles from Oregon. They can't possibly have followed us all this way."

Nick interrupted. "Actually, you flew right to where 'they' are."

"What?! Why?"

She touched Denny lightly on the arm.

"I thought I could hide, but that is clearly not possible. Not from them."

"Who are 'they'?"

Nick perked up. "That is where I think we may be able to gain the upper hand."

Chapter 22

"Every communication, whether it's a phone call, a text or even an email has been recorded and stored in the FBI's Digital Storm database."

Denny laughed. "That's ridiculous. The FBI couldn't possibly record and keep every phone call made."

Nick wasn't laughing. "They can, and they have."

Denny looked at Melissa. "You didn't tell me your friend here was a conspiracy nut."

"Denny, listen to Nick."

He held his hands up. "Okay."

Nick continued as if he had never been interrupted. "Whoever sent someone to kill you had to communicate electronically in order to do so. All we have to do is access the FBI database and find anything that references you or your location on or about the day of the attack."

Denny interrupted again. "Even if we had the resources and capability to do so, shouldn't we be breaking into the FBI if we want to hack their system?"

Nick smiled. "Even though the bulk of the FBI's surveillance system is in Virginia, they still have distributed hubs to keep someone from taking out the entire system by attacking the one location everyone knows about. The hub we are going after is right here in Manhattan."

He clicked the mouse, and the Google map zoomed in to a gleaming glass building in the center of the Manhattan financial district.

"The first ten floors are leased out to legitimate

businesses. It gives the appearance that nothing unusual is taking place. Where we want to go is not up, but down. This is the only building in Manhattan that goes down about ten stories underground. The room we want is halfway down on the fifth underground level. The only access to the underground section is with a single elevator that starts from the second floor lobby."

He turned to Denny. "I think you should be the one to go inside."

Denny's eyes widened. "Me?"

Melissa reacted instantly. "Hold up, Denny is not involved in this."

Nick was insistent. "Of the three of us in this room, Denny is the only one that is the unknown."

She leaned in to Nick. "I will not let you risk his life…"

Denny sat up straighter in the plastic chair. "Karen… Melissa…I'm already involved. I mean, look at me, for chrissake. I want to help. If I can help stop whoever is trying to kill you, kill us, then I want in."

She frowned. "You don't have to do this, Denny."

He smiled at her. "I know. I want to. I was in the Navy for four years after high school. 'See the world,' they said. All I ever saw was the walls around my bunk and the dials and knobs of the engine room. They did teach me how to shoot a gun and take orders. If he can talk me through what I need to do, I'm all for it."

She looked back to Nick.

"Think of some other way. Denny's never trained for anything like this."

Nick gave her a reassuring smile.

"We send him in and within half an hour he'll be back out. The interior of the underground facility is not that heavily guarded. Once he's inside, it's a cakewalk."

She looked back and forth from Denny to Nick and regarded them both. Denny looked ready for anything. It always amazed her how quickly Nick could get anyone ready to follow his orders straight into whatever hell he had planned. He could read people like an open book. If he felt that Denny was capable of helping them, then she would trust that he knew what he was doing.

"So what's the plan?"

His energy increased. He always got excited when he detailed a plan. It was part of what made people ready to follow him into the depths of hell on a moment's notice.

He leaned forward and spun around the piece of paper in front of him. She leaned forward and looked at the hand-drawn map of floor plans for an office building.

"This is my best guess as to how the lower levels are laid out. Denny will enter the building here. He will climb these stairs to the second level of the lobby where he will have to pass some pretty tight security. He will be wired with an audio and video transmitter. I will be outside in a van and can see what he sees and communicate with him. You will be in position here in the lobby ready to move fast in case something goes wrong."

"What could go wrong?" she asked.

"I have prepared for every contingency I can think of. Nothing should go wrong. I can hack the system and set him up with an ID to get him past security. If everything goes smoothly, he will get in. The ID won't stand up to too much scrutiny, so let's hope the guard is lazy.

"As soon as the security guard clears you, he will ask for you to enter in the access code on the keypad at his desk. The code will error immediately if they have changed the algorithm that defines the password. If that happens, he will abort and get out of there as fast as he can. If things go south, Melissa will help get you out of there. If everything goes as planned, he will enter the elevator unchallenged. At that moment I will lose the video feed as he goes underground."

Nick stopped his speech and looked at Denny.

"Are you sure you are up for this? Once you are inside that elevator, our direct support drops off, and you will complete the rest of the mission alone."

Denny paused for only a moment before responding.

"You do not have to do this," she spoke up. "Nick can come up with something else if you don't think you are…"

"We would lose the element of surprise if we change the plan now," Nick cut in.

She shot Nick a glance. The warning she gave was not mistaken for anything other than what it was. She pointed to the other side of the warehouse.

"Can I talk to you over there?"

He dropped his shoulders. As powerful as he was, and with the influence he carried, it always took everything he had to get her to buy into one of his plans. She had always wanted to cover every base before running into the line of fire. He stood up and headed away to another section of the warehouse. She waited until Nick was out of earshot. She looked at Denny.

"You are under no obligation to do this."

"When I was discharged from the service, I had nowhere to go and ended up back at home with a dead-end job and nothing to live for. And then I met you. If doing what this guy says might keep you safe, I'm going to do it. Despite not knowing who you really are, I have spent enough time around you to know you're somebody worth hanging on to."

"There will be no hero's parade for you. This operation is so completely under the radar, only the three of us know about it."

"I don't need a cheering crowd to tell me when I'm doing something right."

She got up before he could respond and moved quickly into the back of the warehouse to where Nick waited patiently for her.

"Who the hell do you think you are? This is not some mission with a highly trained team at your disposal. Denny is a regular guy. He's not like us. He never saw action in the Navy. He was a maintenance engineer on an aircraft carrier. He has never had to make that split-second decision to pull the trigger on another human life. He is not ready for this."

He waited until she had said her piece before he responded.

"Denny says he's ready. And I think he saw more action in the Navy than he's admitting to you."

"He just got the stuffing beat out of him by an assassin. He's physically not ready for this. Look at him. Even I feel the pain every time he moves."

"He is performing a simple task…"

"Give me a break, Nick, you could talk an Antarctic expedition into bringing along an ice machine. He's not making his own choice here. You are giving every red-blooded American boy his wildest fantasy. Become a super spy. He's not living in the real world right now. He's living out a Mission Impossible movie, and you have him thinking he's Tom Cruise. This isn't a movie, and he's not Tom Cruise. Does he even understand how dangerous this simple task of yours will become if he gets caught? I was a highly trained killing machine in top physical and mental condition, and I still almost died three years ago. You are sending a civilian deep into enemy territory."

"Denny is not a civilian."

Damn his disarming nature. This gave her an even bigger reason to stop Denny from following Nick into certain death.

"He was in the god damn Navy fifteen years ago. He might as well have watched Top Gun four hundred times with what he still remembers about those days. Stop feeding him the glitz and glamour of your life. We both know it's the farthest from the truth you can get. Look at him. He needs a morphine drip just to move around. What possible benefit can you get from including him in this plan?"

"Are you done?" Nick said.

She dropped her head. He hadn't listened to anything she just said.

"I have reduced the risk considerably," he said. "I know that sending in someone like Denny could seriously jeopardize this operation, but we don't have much of a choice. He has the greatest chance of getting through security. They use thermal imaging cameras. You can change your appearance, but only plastic surgery can alter your bone structure. You or I would be stopped before we even entered the elevator. We need to do better than that. Denny is our only chance. But moving around in the underground section is only part of the problem. We also have to track the guards' movements. That is where I will need your special skills, Melissa. I need you to plant tracking devices on the guards that I point out to you."

She nodded. Nick was a master tactician, and if he put together a plan, it always worked out. If it weren't for him, she would have died years ago.

She sighed heavily. "When do we go in?"

"First thing in the morning."

Chapter 23

Melissa stared into the darkness at the ceiling. Despite several attempts at counting sheep and many other tricks learned during her time in the service, she was still awake. She finally sat up and looked at the clock. It was just after three o'clock in the morning. She swung her legs over the edge of what was called a port-a-bed and slipped her shoes on. She needed to take a walk outside to clear her head from the memories that kept clawing their way to the surface.

She crept silently past the other two offices where Denny and Nick were sound asleep. The painkillers had put Denny into a deeper sleep than normal, and he snored loudly.

She was on the sidewalk in a matter of minutes and turned around the corner. New York was a different kind of place. The city that never slept, they said. And they were right. After only a couple of blocks, she sensed she was not alone.

Her long dormant training kicked in, and she picked up the pace of her walk. She started making turns down more streets than she cared to count. She did, however, keep count since she wanted to be sure that she made it back to the warehouse. Four years in the jungles of South America enhanced her navigational skills. If she could find her way through those dense jungles without getting lost, she could easily navigate the concrete jungle of New York.

She rounded the corner and saw a neon sign that lit up the street above a single canopy that cast a shadow over the only door along the long, and graffiti-tagged wall. She had found what she was looking for. She broke into a fast sprint towards the seedy downtown bar. She stopped just before the door and looked around. Across the street, a tiny indentation between the buildings housed a large dumpster. She darted across the street and squeezed in next to the dumpster.

Moments later, she saw her shadow round the corner and cross the street. The gait of the walk told her the shadow was a man. Whoever was following her was good, but not better than her. The shadow looked up the street as he crossed. He paused at the other side and began to walk down the street. His focus was on the bar, just as she had intended. She lost sight of him briefly. She wondered if he had continued on and was about to crawl out of her hiding spot when he appeared right in front of her and slid into the shadows next to the dumpster.

At her feet were several bottles that had missed the dumpster for one reason or another. She quietly slid one off the ground that was still fully intact as she silently cursed herself for leaving her SIG P226 back at the warehouse. The bottle neck would have to stand in for a gun barrel on this one.

Her shadow stood without moving a single muscle. If she had gone into the bar, she would never have seen him standing there in the darkness next to the dumpster, even if she knew where to look.

She jammed the bottle into her shadow's back and hooked an arm around his neck to bend him slightly backwards in a single-practiced move.

"One peep and it will be your last," she hissed as she

pulled him farther back behind the dumpster.

She slammed her catch of the day face first into the wall and kept the bottle pressed into the small of his back. A quick search revealed that he had no weapons, but he did have a small tactical flashlight. She spun him around and switched the flashlight on.

She shone the flashlight right onto the face of her shadow.

"Hey, watch the retinas," Nick complained.

She lowered the flashlight and released her grip on the collar of his coat.

"Why the hell are you following me?"

"Why the hell are you hiding from me?"

"I'm not. I just needed to get some fresh air," she said.

"At three o'clock in the morning?" he replied.

"I couldn't sleep," she admitted. "I'm too wound up about tomorrow."

"You'll be fine," he said. "Besides, Denny's doing all the heavy lifting."

"That's what worries me. He's not up for this."

He chuckled and placed his hands on her shoulders.

"This is a simple recon mission. No guns. No glory. Just get in and get out. Zero body count is the rule. The fun comes later."

Down the street, a van pulled up to the curb at the end of the street. Someone leaned out of the open door, dumped a large package on the corner, and then sped off.

He turned her.

"I've kept you a little isolated about what's going on all around us. Let me show you."

He pulled the KA-BAR from its sheath above his left boot. He held out the seven-inch fighting and utility knife used by the U.S. Marines ever since World War II, handle first, out to her. "Take a look at this morning's headlines."

She silently kicked herself for having missed it during her hasty search and took it from him.

The mixture of the carbon and low chromium steel allowed the blade to hold an edge very well. The matte black finish on the blade did not reflect any light as it sliced easily through the heavy twine around the bundle. The large bundle relaxed and expanded slightly after the twine was severed. She pulled the top copy of the Early Edition of the New York Times off the stack.

She stared at the bold black letters at the top of the newspaper that stated, "Nation Waits for News of Vice President".

She looked back up at him.

"There was an attack on the Vice President's motorcade the same night you called me."

"Do you think that this has anything to do with why someone wants to kill me?"

"We will find out tomorrow. I promise." He gave her a warm smile and crooked his arm.

She folded the newspaper under her left arm and hooked her right arm through his offered arm. They walked back to the warehouse in silence. Anyone who took the time to look in their direction saw a typical New York couple out for a late-night stroll. Or early morning, depending on how you look at it.

It never mattered in a city that never slept.

Chapter 24

The sun rose silently in the east over a peaceful Pennsylvania countryside. Hartford had not slept at all last night and still paced nervously around the front room of his estate. He still wore the same suit he ran from his apartment in. The only addition was a dull mustard stain on the lapel from the sandwich he made just before sunrise. The mustard had dripped unnoticed onto his coat after only the second bite. The other half of the sandwich sat untouched on the plate at the edge of his desk.

He had called his daughter's phone number all night at half-hour intervals. He even called the operator in the Vermont area to see if there were any troubles with the lines. He feared what might be keeping her from answering.

He tried to reassure himself that there was a logical explanation. She must have taken a weekend trip somewhere and left a day early. That was it. She could do that since she only worked part time at the college. He sat down somewhat relieved at the thought it could be something that simple.

After all, since her divorce, Samantha was trying to live a regular life. And regular people often went away for the weekend. That had to be it.

He looked around his room, which was in a shambles. He had been up all night looking for a tiny slip of paper, which held the number to someone who could save him and the Vice President.

He cursed himself for being so absentminded and

forgetting where he had hidden the piece of paper. And he cursed himself for being foolish enough to think that after three years, the promise of help would still be available.

But despite all his thoughts of failure, he continued to look.

Chapter 25

Melissa sat on the small folding cot that served as her bed in the upstairs office. Nick and Denny were downstairs on the other side of the warehouse going over the floor plan of the lower levels of their target building, or at least the best as Nick could determine from hacking into local city planning databases.

She heard the echo of footsteps on the metal stairs moments before the door opened and Denny walked in. His face was no longer swollen, and the makeup she had applied would hide the bruising from anything but close scrutiny.

"Nick says it's time to go."

She looked at him for a brief moment and then decided she had to ask.

"Why are you doing this, Denny?"

He stared at her for a moment, his hand still on the door.

"To be honest, I don't really know. I just feel that it's the right thing to do."

"I don't feel comfortable with you putting yourself in danger like this."

"Nick said I won't be in any danger. I probably won't even see anyone while I'm there."

"Nick can't plan for everything."

"I can take care of myself. I'm a big boy."

She smiled. "I don't doubt that."

He was determined to do this. She didn't doubt that Nick always managed to get people to buy into his schemes on a daily basis. Some things never changed.

"If it goes bad, I won't let anything happen to you."

It was his turn to smile. "I don't know what scares me more, that you mean that or that you can actually deliver on that promise."

She stood and walked up to him and looked him in the eyes. "When this is all over, you and I will have a heart-to-heart talk. There are things about me you don't know."

He started to open his mouth, but she put a finger on his lips.

"There are things about me that even Nick doesn't know. Things I'm not proud of, but they made me what I am. After you know everything about me, then you can make your final decision as to what happens with us."

She brushed past him and walked down the stairs without turning back. He ran to catch up. He joined her just as she reached Nick by the side of the Ford E-350 Super Duty XL Wagon. She had seen this large silver van parked off to the side the day before. Now it was center stage in the open space of the warehouse. The windows of the silver van were tinted, and she couldn't see inside.

Nick swung the side doors open to reveal what looked like a miniature television studio built inside the van. A long bench with flat LCD monitors ran along the entire left side of the van. Three swivel chairs were mounted to the three separate stations and their corresponding monitors.

"Is everybody ready?"

"As ready as we'll ever be." She hopped into the back of the van and buckled into the first of the swivel chairs. She felt like she had climbed into the space shuttle instead of a van.

Denny jumped in and sat next to her in the next station. Nick regarded them for a moment before he closed the door to the van. He walked around the front of the van and climbed into the driver's seat. The 6.8L Triton V10 engine started with a meaty roar, and he backed the E-350 out into the crisp morning air. The powerful engine idled as he rolled the warehouse door closed and jumped back into the van.

She looked over at Denny. He had been persistent in his pursuit of her, and she never once considered his unwavering attention crossed the line into stalking. He just showed up every day at the same time at the motel restaurant and ordered a cup of coffee along with a request for a date. After three months, she felt that the only way to get him to stop pestering her was to finally give in. He seemed harmless enough, and if need be, she could take care of herself.

He reacted to her approval for a date as if he expected it. He probably came in every day thinking that this would be the day she said yes. He agreed to pick her up in front of the motel at seven o'clock that night.

He was a perfect gentleman.

She watched him as they sat in the van. She still felt the same feelings for him she had felt only two days before. Love was not something you could turn on and off like a switch. She had lied to him since the day they met, and he deserved to know exactly what she was and what she had done. Only then could they go on with their lives, whether it was together or separate.

It was a choice they would make together.

Chapter 26

Melissa sat in the lobby of the building. The main section of the building was not heavily secured. It almost made the second floor guards seem out of place. It was good that the main lobby did not have metal detectors, she thought, as the silencer dug into the small of her back. She was able to house the X-Five in the shoulder holster, but with nowhere else for the sound-suppressor, it was stuffed into the back pocket of her pants. She had nearly forgotten about it when she sat down, but it quickly reminded her that it was there. She almost gave out a small yelp but stayed quiet and hid the discomfort from registering on her face.

Nick had gone over the plan while they drove the ten minutes to the target building. She would sit in the main lobby of the building, and as the guards entered to begin their shifts, she would plant a micro tracking device on each guard. Once both guards were tagged, Denny would be clear to move in. Nick would monitor everything from the equipment in the van, stay in constant communication with Denny, and talk him through what he needed to do.

Nick handed her and Denny each a Mir 21 Covert Earpiece that was linked to their cell phones. The earpiece, once inserted into the ear, was nearly invisible. If someone knew what he was looking for and shone a flashlight into the ear, he might see it. Otherwise, it would go completely undetected. Nick would conference them in together for complete communication through the PBX system installed into the inside wall of the van.

She sat in the main lobby and turned a local tourist map of New York in all sorts of directions. Her earpiece crackled.

"One guard is heading your way," Nick reported. "Six foot two, a hundred and ninety pounds. He's wearing the red and gold uniform. Can't miss him."

She folded her New York map and stood up. She could see the guard approaching through the windows that enclosed the main lobby. She headed for the front doors of the lobby on an intercept course with the guard. Just as the guard entered the lobby, she was blocking his path. She gave him her sweetest smile.

"Excuse me, do you work here?" she batted her eyes.

The guard glanced around, unsure of how to answer that.

"I need help with directions."

She unfolded the map and spun around to be right next to the guard.

"I'm trying to get to the nearest subway terminal, but I can't tell which way I'm facing."

He smiled and responded exactly as she wanted.

"Of course." He took the map and turned it ninety degrees. Melissa brushed the back of his shoulder just to the side of the neck and placed the tiny microdot tracker that was the same color as the maroon shirt. He must have felt something. Melissa was too far out of practice. He quickly looked around and then right at Melissa. She smiled her best disarming smile and tried to turn the map the opposite direction.

"Like this?" She inquired.

He looked at her a moment longer, then back to the

map. He twisted it around.

"No, we are here," he said, pointing to the building's location on the map. "The subway terminal's there."

Melissa looked at the map and then looked out the windows of the lobby. His shoulders dropped. Melissa was sure he was concerned about being late for work. She pointed to the left.

"Down that way?"

His look softened, relieved that she understood.

"Yes," he said. "Go that way two blocks and turn left. You will see the stairs going down to the terminal."

"Thank you," she chimed as she walked out the doors and followed his directions.

Four minutes later, she was back inside the main lobby of the building wearing new clothes with a bike messenger pack slung over her shoulder. She was standing in front of the large sign that showed the names of all the companies and their corresponding floors. The second guard drove into the city and wouldn't know where the subway terminals were located, so she needed to take a different approach to get close.

She would approach him as he entered the lobby and ask which floor a company was on. He wouldn't know, and being the ever helpful guard, would take her over to the board listing. She would hand him her bag as she dug out the exact name of the person she was delivering to. As she was taking back the bag, she planned to plant the tracking device on him at that time.

She had left the bicycle just outside the lobby doors. The bike leaned on the right side door so that anyone going into the building would have to use the left door. A majority of the population was right-handed, and this tended to be the most used door. Her choice of doors caused the greatest inconvenience for someone trying to get into the building.

Her earpiece crackled again with Nick's voice.

"The guard is heading to the door. He's checking out your bike. He just moved it away from the door."

She changed her original plan and spun around. She ran across the lobby, pushed the door open and stepped outside.

"What the hell are you doing to my bike?" she demanded. She reached the guard in two large strides, approached from behind to grab the bike with one hand, and slipped the microdot tracker on his back just below the neck with the other.

He stiffened and spun around.

"Do not touch me!" he ordered.

"Don't frickin' touch my bike!"

"You left it leaning on the door."

"I was only gonna be in there a second."

"Don't leave your bike leaning on the doors, it's a safety hazard."

She checked her bike over and climbed on.

"Moron," she spat over her shoulder as she pedaled away.

She looped the block once and pulled up next to the van. Denny opened the side door and stepped out. He either wasn't nervous or he hid it well.

"You ready for this?" she asked.

He smiled silently. He was nervous.

"Go get'em, tiger."

She patted him on the shoulder a little too hard as a test. The painkillers worked. He barely flinched. She tossed the bike behind some nearby bushes as he crossed the street towards the building. She pulled herself into the van and took the seat next to Nick. He glanced at her briefly. He turned back to the video monitors.

"So far so good."

Chapter 27

"I'm going into the building now," Denny informed the two waiting in the van.

"Only tell me significant events. We can't have anyone see you talking to yourself." Nick replied.

"Got it," he said as he reached the building entrance.

He pulled the door open and walked inside. His hands weren't sweating, and he felt confident. He walked up the stairs to the second floor and circled the lobby area. Up ahead a single door sat apart from the rest. It was solid wood unlike the glass-paneled doors leading to the other offices. The stenciled title on the door labeled it as the security office for the building.

He turned the handle and opened the door as if knew where he was going and did this every day. He walked into a small room. At the other end of the room, the guard who had moved the bike sat at the metal desk.

"Can I help you?" The guard looked him up and down.

He remembered exactly what Nick had told him to say.

"I'm with section seven."

"ID, please."

He handed the ID, manufactured just this morning with one of the machines in the warehouse, to the guard. Nick had definitely been preparing for this for quite some time.

The guard looked back and forth between the ID and his face.

He seemed to agree with what he saw and slid a keypad across the desk to him. Nick had spent an hour this morning going over what he thought the code would be. He made him memorize the code and had tested him several times on the short drive over. He excelled at memorization and swiftly entered the code into the keypad.

The half-second the system took to verify the code seemed to stretch for hours. The amber light on the top of the keypad changed to red. He was ready to make a run for it, but the light quickly changed to green. The guard slid the keypad back. He observed the guard's right shoulder muscle relax and drop slightly. No doubt, the guard's right hand had just released the grip of a pistol that was mounted under the desk. If he failed to enter in the correct code, the guard would have been ready before he even started to run.

The covert earpiece crackled and Nick's voice spoke into his ear.

"It looks like you are going to have some company in the elevator."

The door opened behind him and he turned. He immediately recognized General Archon from pictures Nick had shown him while they went over the plans earlier this morning. General Archon was not supposed to be here today, and he worried he would be discovered as Archon walked into the room and up to the guard.

The General received a very different greeting than he had. The guard stood immediately and did not ask the General for ID or request an entry on the keypad. He walked over to the double doors of a free-standing storage unit. The storage unit was a gray metal unit that looked like it belonged in a locker room instead of a security office. He had noticed it when he first entered and had decided that this small room also served as a changing room for the guards. That would explain why both guards wore their uniforms to work instead of changing here.

The guard opened the doors to reveal that they had been hollowed out, and instead of the expected shelves and hooks, there were elevator doors located directly behind it. The guard pulled a key attached to a chain from his belt and inserted it into the lock by the side of the elevator. The doors slid open and General Archon stepped inside.

Denny paused. He hadn't gotten the abort order from Nick and couldn't decide if the danger had increased with General Archon's unexpected appearance in the building.

The General looked at him impatiently.

"Are you coming?"

He took a step forward and joined the General. The doors slid closed, and the elevator started its descent. He and the General both watched the numbers on the overhead display as they counted off the floors. He sprinkled several tiny dots that looked like dark red confetti on the floor of the elevator near General Archon's feet.

The cell phone in his pocket beeped to show it had lost the carrier signal. General Archon looked at him.

"Cell phones don't work this far underground," the General said. "Didn't they tell you in orientation that recording devices aren't allowed down here?"

He pulled the cell phone out of his pocket and held it up for the General to see.

"No camera," he explained. "It's a pretty old phone."

"Right," the General remarked. "Turn it off or it'll keep beeping at you. There's no chance of getting a signal down here."

He powered down the decoy cell phone he had brought along in case security detected the carrier signal of the microdot tracker that he had in the same pocket. The van had a strong enough signal to transmit directly to the modified cell phone in his other pocket. He would be able to hear Nick but not talk back. The microdot would transmit his location and Nick could tell him when any of the guards were close by.

The elevator stopped on level four. The General stepped out and headed straight down the hallway without looking back. When the doors closed again, he let out the breath he had been holding since General Archon walked into the security office. He reached down and picked up the confetti he had dropped less than a minute ago. A quick count showed that he recovered two less than he dropped. The General's shoes had picked up the other two.

He hoped that Nick had correctly tracked on his video map that the person who just left the elevator was the General.

Nick's voice broke through the light static.

"Nicely done," Nick said. "I am tracking General Archon's movements. If he gets close, I will let you know."

He smiled. The elevator doors squeaked open and he stepped out into the underground facility. He immediately turned left and walked down the hallway to the file room.

Nick released the talk switch on the panel mounted to the inside of the van.

"That was close," he said. "Denny is able to adapt far more readily than I gave him credit for."

Five of the LCD displays along the inside of the van were already powered on. He set four of them to display a top-down view of each person being tracked.

Melissa watched the dots move around on the screens. The walls were assigned green lines on the display. From the top-down view of the displays, they looked like a maze built for mice looking for cheese. The end of this maze several hundred feet below them offered a bit more than cheese, however.

He had set the dot that represented Denny to the color blue, the two guards to red and the General's overlapping dots were changed to amber. The crude graphics reminded her of the Pac-Man video game from the early eighties.

Chapter 28

General Archon sat at his desk four stories below the
streets of Manhattan. The simulated window behind his
desk always gave off the proper amount of light depending
on the time of day and the season. These false windows
were the brainchild of some architect hired to build the
levels that went down ten stories below the New York
building. Since the human condition was affected by the
availability of natural light, these windows were designed to
simulate outside lighting conditions and fool the brain into
thinking it was several stories above the ground instead of
below it.

He didn't care about fooling his brain. He came into the
office on a Saturday to see if he could discover any
information about Representative William Hartford and
why he refused to report to Site R with the rest of Congress.

He booted his computer system, and while the screen
was warming up, he checked the time logs out of habit. He
noticed the guard at the main security desk had clocked in a
minute late. While this may be acceptable in the private
sector, he prided himself on running a tight ship and
decided to call the guard about it later in the day after he
researched Hartford.

To ensure continual coverage, he staggered the entry of
each employee by five minutes and overlapped the ending
shifts by half an hour. This way there would always be
someone on duty while the other guards clocked in and out.
He glanced at the other report and saw that his earlier man

had also clocked in about a minute late. He looked at his watch. He still had the late shift on duty for another twenty minutes. Since both employees were late, he decided it was better not to wait. He didn't want this to become an epidemic. He lifted the receiver of the phone on his desk and dialed the main security office.

After only a single ring, first level security answered. At least some things were still running perfectly around here.

"Level One Security," said the voice on the other side.

"This is General Archon." He could almost hear the security officer snap to attention. "Send Rawlins and…" he looked down at the time sheet "…Wilson to my office right away. I need to speak to them before the late shift ends its day."

"Yes, sir."

The line disconnected and he replaced the receiver. It wouldn't take long to put the fear of God into these two and bring them back into line.

He longed for the days when he was in charge of active duty personnel. Ever since his injury, which he constantly reminds his superiors that he has fully recovered, he had been relegated to the career smothering position of security chief for the FBI's Digital Storm.

While this was a worthy assignment, he reminded himself, it was not as exciting as combat duty. And the guards who worked for him were always pushing the envelope in what they thought they could get away with.

Denny stopped at the door marked Personnel Records.

He knew that this was not what was kept behind this door. He entered a different code provided by Nick into the keypad next to the door. The lock clicked and he opened the door. He glanced around him and slipped into the room unnoticed.

Melissa watched as the two red dots moved at the same time. They both converged at the elevator. She nudged Nick and pointed to the screens.

"What are they doing?"

"I'm not sure," Nick said. "I don't think that their normal routine would get them together like this."

Nick pushed the talk button on the console and spoke into the microphone.

"Be on the alert, Denny," Nick said. "The guards are moving unexpectedly."

She and Nick watched as the two red dots converged on the amber dot that represented General Archon.

Chapter 29

"Please close the door," the General said as the second guard entered the room. He looked at both of them without saying a word for almost a minute. This time of silence solidified that General Archon was in control, and he was letting them know it. It also had the extra benefit of increasing the fear level of those who stood on the opposite side of the General's desk.

He picked up the report attached to a clipboard.

"Mr. Rawlins," he began.

"Yes, sir," Rawlins stated a little too loud for the small office.

"I see that you clocked in a few minutes late for your shift."

"It was only one minute, sir."

"Could you explain to me why you clocked in a minute late?" He slammed the clipboard down to emphasize his displeasure.

"It wasn't my fault..." Rawlins stammered. "She couldn't figure out the simple directions I was giving her."

"Her? Who her?"

"Just as I entered the lobby, some lady asked me where the nearest subway terminal was. I tried to explain it to her, but she kept getting confused. She kept turning the map this way and that way..." Rawlins paused. "I'm sorry, sir," Rawlins pleaded. "It will not happen again."

He turned to Wilson.

"And what about you?"

"I have no excuse, sir."

He let a smile creep onto the edges of his mouth.

"Then maybe you can give me a reason."

"Had to move a bike, sir."

Wilson was all business. He wished he could hire more like Wilson. In order to maintain the cover of the building above them, they had to rely more on the sophisticated security system to protect the assets contained in the lower levels of the building and use civilian unarmed guards from a local agency. This made sure that no one questioned the security in place at the building.

"And why did you have to move this bike?"

"It was a hazard. She had parked it across the entrance."

His internal alarms sounded. "She?"

"The bike messenger. She left it leaning on one of the doors. I was moving it when she ran out and attacked me."

"Attacked you?"

"Well, not really attacked, but when she grabbed the bike out of my hands, she sort of pushed me. I said some things, she said some things. It was over quickly. But it still made me late, and I apologize for that."

He looked at them both. He turned to Rawlins.

"Can you describe the girl you helped?"

Rawlins scrunched his eyes as he concentrated.

"She was Caucasian. About five foot nine, a hundred and twenty pounds, sandy blonde hair, blue eyes."

Wilson's mouth opened in shock. The General noticed.

"Something wrong, Wilson?"

"That's how I would have described the bike messenger."

Denny looked around and didn't see any computers in this room either. This was the third room he had tried and with each failure, he became more agitated. He silently cursed as he thought about spending more time wandering around down here with General Archon also wandering about. The longer he was down here, the greater his chances were of being discovered and captured.

He needed to find a computer and connect the satellite modem Nick had provided to the USB port. He peeked into the hallway. It was empty. He stepped out of the room and moved on to the next door. This one was locked, but he made short work with the pick kit, and the latch clicked its surrender in less than fifteen seconds. He opened the door hoping that this room held the computer that Nick was looking for. As far as he was concerned, he would accept any computer at this point.

"Did she touch you as well?" Archon asked Rawlins.

"I thought somebody touched me when I was showing her the subway on the map. I looked around and didn't see anyone near me. She was looking at the map and hadn't reacted, so I dismissed it."

He told both the guards to turn around and stand still. He went up behind Wilson and ran his hand along the shoulders and around the neck. He pulled his hand away and something the same color as the guard's uniform was sticking to his hand. He looked at it closer and saw that it was a micro tracking device. He ran his hand along Rawlins' uniform and got another one just like the first.

He remembered that he rode in the elevator with someone he didn't know. He stood with his back to the wall and the other man stood in front of him the entire time.

Unless.

He lifted his shoe and saw the dot that was the same color as the guard's uniform stand out against the black tread of his boot. He pulled it off and set it on the table with the other two transmitters.

"What floor did the new visitor go to?"

"Which visitor?" Wilson asked.

"The one who rode in the elevator with me," he demanded.

"Mr. Bloom?" Wilson asked. "Um, Five, sir."

That was the same floor as the archive. If someone gained access to any computer on that floor, he would have immediate access to everything in Digital Storm.

"Is there anyone else here?" he asked.

"Only you and the visitor from section seven. It has been a pretty quiet morning."

"It's about to get a lot noisier." He tossed the three microdots onto the desk. He radioed the other guards and ordered them to guard the entrance to the main elevator and restrict access to everyone, no exceptions. He looked at the two guards before him.

What he really wanted was a team of highly trained soldiers. He looked at these men who were nothing more than glorified crossing guards. He had no choice but to use them. This was a numbers game, and these were the only numbers he had to play with.

"Either of you ever shoot a gun?"

Chapter 30

Nick stared at the colored dots on the screen.

"What are they up to?" Melissa asked.

"I don't know. Looks like they gathered in the General's office."

"But why those two specific guards?"

She stared at the dots overlapping each other. The fifth display lit up and Yahoo! Messenger popped up on the screen.

"Hello, Nick"

"It's Denny. He found the computer," he said. "Let's see if it's the right one."

He pushed the talk button on the panel. "Denny, hit control escape and let me access the hard drive."

He spun the swivel chair and flipped a keyboard down from the side panel. He watched the screen, and as soon as a blinking cursor appeared, he started typing. The screen lit up and was immediately replaced by a password screen. He hit the talk button on the panel.

"You found it. The mission's over. Come on out."

She saw the amber dot separate from the two red dots. She rapped him on the shoulder and pointed to the screen.

"Look," she said. "The General's moving."

He looked at the monitors. He saw that there was still an amber dot overlapping with the two red dots that remained stationary, with another amber dot on the move.

"He found the tracking devices," he said. He still had his finger on the talk button and Denny heard him.

Where are they?

They watched as the single amber dot rode the elevator to the fifth level.

"He's on the same level as you," Nick said. "He found the guards' tracking devices but not both of his. Find somewhere to hide, and I will let you know when it's safe to move." He released the button.

"How do I get in there?" she chambered the first round in her X-Five and screwed the sound-suppressor onto the threaded barrel.

He looked at her with full understanding. She had to get Denny out of there. They couldn't let General Archon get to him first.

"The ventilation system. Once you are inside the lower sections, there are no cameras to worry about. I can lead you right to Denny with the tracking dot."

Denny slowly opened the door to the computer room by half an inch. A few feet down the hallway stood one of the guards. He faced away from him. The door hinge creaked, and the guard spun around. He looked right at the door. He left the door partially open and looked around for somewhere to hide. The room was small, and there was no other way in or out.

And no place to hide.

He spotted the fire extinguisher. He lifted it quietly off the holder. He could hear the guard just outside the door. He stood behind the door and raised the extinguisher above his head. The door slowly swung open. A head peeked around the corner, and he brought the extinguisher crashing down on it.

The guard went immediately limp and hit the floor with a thud. He pulled the guard into the room and closed the door. He checked the guard and found a SIG-Sauer P229, safety still engaged. His Mir 21 earpiece crackled and hissed.

"Melissa's coming in to get you. Stay where you are, if you can, and I will direct her right to you."

He went to the computer where Yahoo! Messenger was still on the screen. He placed his hands on the keyboard and typed.

"I will stay here as long as I can."

He could hear the hard drive whine as the computer accessed a program. Clicking noises came from behind the far wall that sounded like old tape storage devices as they spun and stopped.

Melissa removed the sound-suppressor and placed it in her jacket pocket. She needed to rappel down the ventilation shaft and couldn't holster her X-Five with the silencer attached. She moved purposefully and as quietly as possible as she lowered herself down the vertical shaft. The metal walls of the shaft bent and flexed under her weight. The rope she clung to was not designed for rappelling and was too thin for the clamps to work perfectly. If it weren't for the half-inch seams in the shaft where the sections had been welded together every three feet, she would have nothing to control her descent.

She reached a cross-section in the shaft. She paused and

waited for Nick to tell her where she was.

"You are at the third level. There is a stairwell just at the end of that cross shaft that will get you down to the fifth level."

She decided it was easier to move around freely in the stairwell then risk being discovered in the ventilation shaft. If she was spotted, she couldn't draw her pistol out before she was shot. She unclamped herself from the rope and slid sideways into the shaft. She slithered along like a snake and stopped every few inches to listen for anyone moving in the hallway just ahead.

At the end of the shaft, she listened again. She gave a test push on the mesh grate to see how much force it would require. The grate was loose and fell away from her.

Chapter 31

General Archon could not believe that someone had managed to infiltrate the underground section of Digital Storm. Only a select few even knew that the FBI had moved the entire system to New York from Fort Meade, Maryland.

He had sent Wilson down to the lowest level and instructed him to open every door and work his way up. He went to the upper underground level and was working his way down. Rawlins was to stay on level five in case Wilson or he flushed the intruder out of hiding. To increase his advantage, he had provided both the guards with SIG-Sauer pistols. There was no way the intruder could be armed.

He had almost checked all the rooms on level three when he heard a loud clattering sound from around the corner. He raised his SIG-Sauer P229 and released the safety.

He rounded the corner with his gun straight in front of him like a natural extension of his arm.

A ventilation grate had fallen to the ground.

He peered into the open shaft.

It was empty.

As soon as the grate hit the ground, Melissa moved fast. She did not want to be caught in the ventilation shaft if someone had heard the grate fall and came running.

In the hallway, she listened. She didn't hear anything and had a choice of left or right. She chose left. She peeked around the corner and saw the hallway was empty. The stairs were just at the other end. She crept down the hallway and never heard the General approach the open vent shaft.

She paused at the stairwell door and listened hard. She opened the door and listened again. The stairs were made out of cement, and the sound wouldn't travel like it did on steel stairs. She heard nothing and entered the stairwell heading down to level five.

General Archon peeked around the corner and saw the door closing to the stairwell. He raised his walkie-talkie.

"Wilson report," he said just above a whisper.

"Just finishing level eight, sir."

"Rawlins report."

There was no answer.

"Rawlins report," he said a little more forcefully.

Rawlins didn't answer. Or couldn't answer.

Either way, whoever just entered the stairwell was not one of his men.

Melissa reached the landing for level five just as her earpiece crackled to life.

"Denny is still in the same location," Nick said. "Go out the stairwell to your right. He's in one of the rooms about thirty feet down the hallway. The door will be on your right."

She paused at full attention. Did she just hear a doorway close above her? She held her breath and strained to listen for any sound of footfalls in the stairwell.

"Melissa, why aren't you…"

She pulled the Mir 21 Covert Earpiece out of her ear and shoved it into a pocket. She focused again on the stairs above her. There was no sound.

She turned back to the door and opened it slowly. She looked left and right. The hallway was empty. She exited the stairwell and turned to her right. She counted out silently to herself approximately thirty feet and paused as the stairwell door clicked shut again behind her. She started to turn her head when a commanding voice told her to do something else.

"Let me see your hands," General Archon said.

She raised her hands above her head.

"Turn around."

He had snuck up behind her. She was definitely rusty. Back in the days when she was hunting her former squad mates, this would never have happened. At least her gun wouldn't be strapped securely in the shoulder holster.

She spun around slowly on the balls of her feet. As she spun around, the door to her right opened slightly. She saw Denny step back away from the door and farther into the room.

General Archon moved a few feet closer. He was still at least twenty feet away. He continued to move close enough that a reaction shot wouldn't miss her but far enough away that she couldn't rush him.

She wasn't going to give him that satisfaction and duck-rolled into the partially open door. Her weight slammed into the door, and it swung the rest of the way open. No shots splintered the doorframe. In fact, she didn't hear the

General fire a single shot. She kicked the door closed.

She pulled her own gun out and thumbed the safety off. She could hear the General calling for backup. She looked around the room and saw Denny standing by the computer.

She glanced at the guard on the floor.

"Is he dead?"

He pointed to the dented fire extinguisher. "I don't think so. I hit him with that." He held up a SIG-Sauer P229. "And got this off him."

Excellent. Two guns were always better than one. Until help arrived for the General, they had him currently outnumbered and outgunned. She needed to make her move now if there was any hope of escape. She looked around again for any way out of the small room.

He could tell she was looking for another way out.

"The only door is the one you just came through."

That meant that they had to go back out the way they came. The guard moaned, and she knew exactly how she was going to achieve her objective.

General Archon backed away from the door she had just entered. As luck would have it, this was the only room in the entire underground facility he didn't want her anywhere near. And now she had barricaded herself inside. He couldn't let her walk out without a fight, she would be too suspicious.

He still had at least another minute before backup would arrive, and then she would be forced to inspect the room for another way out. If she accessed the computer, she would be connected to Digital Storm. Even though she wouldn't be able to decode the password, just knowing it existed made her more dangerous than before.

He was still trying to figure out how to get the woman out of that room when the door opened and Rawlins shuffled out.

Melissa had her left arm around the guard's neck and forced him out into the hallway. He probably had a concussion and was unsteady when he walked. She turned left and saw General Archon down the hallway. She raised her gun with the silencer attached and aimed it right at him. He didn't make a move, and she didn't hear anyone else around. At the moment, he was still outgunned.

"Come on, Denny."

He stepped out, and when he saw the General, he raised his gun to point right at him. General Archon put his own gun down to his side but didn't drop it.

"Drop your gun, General," she tightened her grip on the guard.

"I don't think so."

"Is your guard's life worth your lack of cooperation?"

The guard flinched and she hugged his neck tighter.

"His name is Rawlins, and you won't hurt him."

"What makes you so sure?"

"I won't let you."

When Archon took an almost unnoticeable step backwards, she unconsciously took another step towards him.

"Whatever you think is happening, you're wrong."

He slowly took another step back while he spoke.

"What I see is someone trying to gain access to Digital Storm."

"It's not what you think."

"Then what is it?"

She heard the ding of the elevator, and she gripped Rawlins harder around the throat. His face turned red from the increased pressure.

He held his hand up and stopped whoever was coming down the hall from getting any closer. It was then she noticed that she had moved away from the door and had traveled several feet down the hallway. She had used the same tactics on several occasions to get her target right where she wanted. Only this time, she was the target. It had been too long since she thought like a soldier.

She glanced at Denny. He was holding his gun steady and had stayed right alongside her. She had given him careful instructions back in the room, and so far, he was carrying them out perfectly. She hoped that if things got worse, he would be ready for action.

Now that she was paying attention, she noticed that the General had become more relaxed with each step he led her down the hallway. Was he leading them into a trap? She glanced at the doorway over her shoulder. Or was he leading them away from something?

"My guards have arrived, and you are outnumbered," he said. "It's time you gave up."

"Sorry," she replied. "I still have a hostage."

She watched as he instructed his men to stand down and

stay out of sight. He turned back with an easy smile.

She tested her theory and took two steps backwards.

His eyes darkened and his jaw muscles tensed. This confirmed that he was leading her away from something. Could it be the room with the computer in it?

He refused to take a step forward with her.

"I'm sure we can work this out peacefully," he stated. "I don't want to see anyone hurt."

She took another step back.

"Be reasonable." He spread his arms in a pleading gesture. "I can give you my assurances that you will be treated fairly."

She took one more step back and stood by the open door of the computer room again. She could see by the look on the General's face that she had guessed right. Then his eyes focused to something behind her for less than a second. Denny noticed the change in the General's eyes and glanced behind them.

"Behind you, Melissa!" Denny roared.

He fired two rounds at the General while she let go of her hostage and spun around. The other guard must have come up the back stairwell. He had just raised his gun to fire when her X-Five quietly spit twice. The impact from the bullets slammed the guard into the wall, and he slid down to the floor.

His first shots missed General Archon as he ducked and rolled sideways out of the main hallway and out of view. She rolled her hostage into the computer room. He fired two more rounds down the hall to keep everyone out of sight and slammed the door shut.

The other two guards ran towards the corner of the hallway with their guns ready.

"Do not fire," Archon barked. "Do not return fire."

The two guards were stunned and halted their advance.

"They're trapped in the computer room." He stood back up. "There is only the one door, and they can't get out any other way. We have time on our side. We can wait them out."

He peered around the corner down the hallway. Wilson lay on his back at the other end and didn't move. He was glad he had issued bulletproof vests for each guard. Wilson was lucky. The woman, her partner called her Melissa, had hit him with only two shots to the center. She'd held a guard hostage and would have felt the vest under his uniform. It would be an easy assumption that all the guards had vests. Despite this obvious knowledge, she had fired directly to the center of Wilson's vest.

He looked up at the bullet holes in the ceiling. Her partner had aimed above his head. Even if he hadn't ducked, those bullets would have missed him completely. What was their game? He had her trapped in the computer room with no way out. He turned to his two guards who waited tensely beside him.

"Jens, you go around the other way and pull Wilson to safety. Take position on the corner."

"Yes, sir."

Jens disappeared around the far corner. He looked at the other guard.

"Roberts?"

"Yes, sir?" Roberts replied.

"You and I will take the room by force."

"Yes, sir!"

He smiled. Roberts also behaved like he was in the military instead of just administrative security. Just like Wilson. He decided to test him on his tactical skills.

"How do you suggest we proceed?"

Roberts looked at him for a moment. His brain must have been working through multiple options.

"What are the objectives?" Roberts finally asked.

"Capture. Eliminate all possibility of collateral damage." He let Roberts digest the information he had just provided.

Roberts peeked around the corner and saw Jens had already pulled Wilson out of sight. Roberts leaned back and looked directly at him.

"Gas," Roberts said.

He smiled. "There are CS Canisters in the armory on three. Get four gas masks. Once we have control of the room, I want a mask placed on Rawlins."

He watched as Roberts headed for the stairwell and not the elevator. Roberts had a definite future in security. Who knows, maybe he would even consider offering him a position when he got out of this desk job.

He smiled to himself. Today was a blessing in disguise. Saving the FBI database from these intruders would show that he was still capable and ready for active duty.

He looked around the corner and saw Jens looking back at him. He motioned for him to approach the closed door while he approached from his side. They each came within a foot of their respective side of the doorway and stopped. It was time to start the psychological aspect of warfare.

"There is nowhere to go," he began. "You need to put down your weapons and come out. If you come out now, I will listen to whatever you have to say. If you make me come in there after you, I guarantee I will not be so generous."

He waited. There was no reply. He put his ear against the wall and strained to listen in the room. He could hear shuffling and a slight moan. They still had Rawlins with them.

"Let my guard go. He needs medical attention."

He waited and listened. He needed to buy time for Roberts' return with the CS gas.

"Let's talk about why you are here. I will let you ask me one question. I will answer any question you want. No tricks, no lies, only truth. I can hear you through the doorway if you speak loudly."

No response from the closed room. They must be preparing for their last stand. Whatever they had planned, it wouldn't work. They were more than sixty feet underground and trapped in a tiny room with no hope of escape.

Rawlins returned with two canisters of CS gas and a flashbang grenade. For the size of the room, one would be more than enough to provide a lethal dose of the volatile substance. When he pulled the pin on the grenade, he would have a two-second delay before the compound inside was expelled and everyone not wearing a gas mask would wish they were dead. Then he would regain control of this situation and use it to get promoted back out of this place.

Still, he did not want to risk damaging any of the equipment in the room that the release of the CS gas might cause. It was better to get them to give up without a fight. He needed to make them feel like the only option was surrender.

"I have five armed guards on each side of the hallway and will be launching gas grenades into the room if you do not surrender."

They must be working off each other's misguided bravery. He needed to break that team up, and quickly.

"Mr. Bloom, if that even is your real name," he began, "I know that you may have been told you have a lot of reasons to stand and fight, but I don't want to see you getting hurt because of stupidity. If you toss out the gun you pulled off my guard, I will toss in a gas mask for you. I don't know what you were told to get you to break into a United States military facility, but it's not worth your life to keep fighting. Toss the gun out, and I will take your compliance into consideration."

Silence.

They were both fools. It was time to end this standoff right here, right now.

He backed away from the door and motioned for Jens to follow. They paused at the end of the hallway.

"We're going in," he whispered. "Roberts, you get that door open so I can toss the flashbang. Jens, after the flashbang blows, you go in first and take the right. Roberts will follow and take the left. Fire only if you are immediately threatened. Be sure to pull the trigger only if you can hit flesh. I do not want any of the equipment in that room damaged. If you meet resistance, pull out and I will toss in the gas grenade."

General Archon grabbed one of the gas masks and strapped it over his head. Roberts tossed a mask to Jens and put his own on. They would form the three-man entry team. He wondered if these young boys had any formal training or if their tactical understanding came from playing video games.

He counted down from three and pulled the pin. Roberts was ready, and he rushed the door. A single kick sent the door swinging inward, and he tossed the flashbang. The loud explosion and resulting smoke filled the room quickly.

Jens rushed in and spun to the right. Roberts followed immediately behind him and covered the left of the doorway. They shouted for compliance and swept their weapons back and forth around the room. General Archon held his weapon on the open doorway with one hand and was ready to toss in the CS gas grenade with the other.

Nobody fired.

In fact, nothing happened.

The General approached the doorway. He could see clearly into the room as the smoke quickly dissipated from the powerful ventilation system installed to cool the computer equipment.

The only people in the room were his guards. Jens helped Rawlins sit up. The General leaned down to Rawlins and shouted close to his ear.

"Where are they?"

Rawlins had been temporarily deafened by the flashbang and was so disoriented he didn't respond. Archon stood up and looked around. The only way in or out was the single door that led to the hallway. The same door they went in.

The General glanced at the vent openings in the ceiling. The upgraded ventilation system was built for security as well as ventilation, and the openings were designed to be too small for a person to climb through. They were not the same size as the vent on level three that Melissa had used to get in.

General Archon stared in disbelief at the empty room.

And he felt his chances of getting a better assignment dissipate as quickly as the smoke. If he let them escape, his career would suffer a fatal blow.

And he couldn't let that happen.

He spun around to face the only three other people who knew that this had even taken place.

"Gentleman, we are going to fix this."

Jens looked at him. "Sir?"

"If anyone else finds out what happened today, we will all spend the rest of our lives in misery and despair. Do I make myself clear?"

Jens and Roberts looked at each other and then back at the General.

Jens responded for both of them. "Perfectly, sir."

Chapter 32

Melissa hefted herself out of the ventilation shaft and into the morning sunlight that reflected off the side of the building. She unclamped herself from the rope and reached back down into the mouth of the dark tunnel. She pulled Denny out of the shaft and unclamped him from the rope. Even though the rope was not originally designed for climbing, it was still strong enough to support their combined weight. For that, she was grateful, or they would never have both made it out of the building in time.

She looked to where Nick was waiting with the van and let a gasp escape from her lips.

The van was gone.

She looked around her quickly.

The van was nowhere in sight.

"Where's the van?" Denny also looked around the empty street.

"I don't know," she tugged at his jacket and pulled him away from the building. They couldn't stay here.

They crossed the street and walked down half a block. She kept glancing over her shoulder looking for Nick and watching the building entrance all at the same time.

The third time she looked back, General Archon stepped out into the sunlight and looked up the street away from them. She pushed Denny down behind a parked car and crouched next to him. She peeked around the bumper of the car and watched as the General looked in her direction and then back the other way.

The General watched for a long minute, then turned around and went back inside the building. She stood back up and briskly walked around the corner. Denny caught up quickly and fell in step next to her.

"Where are we going?"

"To the warehouse." She stared straight ahead as she walked.

"You think Nick went back there?"

A light screech of tires stopping suddenly on the asphalt sounded next to them, and they both turned their heads at the same time. Nick looked out the opened window of the van at them.

"Well, don't just stand there, get in."

Chapter 33

Melissa and Denny sat in her room above the warehouse. Nick had spent the better part of an hour trying to hack the password to gain access to Digital Storm. With no success.

"Have any of his plans ever failed before?" he asked.

"None."

"None?"

She let the hint of a smile form at the corners of her mouth.

"Well, one of his plans never went the way he wanted."

"What was that?"

"He tried to recruit me into The Council."

"What happened?"

"Nick provided the information I needed to wipe out The Council instead."

"So you put him out of a job?"

"Yeah, I guess so."

"And he's not holding it against you?"

"To tell you the truth, I think he had been trying to figure out how to get out for a while. In some crazy convoluted way, I actually helped him."

"You think he can find out who tried to kill you?"

"If Nick thinks he can, then he can."

His eyes bored into hers. "Let's say he finds out who sent someone to kill you. What then?"

She smiled. "I ask them to please leave me alone."

"And if they won't."

She stopped smiling. She stood up and walked back

downstairs to Nick. Denny knew he must have crossed some line as he didn't follow her.

She walked up to Nick who was hunched over the computer muttering to himself.

"Any luck?"

He spun around. "I'm going to have to bring in someone else on this one, but I don't know who to trust with this just yet."

Before she could respond, a phone on the desk rang.

Startled, he and Melissa looked at each other. She looked back at the phone. "It can't be for me. This is your place."

He lifted the handset and held it to his ear. "Hello?"

He suddenly looked at her and then held the phone out towards her. "He asked for you."

She took the phone. "Hello?"

"Melissa Stone?"

"Who's asking?"

"You gave me your number a couple years ago and said if I ever needed your help to call you. And I need your help now more than ever."

"Who is this?"

"My name is William Hartford."

She almost dropped the phone.

He stood up in response. "What is it?"

She waved him away, "Keep talking."

"I have the Vice President with me..."

"That's not possible."

"He was replaced with a duplicate for the attack. He's alive and I have him."

"What do you want?"

"You misunderstand. I am not holding him prisoner. We are both prisoners."

Chapter 34

Melissa and Nick had argued for half an hour about how to remove the guards wandering all around the estate. He insisted that it was too dangerous to leave them alive. But when she finally told him that she would kill only if necessary or else he could find someone else to go in, he conceded that leaving the guards alive would still be acceptable as long as she promised that they would rescue Hartford and the Vice President before any of them managed to escape. She ensured him that none of the guards would get loose until someone found them.

She spent the early hours of the morning collecting guards. By sunrise, they were all bound and gagged in the barn. The last one suspected something when he couldn't contact the other guards with his radio or personal cell phone. She was getting tired by the time she went for that last guard. He put up a big fight and lost a boot in the corresponding struggle with her. She had won the fight, and the last guard sat bound and gagged staring at the other guards who all stared back at him.

As soon as the last guard was captured, he switched on the jamming equipment that prevented cell phone service within a two-mile radius. At the same time, Denny cut the power and phone lines to the estate.

Nick sat in the running Ford E-350 Super Duty XL Wagon to monitor the situation and be ready to make a hasty getaway when they needed it.

Denny was stationed at the entrance to the estate with a

mounted grenade machine gun. He could take out anything that tried to get in.

Henderson woke with a start. The sun sliced into the room through the slit of an opening in the drapes. His alarm should have gone off long before the sun rose. He looked over and saw the clock was dark. He sat up and listened. The room was absolutely silent.

Too silent.

He didn't hear any of the ever present electronic hums in modern homes. Electrical appliances still draw power even when they are turned off and he didn't hear any of the quiet electrical noises he expected. He slid out of bed and walked softly to the window where he used a single finger to push the drapes open slightly along an edge. He looked out onto the expansive grounds of Hartford's Pennsylvania estate and saw nothing. He watched for ten full minutes. His team was supposed to be patrolling the grounds. He slowly let back the drapes and paused when he saw the empty combat boot lying by the barn.

He reached for the phone by his bedside. No dial tone. He slid the cell phone out of his uniform coat pocket. No signal.

Someone was attempting to rescue the Vice President.

But worse than that, Hannah hadn't called to warn him about the morning invasion.

Two scenarios flitted across his mind. One, she didn't know about it, which meant she was not in control as much as she claimed. Or two, she was unable to get in touch with him before the lines were cut and the cell phones were jammed.

Either way, he still had a job to do, and Hannah had hired him because he could think on his feet and under pressure.

Melissa lowered her binoculars and pushed the talk button on the walkie-talkie. Nick had modified the signal so that they could still communicate despite the cell phone jammer.

"We still have some guards inside the house. I saw one look out the second floor bedroom window. He must have noticed by now that the guards are missing and the power's out."

"Hartford said he would move the Vice President into the basement as soon as the power was cut," he replied.

"I'm on my way." she turned off the walkie-talkie and stuffed it into the pack on her shoulder.

She stepped to the back of the barn and pushed aside a storage bin from off the floor grating. Hartford had mentioned that under the storage bin was a tunnel that traveled underground straight towards the main house. She could have slipped past the guards through this tunnel, but she needed to exit faster than she entered. It was best to take care of them before she went into the house.

She lifted the grate, dropped into the tunnel and pushed the grate back into place. She dug in the pack slung on her shoulder and removed a flashbang grenade. She wound a string around the grate edge and tied it to the grenade.

It didn't have the power to kill, but it would slow down anyone who dared follow her.

After waking the rest of the guards sleeping in the house, Henderson took them down to the basement. He unlocked the gun safe, removed Heckler & Koch MP5SDs, with integrated silencers, from the rack and handed them to the other guards. This house was the ultimate arena for close-quarters fighting, and the MP5SD was the undisputed champion of close-quarters combat.

He then pulled several handheld walkie-talkies and tossed them to the guards. One of the guards tried his radio and received only static.

"Keep the radios on but stay inside the house until communication is restored. Do not do anything until I give the order, is that clear?"

In unison, the guards responded. "Yes, sir!"

"Do not engage the enemy unless you have absolutely no other option."

"Yes, sir!"

"Now, go."

As the guards left to take their assigned posts throughout the house, he switched on the security camera screens. They were operated by a battery backup that automatically switched on when the power was cut. A quick glance at the meter levels showed he still had another fifteen hours before the batteries died. It didn't matter. Whatever happened would take place long before the security system shut down.

He felt confident having the home field advantage. He

would watch the video screens, and when they showed someone approaching the house, he would leave through the secret tunnel that led from the basement to the barn sixty feet away, and then he could come up on the intruder from behind.

He watched as several screens lit up in the semi-darkness of the basement. The video feeds filtered through software that showed a brilliant red wash on the screen when movement happened within view of any camera. The full color displays showed the view outside the house, quiet and serene.

They completely misrepresented the danger he was in.

Hartford's muscles ached. He crouched in the tiny utility closet with the Vice President and waited. Melissa had warned him that a house guard could make it to the basement before she did, but it still surprised him when the lights flickered on under the closet door and he listened as the guards armed themselves and headed back up into the house.

He prayed that she was able to do what she promised and rescue him, despite the heavily armed guards.

The Vice President snored softly on the floor. He had been under heavy sedation since the switch on the night of the attack on his motorcade, and he wasn't sure if he could keep carrying him if the sedation didn't wear off enough before help arrived.

Shadows flickered under the door as the guard activated the various pieces of equipment in the basement. If the guard opened the closet door for any reason, it would be over for him and the Vice President. They would not be given a second chance to escape.

Melissa dug the flashlight out of the pack and switched it on. The light faded down the tunnel into the distance. She mouthed the flashlight and held it steady while she unscrewed the silencer from her pistol. With the guards under wraps, she didn't need to be stealthy anymore. She preferred the better accuracy and punch that the X-Five delivered without the sound-suppressor attached.

She continued through the tunnel. She came to a small intersection. Apparently, there were underground tunnels connecting more than just the house with the barn. She continued on in the direction that led to the house.

At the end of the tunnel, she reached a half-height steel door. The handle was tight with rust in the cool damp air of the underground tunnel system.

She mouthed the flashlight again and grabbed the circular handle with both hands. She grunted with all her strength. The handle refused to budge.

She tucked the flashlight into the spokes of the handle and positioned it like a lever.

She pulled down on the end of the flashlight and hung onto it with all her might.

The handle groaned its resistance. She shifted down, and the wheel gave slightly with a muffled squeak. She kept the pressure on the flashlight, and the wheel turned again.

Henderson heard a faint scraping sound come from the direction of the tunnel. He took his eyes off the screens and shone a flashlight onto the steel door. His eyes adjusted to the darkness as he heard more scraping sounds. He repositioned the flashlight beam and watched the handle turn slowly.

The tunnel had been compromised.

He thumbed the MP5SD's fire selector to full auto. The door was shorter than most doors. Whoever was coming would be off balance from having to crouch through the low door.

He trained the MP5SD on the slowly opening door.

Melissa opened the door a little more than two inches and then stopped. There was light coming from the other side of the door. She switched off her flashlight. The light from the room was not bright like the vertical spill of an overhead light but more horizontal like a television set. Or a computer monitor.

Denny had shut down the power to the entire house. That meant that if this room had power, there was a battery backup that fed the computers in this room and allowed it to continue to operate in the event of total power failure. That also meant that one or more guards were in this room.

She crouched with her hand still on the door. She opened her mouth wide to let each breath escape noiselessly as she strained to hear anything from the other side of the door.

She refused to move for five minutes. Every muscle screamed for mercy. She didn't dare move. The slightest noise would echo like a cannon blast in the silence of the basement. She hadn't heard anything for those five minutes and was only assuming that armed guards were on the other side of the door. If they weren't, she was wasting valuable time. If they were, how long would they wait?

Her muscles screamed in agony.

She couldn't wait any longer.

She slowly pushed open the door with her flashlight, ready to jerk her hand back should anyone start shooting. The door was situated in a corner of the room, and she couldn't see all the way inside without actually entering the room.

She internally applauded the guards for not firing on the opening door. If they watched that door open, they would wait until someone stepped through before firing.

She turned away from the door and risked turning her flashlight back on. The dirt walls would reduce any glare from the light, and she hoped no one heard the click of the switch. She shone the light into her pack and fished out a grenade. She looked at the bright neon green band painted on the bottom of the grenade and smiled.

Anyone who spent time in the military or law enforcement would easily recognize the significance of the colored bands painted onto every grenade. Each color had its own code. The bright green band at the bottom of this grenade designated it as a diversionary device called the flashbang. It derived its name from its explosive properties. It emitted a flash and a bang.

The flash emitted was brighter than a million candles, and the bang registered a deafening 170 decibels.

The flashbang would blind and deafen everyone in the room with little hope of limiting the effects.

The flashbang was designed not to kill, but was an effective diversionary tactic to momentarily distract and disorient any potential threat. If there was ever a time when she needed to distract someone, it was now.

She turned her flashlight and shone it through the door into the room. She tossed the grenade and adjusted the flashlight beam. She had to make sure he saw the green band on the grenade within seconds of it hitting the ground.

If Henderson hadn't watched the door open so slowly, he might have dismissed the sound as some woodland creature in the tunnel. There was no doubt that someone waited just on the other side of that door. He strained to hear over the small hum of the fans that cooled the monitors situated around the desk.

But even after the door was fully opened, nothing happened.

He kept reminding himself that he watched the door slowly open and that meant that someone was there. The more time passed, the more his brain wanted to say it was only a trick of the light. This must be what prisoners in solitary confinement went through. He was starting to believe that he had imagined the whole door incident and that it must have been open the whole time when a light shone into the room from beyond the door.

The light moved around and stopped on the floor about ten feet from the door. He heard a light thud on the hard-packed dirt floor. The flashlight moved slightly to reveal a grenade had been tossed into the room.

He immediately recognized the green band. This designated the object as a flashbang grenade, and if he had any hope of limiting its effects, he had to react quickly.

He dropped the MP5SD and slammed his eyes as tightly shut as possible and covered his ears. In this enclosed underground space, his attacker would have to do the same.

Melissa heard the clatter of something metal hit the dirt floor inside the room. Her diversion had worked. She moved swiftly into the basement room. She wasn't worried about making noise. The tightly packed dirt would muffle her footfalls, and if she was correct, the guard would be suppressing any sound she made all by himself.

The threat of violence was always more effective in subduing an opponent than violence itself.

To her surprise, only one massive guard was in the basement.

She holstered her SIG-Sauer and scooped up the MP5SD. She pushed the guard over with a foot and pointed the MP5SD at his head.

The guard yelped in surprise as he hit the floor and looked up at her. True fear showed for the first time in his eyes.

"Knock, knock," she said.

Chapter 35

The door to the barn creaked open, and a lone figure slipped in. He stepped around the various tied up guards and stopped at an older guard.

He slipped the gag off the guard's mouth. The guard worked his jaw and looked at his old friend with a sigh of relief.

"Thank god you're finally here."

"Tell me what happened."

"Some girl snuck in during the night and grabbed us one at a time."

"You're telling me that a single girl did all this?"

"I am ashamed to say so, but, yes."

The man shook his head. "Hannah will not be pleased. She hired you for a simple task, and you failed her."

"What do you think she will do?"

"I think that she will have to start downsizing her operation."

"You mean…?"

"Yes, she will have no choice but to terminate each and every one of you."

Before the guard could even yelp in surprise at seeing the silenced pistol pointed right at his face, his head exploded.

Chapter 36

Melissa tightened the zip ties a little too much around Henderson's wrists and ankles. After she bound him, she sat him up on his knees. He kneeled in the familiar position as if he expected to be executed. She sat in the chair by the computer monitors and stared at him for a long time.

He was tired of waiting for her to say something, so he spoke first.

"What now?"

"You tell me where the Vice President is and maybe I'll let you live."

She could see the defiance flash across his eyes.

"I don't know what you're talking about."

She knew that she had to show him she was more dangerous than he currently believed.

She leaped up from the chair she was sitting on, grabbed it, and threw it violently across the room. "Cut the bullshit! All your little friends are dead. If you want to join them, keep lying to me."

He flinched under her sudden outburst.

"Okay, he's in the bedroom at the top of the stairs, second floor."

She smiled. "You must think I'm a fool. That's your room."

For the first time he appeared shocked. He quickly hid it, but she knew that she had gotten her point across. She had insider information. And anytime the enemy knew anything about your base camp, they were very dangerous indeed.

"I don't know."

She moved in closer. "Nice try, but you are the head of security here. Where is he?"

"As soon as I noticed my guards missing from the perimeter, I checked his room. He's wasn't there."

She stood back up.

"Now we're getting somewhere."

Chapter 37

Denny rubbed his cold hands together. Water vapor escaped is mouth with each exhale.

He didn't know how much longer he could lie on the freezing ground and hoped something would happen soon. He had watched the only access road to the estate for half an hour, and nobody had used it in any direction.

His walkie-talkie crackled to life. "Denny, do you read?"

Nick was calling. Maybe it was finally time for some action.

"Loud and clear," Denny responded.

"Any activity on the perimeter?"

"Negative. All quiet on the western front."

"What about the barn?"

"Can't see it from this position. Do you want me to move?"

"Go ahead and stay where you are, but stay alert."

"Roger that."

He put down the walkie-talkie and cupped his hands while blowing into them to try to warm them against the bitter cold. Hopefully something would happen soon.

Nick tried to reach Melissa again on the walkie-talkie.

"Melissa, come in." He released the talk button and listened to static. "Melissa, do you read me?"

She hadn't come back online since she ceased communication right before going into the underground tunnel. He listened to the static for a second and then dialed her cell phone and listened as it rang several times before the voicemail answered.

"Come on, Melissa, where are you?" he muttered as he hung up.

He couldn't wait any longer, and slung the Heckler & Koch HK416 Enhanced Carbine over his shoulder and set out for the house.

Chapter 38

General Archon had stayed up the entire night waiting for the break that would help him save what was left of his career. Rawlins had heard the man call the woman by the name Melissa. It wasn't much to go on, but it was all they had. That and Digital Storm. And his men had agreed to keep the intrusion under wraps to give them a chance to fix the situation.

His contacts in the civilian sector also meant that waiting on the roof of the nondescript building in the middle of Manhattan was the Sikorsky X2 TECHNOLOGY Demonstrator helicopter. This one-of-a-kind experimental helicopter prototype was developed by the Sikorsky Aircraft Corporation and could easily reach a top speed of nearly 300 miles per hour, nearly double the speed of any other helicopter in the world.

He would have preferred a mach capable fighter jet, but with the lack of a runway in the middle of Manhattan, this was the best he could do. And as soon as Digital Storm located who had infiltrated one of the most secure locations in the United States, he would catch up to them in no time.

He sat at his desk and rubbed his bloodshot eyes as each new report flickered on the monitor. People sure do use the name Melissa a lot in emails, texts and phone calls over a twelve-hour period.

His desk phone rang, and he snatched up the receiver with the speed of a rattlesnake striking its prey.

"Tell me something I want to hear."

"DS picked up a call that used the name Melissa thirty seconds ago."

"I have been watching the reports on my monitor. That call was made in Pennsylvania."

"I think this is the one you are looking for, sir."

"It matched none of the other criteria. Only the name Melissa. And that was faint at best."

"But it's where the call originated from that makes this one unique."

He was far too tired to play games. "Out with it!"

"The call was made from a cell phone within the boundaries of Representative William Hartford's estate in Pennsylvania."

He sat up straight. This was it. All the pieces were falling into place.

First the attack on the Vice President.

Then William Hartford failing to report to Site R.

Later someone infiltrating Digital Storm.

And now a phone call from Hartford's Pennsylvania estate referencing someone named Melissa. There was too much coincidence to think it couldn't be the very same Melissa who was here yesterday.

He had just stumbled across the biggest chance of his career. Soon he would have his pick of assignments and would never have to sit at a desk again.

Chapter 39

Melissa had been getting nowhere in her questioning of Henderson when she noticed the computer-enhanced bright red flare on the screen that signaled movement outside and looked directly at the monitor. She turned back just as he stood up quickly and smashed his head right into her nose. She stumbled backwards as blood gushed from her nose.

His head hurt from the strike, but he had to make his escape before whoever was approaching the house showed up and he became outnumbered.

He hopped forward on his bound legs. He propelled himself forward and drove her into the wall. Her head cracked against the wall, and she slumped to the floor.

He rolled over to the pack that she had carried in. He lifted it with his hands bound behind him and dumped the contents all over the floor. He found the knife he was looking for. He lifted the knife and jabbed it into the top of the table. On the third attempt, it stuck solid in the surface. He sawed the zip ties against the blade and freed himself. He rubbed his wrists and pulled the knife out of the table to cut his legs free.

He scooped up the MP5SD and gathered the spilled contents of the pack. He stuffed them all back in the pack and slung it over his shoulder. He aimed the MP5SD at her moaning form.

A quick burst, and she would no longer be a problem to anyone.

The utility closet door burst open and William Hartford

slammed full force into Henderson. The collision skewed his aim, and the MP5SD chewed into the dirt floor around her with all thirty rounds before clicking empty.

Henderson swung around and grabbed Hartford by the neck. He spun him around and tossed him over the desk and into the security monitors.

The LCD monitors cracked under the impact, and Hartford crumpled to the ground whimpering, shattered LCD panels collapsing down on top of him.

The stairs leading down to the basement were old and made of wood, and the top stair creaked anytime someone put his weight on it.

Henderson heard it creak now.

He ran to the tunnel opening and looked back to see feet coming down the stairs slowly. He closed the door to the tunnel as quietly as he could and ran through the low underground tube.

Chapter 40

Melissa felt the water touch her lips. She tried to focus on the room around her, but her head hurt with blinding pain. She hungrily gulped down the water. It soothed her dry throat.

She blinked several times before the room finally came into focus. The room spun around again and she closed her eyes. Another gulp of water, and she opened her eyes again.

The figures standing around her slowly came into focus. She half expected to see her captors standing over her in the dense jungles of South America. Instead, she was pulled back to the present as Nick moved in close and smiled.

"That's quite a bump."

She remembered what Henderson had done, and she tenderly probed the back of her head. Her hand came away clean. No blood. The walls were made from the same packed dirt as the floor, and it absorbed most of the energy when she hit her head against it. This knowledge didn't make it hurt any less.

"Vice President..." she croaked.

"He's safe."

Hartford moved into her field of vision. "Henderson almost killed you."

"Henderson," she looked around the basement.

"If he's the one you tangled with, he must have heard me coming and went out the back door." Nick glanced at the steel door set in the back of the dimly lit room.

"–Guards," she sat up and leaned against the wall.

"You took care of them."

She pointed to the same steel door in the corner of the room.

"No – all alive – end of that tunnel."

"Then we better get out of here."

Chapter 41

Henderson reached the grate that led up to the inside of the barn and spotted the string leading to the flashbang grenade. He jammed a thin stick into the pin slot and removed the grenade. He pushed up the grate and pulled himself up out of the tunnel, replaced the grate, and turned around.

He did a double-take as he stared at his entire security team.

All shot in the head execution style.

His muscles bunched up, and he grabbed a walkie-talkie from one of his dead guards. This girl would pay for what she had done.

He switched the walkie-talkie to the new frequency.

"This is Henderson, anyone read?"

All at once, his remaining five men in the house responded.

"Get out of the house and surround it. Each of you take a spot around the house at seventy-five degree arcs. You have fifteen minutes to get into position. When I toss a flashbang into the air that will be your signal to move in. And I want them taken alive."

Chapter 42

Nick looked around the room, and his eyes stopped at the shattered monitors. One of them still worked, and he could see the bright red flare of movement on the cracked screen. He left Melissa leaning on the wall and stepped closer to focus his attention on the screen. Through the bright red glow, he watched as an armed guard stepped into view around the house right before the monitor sparked and blinked off. They had surrounded the house and blocked all avenues of escape. He went back to her. They had only one chance to escape.

"Can you walk?"

Her head rolled around. She was exhibiting the symptoms of a mild concussion. He held her up and looked into her eyes.

"Focus on me."

She shook her head once and looked at him. Her pupils were the same size. This was a good sign that she would recover quickly.

"How do you feel?"

"My head hurts."

"Can you run and shoot a gun?"

She smiled. At least she still had her sense of humor. He knew that she couldn't hit anything she shot at for at least an hour or more. They needed to carve an escape route out of the wall that Henderson had built around the house. He moved in close and held her gaze.

"Does Henderson know about Denny?"

"I don't think so."

"Don't think so or don't know so?"

"I didn't tell him about Denny."

He pulled the walkie-talkie from his pocket and switched to the second channel.

"Denny?" He released the button on the walkie-talkie.

"Yeah?"

"We are trapped in the house and need you to make a path for us to get out."

"Any particular spot?"

"We'd appreciate a straight run to the van."

"I'll let you know when I'm in position."

He pocketed the walkie-talkie. He glanced at the shattered monitors. They were operating blind. He turned to the Vice President who was breathing heavily as he leaned against the wall. The medication was starting to wear off, and he was drinking water to perk himself up.

"Can you run, Mr. Vice President?"

The Vice President looked at him and let out a slight smile.

"I could if my life depended on it."

He didn't smile back. "It does."

Denny shifted the weight on the Heckler & Koch Grenade Machine Gun before he dropped the tripod stand again. The HK GMG was designed to be portable via a two-man team, but he was only one man and had to carry the tripod while he shouldered the weight of the sixty-four-pound machine gun across his back. He dragged another eighty pounds of HEDP (high-explosive, dual-purpose) M430 cartridges behind him in the ammunition belt.

He spotted the van and dropped the tripod on the ground. He let the HK GMG slide to the ground and then arched his back. He hoped he picked the right spot, because he didn't want to lug that piece of heavy artillery around again.

He unfolded the tripod, mounted the GMG, and loaded the ammunition belt. He pulled the cocking lever and sighted down the barrel towards the house in the distance. He had a clear shot through the trees.

He pulled the walkie-talkie from his pocket.

Melissa was feeling better. Her head still ached, but the dizziness had worn off, and she could stand and walk without the room spinning around. She was ready to make a run for it when she needed to. Nick's walkie-talkie crackled, and Denny's voice came through loud and clear from out of Nick's pocket.

"In position."

Nick pulled the walkie-talkie out and pressed his thumb on the talk button.

"Roger. Can you see the barn?"

"Negative. I have a great view of the house. The barn must be on the other side."

"Good. We'll let you know when we need you to open a door for us."

Nick pocketed the walkie-talkie. He grabbed his HK416 Carbine and looked at the ragtag group.

"Is everyone ready to make a grand exit?"

Chapter 43

Henderson pulled the pin on the flashbang and counted to three. He wanted it to go off as high as possible. He stood and pulled his arm back. He launched the grenade high into the sky. It spun as it arced up. He ducked down away from the grenade, he didn't need to be blinded right before the assault.

Denny saw the small black dot spin up into the sky. It flashed and left a small spot in his vision. He felt like he had looked at the camera when the flash went off. He heard the pop a moment later.

That was a flashbang. He knew that Nick would have called him on the walkie-talkie. This wasn't his signal. This was Henderson signaling his men to move in.

He wasn't about to let that happen, but he didn't want to hit the house until he knew Nick and Melissa were out. He had to create a distraction to stop the impending assault, and he had the best distraction money could buy right in his hands.

He swung the HK GMG away from the house and pulled the trigger. From this distance, they would not hear the launch of the 40 mm grenades before multiple high-explosive charges detonated right in the midst of them.

Henderson stood as soon as the flashbang detonated. He

moved towards the house. He saw his team on both sides of the house advance in as planned. His enemy was outmanned and outgunned. If they knew what was best for them, they would give up right away before things got out of control.

A strange sound hummed overhead. He paused as he searched the sky and tracked the sound. The guard to his left heard it, too, and stopped his own advance on the house right before he exploded.

Melissa had heard the small pop just as they hit the top of the stairs from the basement. It sounded like a flashbang being set off outside.

Right after the initial pop, Nick crouched and slid to hug the wall of the hallway. He had his HK416 aimed at the front door. He lifted his head to peek out a window just when the glass shattered inward. Layers of dust lifted off the furniture as multiple explosions rocked the house from every possible direction. The loud explosions messed with her already shaky equilibrium, and she was thrown to the ground. The thundering stopped and he scrambled across the floor towards her. He looked at the Vice President and Hartford.

"This is our chance. We need to get out of here now."

Nick pulled her to her feet and headed for the front door. He pulled the door inward and looked out. The smoke started to clear, and guards yelled in panic and pain from every direction. He pulled her out of the house after him. She ran alongside him as they dropped from the porch, the Vice President and William Hartford right behind them.

She spotted the guard to her right just as he pulled the trigger on his HK416. The guard collapsed in a spray of red.

She finally gained her balance and pulled away from his grasp. Something hummed overhead, followed by explosions that tore into the house behind her.

She ran in the direction of the van as fast as her unsteady legs would take her. Explosions and screams echoed behind her. Bullets tore into the trees and bushes all around her as the guards regained their senses and opened fire on the escaping prisoners.

A grenade slammed into the propane tanks on the side of the house. The resulting detonation sounded like World War Three had started as the house splintered into a million pieces. The force of the explosion threw everyone to the ground. She rolled over and looked back. The house was gone. Pieces of wood and cement landed all around her.

A lone guard crawled up shakily out of a pile of smoking debris. He saw her and raised his gun. She didn't have time to react, and was bracing for death, when his torso shredded apart in a red mist, and he disappeared back into the rubble.

She dragged herself to her feet and continued to run for the van. She hoped she was going in the right direction because the Vice President and Hartford had regained their footing and were following right behind her.

She heard more shouts as guards continued their pursuit. She could see the van up ahead and ran right past Denny.

She stopped at the van and turned around to help the Vice President and Hartford into the van. Several guards were running right towards her. They stopped as they spotted Denny on the ground with the grenade machine gun. He pulled the trigger. Body parts flew in every direction as the grenades slammed into the guards and detonated.

Nick ran in from the forest to her left and jumped into the driver's seat.

"Get in, let's go."

She held the side door open and yelled to Denny.

"Come on," she screamed.

Denny spotted Henderson running at them through the forest. He swung the barrel of the GMG around and pointed it at Henderson.

Henderson froze.

Denny pulled the trigger and nothing happened.

He jerked at the cocking lever. The feed belt jammed and rendered the grenade launcher inoperable. He jumped up and bolted for the van. Henderson raised his MP5SD.

She never heard the silenced machine pistol fire but watched in slow motion as his face contorted with pain. He arched forward from the multiple impacts of 9mm rounds, and his eyes darted back and forth to seek her out.

Their eyes connected through the forest. Emotions, hopes, fears, and truth communicated instantly between them. She watched Denny's eyes lose focus and glaze over as he pitched forward face first into the dirt.

"No!" she screamed.

Nick jammed the gear shift into drive and smashed the gas pedal into the floorboard.

The van lurched and almost threw her out the side door. She watched as Denny's sprawled body receded into the distance. Henderson ran past Denny's lifeless form and aimed his MP5SD at the van. Bullets sparked as they ripped into the side of the van and forced her to duck away and flatten herself on the floor while she yelled for the Vice President and Hartford to do the same.

Nick yanked the steering wheel and almost tipped the van over as he turned onto the main road. Two wheels lifted before they slammed back down to the pavement. He pushed the gas pedal flat on the floorboard and roared through the Virginia countryside at ninety miles an hour.

Henderson emptied the entire magazine of his MP5SD into the back of the escaping van before he threw the spent machine pistol to the ground in a rage. Hannah had put her faith in him to keep Hartford in line and the Vice President under wraps.

And he had failed on both accounts.

If Hannah ever found him, she would not treat him kindly.

A hollow thumping sound echoed through the trees, and he looked up as a twin-rotored helicopter, unlike any he had ever seen before, circled around the estate and descend towards the destroyed house.

He didn't wait around to see who had arrived late to the party. It was time for him to drop off the face of the earth.

As he ran through the thickening woods at the edge of the Hartford estate, he prayed that Hannah would never find him.

Chapter 44

Melissa sat on the cot in her room above the Manhattan warehouse. She stared at her hands while Nick paced back and forth in front of her. He paused every now and then and muttered to himself.

Finally, he stopped pacing and sat down on the cot next to her.

She looked at him, tears rolling down her face. "He's dead."

He placed a hand softly on her knee. "If there is anything I can do."

Her eyes darkened. "I told you he was not ready."

He took his hand away. "If you want to play the blame game, I'm ready, but not right now. We have the Vice President and the Speaker of the House driving a phony delivery van to your house to pick up your family. But, coming back here is not a good idea. And unless we can think of something quickly, we just might get accused of kidnapping them in the first place. And I don't want anyone to think I was involved in any of this from the beginning."

"We weren't."

"And I'd like to keep it that way. So what do we do?"

She wiped away the tears. "You're the mastermind."

"We need some place to hide them until we can be sure they are out of danger. But I don't have anywhere like that."

She stared at the wall. She had wanted to keep this one last place sacred. Somewhere she could go that nobody knew about. She had even purchased the land through a false identity that couldn't be traced to her. She looked at him. She had never seen him like this, and she doubted she ever would again.

For the first time in his life, he needed help from someone else.

He needed help from her.

She cleared her throat. "I have a place."

He jerked out of whatever thought he was in the middle of and looked at her. "What?"

"I have a place where the Vice President and Hartford will be safe."

"And what about finding out who is doing all this?"

She looked at him. "Robert can tell me."

He stood up abruptly and shook his head. "Robert's out of the business. He can't help us."

"He might still have…"

"No! We can't use him."

He stomped through the door and slammed it shut after him. She stood up and listened as he stormed down the metal stairs. The sound of his feet striking the metal steps reverberated through the metal walls of the second floor office. He was holding something back, or hiding something. She needed to get additional help if they were going to find out who was after the Vice President. Even if he didn't want that help.

She stood up from the bed and switched the lock on the door. He would have heard the lock engage. He had a key, but she was betting that he wouldn't use it until tomorrow morning.

She looked down at her blood-stained clothes and the

pile of new clothes on the desk. She stripped off her clothes and put on the fresh ones. She inspected every seam and fold before she put the new pants and shirt on. The new jacket had a tiny separation in one of the seams. She left that jacket on the desk. The new shoes he provided would also have a tracking device implanted in the soles, so those also had to stay in the room.

She used her blood-stained shirt to wipe as much blood from her jacket and shoes as she could. She tied her shoes tight and spun the jacket onto her back. She looked down at herself. Only if someone looked too closely would they notice the faint blood stains. This was not the first time she wandered around in blood-stained clothes, and it would probably not be the last, she thought.

She opened the window and edged herself out over the windowsill. She bent her knees slightly as she hung from the edge of the window. She let herself drop and crouch-rolled when she hit the ground to reduce the impact and convert the downward momentum into sideways energy.

She stood and looked up at the window fifteen feet above her head. She wouldn't be able to get back in the same way she got out. She had also locked her office door from the inside so she couldn't sneak in the front way either without having to make a lot of noise. I'll cross that bridge when I get to it, she thought.

She walked out to the street and traveled several blocks, checking behind her occasionally to make sure she wasn't being followed.

She spotted a taxi with its light on heading her way. She stuck her arm up and hailed the taxi.

Every night, Robert took his wife Marcie to St. Francis Hospital. While Marcie endured her cancer treatments, he crossed the street to Hamilton Park and sat on the same bench. He had done this for so long he became part of the local culture and would share his wisdom with anyone who sat by his side.

Three years ago, when she went against The Council, she found Robert sitting on that bench. He had introduced her to Nick as well as providing her the support for weapons and vehicles she was in constant demand for. Robert "retired" soon after. His wife had taken a turn for the worse, and he wanted to spend every moment he had left with her.

Whether Nick agreed or not, she had to speak to Robert. She counted on him still sitting on that bench by the time she arrived. What she didn't know was that he no longer had a reason to go to St. Francis Hospital.

Marcie had died two years ago.

Chapter 45

Melissa sat in the taxi and watched the scenes blur by outside the windows. She observed life from a distance, separated from what could only be considered a normal life. She had tried to lead a normal life in Oregon, but a normal life was apparently not something she was allowed to have. The gods above had decided that her life must be full of turmoil and desperation.

What did they want from her?

What did she want from them?

What does everyone want? To be happy? She reflected back on her life and saw happy moments. These were quickly replaced by an overabundance of pain and suffering throughout her life. Her parents died when she was in high school. She chose the military life in an attempt to replace them. The U.S. Army became her new family, and that family turned on her and left her for dead in the jungles of South America.

She sat up in the taxi. She just realized how far down into hell she had traveled in order to bring her to the point where all she wanted was revenge. She emerged from that jungle a different person. Every ideal that she had held dear had been replaced with a thirst for revenge. Her experience in the jungle had changed her very spirit and made her something less than human.

Something primal.

She had become an animal.

What did she hope to gain by talking with Robert?

Did she want him to tell her that what she had done was okay? That she could still be saved?

She almost ordered the taxi to turn around. She feared that he would shun her. He would not recognize what she was now. What she had become.

The taxi stopped and jolted her out of her introspection. She looked up. The gods were once again guiding her every step. She stared into Hamilton Park.

She paid the taxi and glanced at her watch. It was just after five o'clock as she walked into Hamilton Park. It was time to stop running. He would help her. This was her sacred grove. Here is where she could rediscover her true self.

She paused behind a tree and looked across the open space to the bench he should be sitting on. She saw a frail old man feeding the pigeons from that bench. Her heart sank. This thin shadow of a man could not be him. Despite everything, he had always stayed strong. He had told her he kept his strength for Marcie. She needed to see that he stayed strong so that she could also be strong and defeat the cancer that threatened to destroy her.

She walked over to the bench and sat down on the other end of the bench from the little old man. If he wasn't there to guide her, maybe his spirit was still in the bench and she could have an internal dialogue with him.

She remembered the times when she met him at this park for information and supplies to carry out her personal war. She closed her eyes to let the fading sun warm her vision. She pictured herself sitting there on that very bench many years ago. She turned her head in her mind to see him sitting on the bench. He sat there smiling back at her.

She smiled back and suddenly felt warm. In her chaotic life, he had always been the steadfast post she could lean on. He had told her, on many occasions, he would always be there when she needed him.

He opened his mouth to speak, and she heard him as if he was sitting right next to her.

"I was told you were dead," he said.

Her eyes popped open. She hadn't realized that she had actually turned her head and faced the frail old man while she reflected on her past.

It was only then did she look directly into the eyes of the old man. The body was not like she remembered. It was thin and weak. But the eyes still held the power and wisdom she had come for in the past.

Robert's piercing eyes inspected her face. "It looks like whoever tried before is still trying."

She instinctively touched her swollen nose. Her mouth hung open, unable to utter even the simplest sound. He understood and gave her a slight smile.

"When Marcie left," he began, "I no longer had to show that I was strong enough for the both of us. It's funny, here I was being the strong one, and it turned out that she was much stronger than I ever was. As soon as she passed on, I fell apart."

He lifted his thin arms.

"Look at me now. Most people follow within a year of the death of their spouse. I must admit I was determined to fall right in line with the average person. And then Marcie came to me in a dream while I sat here on this bench. She told me that I was still needed. She said that my purpose was not to be strong for her, but to share what I have with those who were young and still searching for answers. For over a year, I sat at home feeling alone. After Marcie gave me a wakeup call, I returned to this bench. I come here every day, unless it's raining. Here, look at this."

He leaned forward and she saw the shiny bronze plaque bolted to the bench right behind his back. She leaned in and saw the words "Reserved for Robert the Wise" etched into the bronze. He sat back and looked at her.

"Either you really are dead and have come to give me some wisdom from beyond, or I am dead and you are here to greet me."

"Neither of us are dead, Robert."

"Too bad." He tossed the last of the bread crumbs to the pigeons all around his feet.

"I need you now more than ever, Robert."

"I am no longer in the game. I cannot provide what you need. You must find someone else."

"I don't know who else to trust."

"You want me to tell you who to trust?" he asked.

"Yes," she stated.

"Trust yourself." He jabbed a bony finger into her shoulder. "Once you do that, your eyes will open to a whole new world. A world where everything is clear."

"I can't trust myself," she said. "I have done too much and don't know who I am anymore."

"You can be redeemed," he said.

"I turned my back on everything you taught me and did something more terrible than even you could ever imagine."

Robert's eyes sparkled with a glint of understanding.

"It is not me you should be telling this to."

"Then who. Who do I tell?"

"You have to live your life over again and make new choices. Through those choices you can forgive yourself."

"No," she replied. "I can't...I can't forgive myself for what I have done."

"Then I forgive you," he said quietly.

"I haven't done anything to you."

"If you have not been true to yourself, then that affects all of us."

"What I have done is unforgivable."

"That's the beauty of forgiveness. And the misconception. Forgiveness is so easy to give out, we often feel that there must be some catch, something we are missing. I can tell you that forgiveness is easy to give, and even easier to give to ourselves. But there is a catch. To be truly forgiven you must learn from your mistakes and grow as a person. We all reach out to grasp at something to hang onto, something that will make us better than we are. But we don't always choose the correct path along the way. When we stumble, it is only forgiveness that can return us to the path that leads us to become the ideal person, the person we strive to be."

"It's too late for me."

"You are not dead yet."

He stood up and leaned heavily on his cane. He turned to face her.

"I will tell you this. Too many times we search for the enemy in the distance when instead we should be looking a little closer to home."

He turned and walked away without looking back.

She watched as he walked slowly out of the park. He leaned heavily on his cane and shuffled as he walked. She knew the hidden strength that burned vibrantly under that frail body. Despite the obvious toll that age and stress had taken on his body, he still walked with a sense of purpose that most people lacked.

Across the street from Hamilton Park, the black van with tinted windows continued its silent vigil. The driver held binoculars to his eyes as he watched Melissa. The old man with her stood up slowly and shuffled off, leaving her alone. The driver lifted a walkie-talkie to his mouth.

"This is Eagle Five. Visual contact with the target achieved."

"Roger, Eagle Five. Please stand by." The walkie-talkie crackled.

"Please confirm location."

"Target is sitting on a bench at Hamilton Park in New Jersey. She has apparently evaded her counterpart to come here. We have noticed no one else around. She talked with an old man for a few minutes and then he left. She is alone."

"Eagle Five," said a new voice. "This is General Archon. Don't do anything until I get there."

Chapter 46

Wilkes blended perfectly into the Vermont countryside and was easily concealed within the wild forest just outside the small colonial-style house. The binoculars looked small in his powerful hands as he held them to his face.

He had changed into his much preferred woodland camouflage BDUs, the standard Battle Dress Uniform of the United States Marines. His orders were to sit and wait for further instructions. His unique training from the Marine Special Operations Command Force Recon gave him the skills to wait indefinitely.

When Hannah called him back with further instructions, his first visit was to Hartford's daughter. Now she was tied up in the trunk of a Toyota Camry hybrid parked less than half a mile away. He shot two holes in the side of the trunk to scare her into staying quiet and provide air holes to prevent her from suffocating. It really didn't matter if she made any noise. He had parked the Camry far enough away from the road that she would never be heard.

He found blankets that would keep her warm during the day, but by nightfall, he would have to move her unless something happened soon. He propped the pre-paid cell phone on the ground right next to him. He needed to be ready when the call came.

He removed the needle from its holder in the case and stared at it. It was going to be a long night, and he needed to stay alert. He stuck the needle into the rubber lid of the small bottle and extracted an appropriate dosage of the clear liquid.

He gritted his teeth as the needle pierced his skin and the liquid burned through his veins. Within moments, he felt more alert. His body temperature increased as the stimulant medication spread through his system. Even in the cold Vermont weather, he could now wait as long as he needed.

Stimulant abuse was the official reason he had been kicked out of the Special Forces. Nobody understood how much they helped make him a better soldier.

Chapter 47

William Hartford glanced at his reflection in the mirror of the USA Couriers delivery van he was driving. His graying hair had taken the dye and was now a sandy orange color. It was dyed to match the color of the false mustache. He touched the mustache again. The glue held well, and the mustache no longer itched.

Melissa had called him during his long drive to Vermont and given him the GPS coordinates of a cabin she owned on the Tug Hill Plateau in the Adirondack Mountains. It was a remote location, and he and the Vice President would be safe there until she contacted them.

He turned the delivery van onto the street where her family lived. The woods were heavy in this part of Vermont. The houses were nestled in little clearings amongst the trees. The forest was so thick in some areas, houses no more than fifty feet apart felt as if they were alone in the forest.

The road he traveled must have started as an old dry creek bed. It snaked back and forth as he wound the van through the forested mountains that shot up behind the single row of houses on either side.

The house was being watched, and if he stayed too long, he might become a prisoner himself. He looked around as he drove. This was such a peaceful place. It seemed a shame that he would have to take them away from all of this.

He turned into the driveway and pulled as close to the front door as he could. The large metal delivery van would shield the front door from view. He planned to get the family into the van as quickly as possible and leave.

He grabbed a large box and stepped out onto the driveway. He walked up to the front door and rang the bell.

He drummed the sides of the box nervously. He resisted the urge to look around. If he was being watched right now, he had to look just like any other parcel delivery driver dropping off a package.

He rang the bell again.

Now he was worried. He fidgeted while he waited for the door to answer.

Rebecca, Melissa's ex-husband's new wife, opened the door.

"Hello?"

"TEO T'WAWKI."

Rebecca stopped talking, her mouth hung open in mid-sentence. He knew he had said the strange word correctly. Melissa told him it was internet chat room shorthand for "The End Of The World As We Know It" and had become the safety word that would give anyone full cooperation of the family in an emergency.

He stepped in closer.

"Get Andrew and Billy, we have to leave right now."

"What?"

"Your lives are in extreme danger," he interrupted her. "I have to get you out of here!"

Rebecca's eyes darkened.

"The house is being watched. We don't have time. Get them now!"

Wilkes watched the driver with the bushy mustache drive past the house. Five minutes later the same delivery van returned and pulled around to the front of the house. From his position on the hill behind the house, he couldn't see the front door directly, but the large family room windows gave him a view of the entry hallway.

It had been several minutes, and he hadn't seen the delivery van leave yet. He suddenly remembered that this was Sunday. Not a typical delivery day. Maybe this was not a standard delivery.

He heard the van start up and pull away from the house. He trained the binoculars on the van. The driver was alone and didn't look like anyone he had been briefed to watch for. He was ready to focus on the house again when, just before he lowered the binoculars, a boy leaned forward into view to talk to the driver.

This boy was the son of Melissa Stone.

And he was no longer in the house.

He stood up and ran full speed to his car, parked half a mile away. That van couldn't travel too quickly, and he was confident he would catch up to it in no time.

Chapter 48

Hartford removed the itchy false mustache and scratched his upper lip. He drove west on the Theodore Roosevelt Highway Bridge over Lake Champlain. This would take them across the islands to the New York side of the lake and into the Adirondack Mountains. Melissa had purchased a home under a false name on the Tug Hill Plateau just west of the Adirondacks in upstate New York.

Tug Hill comprised twenty-one hundred square miles of heavily forested land and received the heaviest snowfall in the entire eastern United States. The most notable characteristic of Tug Hill, and the reason she wanted a home there, was its relative lack of people.

She told him to take her family there until she contacted him.

He glanced in the rear view mirror. His untrained eye never noticed the gold Toyota hybrid that followed the delivery van onto the bridge.

In the back of the van, Melissa's son fired questions at the Vice President, who did his best to stay cordial. He was a politician through and through.

"Look, kid, your mother saved my life. She's a hero in my book."

"But the news said you're in a coma in the hospital."

The Vice President smiled at him. "Who are you gonna trust? Your own two eyes or the liberal media?"

Wilkes caught up to the van just as it crossed the Theodore Roosevelt Highway Bridge to South Hero Island. Finding the van after more than a fifteen-minute head start had proved easier than he had originally thought. It was Sunday, and there was only one delivery van on the roads.

He tried the phone number and got voicemail again. Something was wrong. William Hartford himself came to rescue the family, which meant that the plan had progressed and Hartford was doing exactly what Hannah needed him to do. He would continue to follow the family and stay out of sight until he received the order to move on to the next phase.

He glanced down at the GPS tracking map and confirmed that one of the dots on the screen represented the van's current location. The trackers embedded in every pair of shoes the boy owned functioned perfectly. He touched the GPS screen to cancel out all the tracking dots still at the house in Vermont. Now he could fall back and take his time. He no longer needed to see the van to find them. He let his foot off the accelerator and put a quarter of a mile distance between them.

He tossed the cell phone on the dash. He reminded himself that he wasn't running the show. He would have to wait to be contacted. It was obvious that this entire operation was carefully planned. He was told that someone would come for the family and take them to a more secluded place. And that secluded place was required for the final phase of the plan.

Chapter 49

Wilkes pulled over to the side of the road when his GPS tracker showed that the delivery van had stopped. He looked at his gas gauge. They must be stopping for gas. He would pull into the same station and top off his own tank before continuing his silent pursuit. He didn't need a fill-up. The Toyota hybrid had used less than a quarter of its fuel, but old habits were hard to break.

He marveled at one of the best cars ever created for surveillance. He could outdistance anyone on a single tank of gas. Stopping for gas wasted valuable time, and he performed this little act a tenth of the time as he did with the gas-guzzling HUMVEE he was used to driving when he was on missions for his employer around the world. While not the manliest of vehicles, the hybrid performed this task exceptionally well.

While he sat, he checked the cell phone. He finally had a signal. The phone had been beeping on and off all day as he would travel between cell phone towers found in the small towns placed sporadically along the outer edges of the Adirondacks.

It was time to try the number again.

He opened the phone. The screen displayed two missed calls. They were both from the same number, and neither resulted in a voicemail message. He was relieved. This was the same number he had been trying to reach for several hours. At least his employer was still alive.

He dialed the number, and the familiar voice answered.

"Where have you been?"

"Cell service is spotty out here at best."

"I am afraid that this morning we lost valuable assets and resources. I have determined the final location, and you are the closest operative. In less than an hour, the package will be delivered, and I need you to set it up. We have less than one day, and we cannot afford to waste any more time."

"Yes, sir. You can count on me."

"Good. I will contact you as soon as I have confirmation that the target is en route to your location."

The cell phone beeped and the call ended. The dot on the GPS tracker started to move again, and he started the car and headed for the gas station that the delivery van just left.

He pulled into the station and up to an available pump. He stuck the gas nozzle into the Toyota hybrid and went looking for the station attendant. He needed something a little more conducive to the rugged terrain of the Adirondack Mountains than the Toyota hybrid.

He walked up to the cashier station. He looked through the two-inch thick bulletproof glass and saw that the booth was empty. He walked around to the back of the little hut. The attendant sat on a rusted folding chair behind the tiny building smoking a cigarette. He saw him come around the corner and immediately dropped his cigarette. He stood up and crushed the smoldering ash with a twist of his foot.

"Help ya?"

"I'm looking for the nearest place to rent an all-terrain vehicle."

"Then you want Bob's. He's just a couple miles down

Route Nine. It's on the right. Right next to the Happy Hound Motel. You can't miss it."

He turned and tossed a "thank you" over his shoulder.

Chapter 50

Wilkes jumped over the fallen tree and almost lost his passenger. He hadn't driven an all-terrain vehicle, otherwise known as an ATV, in a long time, and he was enjoying this. The quad ATV had four wheels and was a much more stable platform than its three-wheeled cousin. He was glad that the boss wasn't around to see him goofing off. Samantha, Hartford's daughter, gripped him tightly as he roared through the forest darting recklessly between the trees. He had considered leaving her tied up in the bathroom of the motel next to the ATV rental shop but decided he would be gone too long, and she might attract unwanted attention. It was better that he kept her with him until Hannah said otherwise.

He stopped in a small clearing near the crest of a hill and unfolded the map he had purchased at the ATV rental shop. He checked the map against the GPS readings and then shielded the setting sun from his eyes with his hand as he looked out over the vast wilderness. It would take another two hours to reach the site he marked on the map, and it would be dark in less than an hour.

He decided that it was time to stop and set up camp. Better to have the fire burning before it was too dark to see anything. He positioned the quad in the direction he needed to head in the morning and shut off the engine. The less thinking he had to do in the morning the better. He shut off the GPS unit to conserve the batteries and tucked the folded map into the mesh pocket at the front of the ATV.

He let Samantha go to the bathroom while he watched and then tied her up again.

He pulled the rolled sleeping bag off the back of the quad and cleared a small area of rocks for their sleeping area. He zipped the bound Samantha into her sleeping bag while he gathered and piled nearby rocks into a circle for the fire. Small branches were abundant, and he soon had flames hungrily licking at the leaves and brush he intended to use to get the fire hot enough to ignite the thicker branches.

He sat down on his sleeping bag and munched on a fruit bar as he watched Samantha. It had been even longer since he spent the night with a pretty girl. He knew better than to try anything since it would jeopardize everything they had worked for. He ate two more fruit bars and lied down. He was not worried that Samantha would try to escape. She was tightly bound and trapped in a sleeping bag. She would never be able to wriggle free of the sleeping bag. And even if she could, her feet were bound so tightly she would never be able to run.

He shut his eyes and set his internal clock for six thirty in the morning. He slowed his breathing to a rhythmic tempo and fell asleep within sixty seconds.

Chapter 51

Melissa hadn't moved from the bench and never noticed the immediate temperature drop when the sun had disappeared behind the buildings for the night. Her thoughts were focused on how innocent she was as a child, the adult she became in the Army, and the monster that clawed its way out of the jungle.

At this late hour, a few people still entered the park, using it only as a shortcut to other places. The park reminded her of the jungle. The jungle is where she had died. And the jungle is where she had been reborn. She had risen from the ashes of her former life completely changed. She had become a creature that existed only for revenge.

The trees around her faded from her vision as she retreated into memories buried years ago. Recent events brought them back to the surface in snippets, but she kept burying them back deep into her psyche.

This time she let those memories envelope her. It was time to face what she had become deep in the jungles of South America. Only then could she cleanse herself. Even forgive herself, as Robert had.

She sat on the park bench and let her mind roll back the clock to a time when she fought on the side of the true and the just. Back to the defining event that pushed her to the edge and right over. It was time to understand what had taken her to the darkest aspects of what she was capable of. If she understood what she had become, then she would be able to defeat her internal demons and hopefully recover who she used to be.

Her memories flooded her. She did not suppress them but let them play in her mind like a movie. She remembered vividly every smell, every sound, every feeling she felt on the day her life ended.

The jungle was alive with sounds all around the Delta Force unit. Sergeant Bell stopped and held up a fist. She stopped along with the rest of the unit. He made a few more gestures with his hands, and the team splintered off the trail. Each team member hid far enough away from the trail to be completely invisible in the deep Colombian jungle.

She looked around and finally heard the voices that had alerted the Sergeant. She was the newest member of the unit and had the least experience in the jungles of South America.

Despite her lack of experience in the jungle, she had proven herself a very capable warrior. Her duty record was littered with honors and recommendations from every unit commander that she had served under. She rose quickly through the ranks and was offered a position in the coveted U.S. Army's 1st Special Forces Operational Detachment-Delta.

She accepted with enthusiasm her assignment in the famed Delta Force and was commissioned to South America. Their primary task, hunt down and apprehend drug lords in Colombia.

She reported for duty three weeks ago and informed the Sergeant about her qualifications and the skills that she brought to his command.

He didn't seem to care about any of that. The next newest member of the unit had been serving with Bell for two years. She felt very out of place with this group of jungle warriors. They were a tight clique and she was kept an outsider by everyone in the unit.

The voices moved closer. She watched the trail through the thick jungle brush. Five men passed by. They spoke in Spanish about their latest football strategies and held their Kalashnikov AK-47 assault rifles casually as they walked. The men continued down the path with no knowledge that they were being watched.

She looked through the foliage and located the Sergeant. She watched him for the signal to move in. He let the Colombian guerrillas continue down the path until their careless conversations could barely be heard. Bell stood up and returned to the trail.

She ran to catch up with the Sergeant and shifted the weight of her backpack.

"Why didn't we stop them?"

"Did you see any drugs on them?"

"No, I…"

He stopped abruptly. She almost slammed into him.

"What is our purpose here?" Bell pulled a cigar from his pocket and stuck it in his mouth.

"We are on assignment to identify, target, disrupt and dismantle any and all drug manufacturing and trafficking"

"I say again. Did you see any drugs on them?"

"No." she looked at the ground.

"You're new here, so I'm going to allow you a little time

to make a few errors in judgment. That time is now over. You screw up out here, we all die. Do you understand me?"

"Yes."

"I'm sorry, I didn't hear you." Bell put a finger to his ear and bent it forward.

"Yes, sir!"

"If you question my actions again, you will be reassigned to KP duty in San Diego. Now, get back into position." Sergeant Bell's eyes burned deep into her's.

She stepped out of the trail and let the team pass. She took up the final position as they moved slowly through the jungle.

Two hours later, he stopped the Delta Force team just outside a small town. The team circled around Bell as he spit his soggy cigar stub onto the ground.

"I will go in and meet our contact. Ace and Beverly come with me. Stone, you stay here. Wallace and Hooch stay with her and keep her out of trouble."

She watched Bell walk in to town with his two most trusted members. She slung her M4A1 Carbine over her shoulder.

"What are you doing?" Hooch grabbed for her M4.

"The paramilitary groups don't operate this close to towns." She pulled back away from the reaching hand of Hooch. "And if you reach for my gun again, Wallace here will have to pre-chew your food."

Hooch glared at her, and Wallace laughed out loud.

She walked a few feet away from the two Delta operators. She had been walking through the jungle for three weeks and still had yet to see any action. She was beginning to wonder if this unit was even trying to achieve their objective.

In another week they would be stopping at a NATO re-supply station. She decided to report that the current Delta Force unit was ineffective. She would request a transfer to any other Delta Unit in the world. They had to be seeing more action than she was.

Wallace pushed Hooch into a wall and waggled a finger in his face. She watched as Hooch finally sat down against a tree. Wallace walked over to her.

"You'll have to excuse him." Wallace picked up little rocks and arranged them into patterns on the ground in front of her. "He's been out in this jungle for four years. When you spend that long without a rigid command structure, you forget your place."

"Bell seems to rule with an iron fist."

"Yes, he does. But it's not like you're used to. The jungle, she writes her own rules. Bell has been out here for seven years, and he understands the jungle and understands the people who have made the jungle their home."

Wallace finished placing stones. He pointed to the one closest to her.

"This is the building where Bell is meeting with his informant. The rest of these buildings are storage or market huts. Ace and Beverly are for public display that he is not alone. He'll call them seven and eight to make anyone listening with interest think that there are six more soldiers around somewhere. If something goes wrong, we cover escape from this point and nowhere else. Look at the layout of the town. We have a clear shot right into the center of the village. The three of us can cover every building by spreading out only twenty feet apart."

"Why was I not informed of this plan before Bell went into the village?"

"He came up with this plan seven years ago when he first entered the town. He has never had a chance to need it. But old habits die hard, and here we sit. If something happened, all I had to do was tell you to cover the town and stay put. Hooch and I already know what to do." Wallace looked down at the rocks. "And now so do you."

Wallace walked back and sat against the same tree as Hooch. She looked down at the rocks. Maybe she hadn't seen much action because Sergeant Bell and his unit have already taken most of the drug lords out in this region. Those left would be armed to the teeth to defend themselves against the mythical Delta Force unit.

She ran through multiple scenarios as she crouched before the map made from rocks. She heard Wallace and Hooch get to their feet. She looked up and saw Sergeant Bell returning. She stood up and swept away the map with her boot.

Bell walked up and looked at his unit.

"We have new intel that someone started a small heroin manufacturing shack about two days east of here. We leave now. Any questions?" Bell looked right at her.

"No, sir!"

That two-day walk could just have easily been a two-minute walk. Every tree that she passed look like the last tree they passed. They took more breaks than normal and marched through the night and arrived in a day and a half.

She never checked her compass, but felt as if they had traveled in circles for thirty hours.

Just before nightfall Sergeant Bell raised his hand in a fist, and the unit froze. He signaled the retreat command, and she lead the unit back fifty feet. The Sergeant gathered the unit into a huddle in the middle of the dense jungle.

"Gentlemen," Bell looked right at her. "We have reached the target area. Just over that hill is the heroin lab. Ace will recon and report back the situation. We'll set up camp in the jungle a hundred feet from this position due north. We move first thing in the morning."

She dropped her rucksack and leaned her M4A1 Carbine against it. She glanced over at Hooch. Predictably, he was eyeballing her and shot his eyebrows up in an invite to join him in his sleeping bag. He had done this every night since she arrived.

She had complained once to the Sergeant.

He responded with male chauvinist quips about women in the military. She hadn't complained again. It was just another reason why she would request the transfer as soon as they hit the NATO supply station.

Before her internal clock could wake her at five o'clock in the morning, someone kicked her foot. She opened her eyes and noticed, in the fading darkness, that she hadn't been kicked, but tripped over.

The quiet shadow hadn't noticed her laying in the overgrowth farther away from the rest of the unit.

He must not have realized he had bumped into a soldier as he slowly made his way towards the rest of her unit. She slid silently out of her sleeping bag.

She fingered the safety on her SIG-Sauer P226 X-Five and stood to a shooter's stance.

"Helada." The shadow froze as she had commanded, and the rest of the unit was instantly awake.

"Manos para arriba." The shadow's hands shot into the air.

"No disparar! Don't shoot!"

Flashlights illuminated the face of a kid no more than twelve years old.

"What are you doing here, Alonso?" Bell walked into the dancing beams of light.

"Mi hermano…my brother is at the lab. Please don't kill him." Alonso still had his hands raised.

"Don't worry, son, you can put your hands down." Bell put his arm around the boy's shoulders. "Where did you hear that we were going to the lab?"

Alonso looked around. She could see the fear in his eyes. He hesitated, and Sergeant Bell smiled as he turned Alonso to face him.

"Tell me who told you…"

The harsh staccato of an AK-47 pierced the darkness.

Everyone hit the ground.

She rolled to her stomach and searched the darkness around her. She spotted the flashes from the barrel as each lethal round chewed into the trees around her. She sighted down her X-Five to just above the muzzle flash and fired a single shot. The echoes continued through the jungle for several seconds after the AK-47 stopped firing.

She scanned the semi-darkness for any movement. She still had eighteen rounds in her modified P226 competition pistol. And she was deadly accurate. She heard movement to her right and swung her SIG-Sauer X-Five towards the sound. Alonso was running away through the jungle.

"We move now." Bell jumped to his feet.

She was on her feet. She rolled her sleeping bag and donned her rucksack in less than thirty seconds. She holstered her X-Five and held the M4A1 at the ready. The unit formed a V-shape and moved through the jungle in the direction that Alonso had run. He would be warning the heroin lab that the attack on the U.S. soldiers was unsuccessful and they were coming.

The unit fanned out into a wider V and simultaneously dropped to a crouch as they crested the hill towards their intended target. Just over the hill, Bell halted them with his raised fist. He slid over to her.

"Stay back here and watch the rear. The last thing we need is to walk into a trap and get surrounded."

She nodded and dropped to the ground. She switched her fire selection on the M4A1 Carbine from full auto to single fire. She could be just as accurate with the Carbine as she was with the X-Five.

She crawled back to the top of the hill and watched for any signs of movement. Behind her, AK-47 assault rifles shattered the silence.

She spun around and sighted through the ACOG scope mounted to the rail on her M4A1 Carbine. Muzzle flashes flared brightly in the telescoped view. She pulled the trigger twice, and the Colombian guerrilla went down. She scanned the jungle for the source of the remaining gunfire, her view blocked by the square outline of the small shed that was the makeshift laboratory for the heroin.

Two M4A1's returned the call of the AK-47, followed by silence. She swung around and searched the early morning dawn for any movement deep in the jungle. After a long minute, she stood up and headed down the hill to join the rest of her unit.

"Look at that, the newbie dropped two." Hooch picked up the AK-47 from where the guerrilla had dropped it. She walked up to Hooch and stopped suddenly, her mouth fell open. She stood in a pool of blood that spread from the lifeless form of Alonso.

"If you hadn't stopped him at the camp, he would have slit our throats while we slept." Sergeant Bell kicked the lifeless form.

"Mierda Pequena." Hooch tossed dirt onto the boy.

Ace ran out of the small rusted shed.

"We hit the jackpot this time." Ace handed Bell a small bag of white powder. "Their own tests showed this was about ninety-five percent pure."

"Not bad for a shit-hole like that." Sergeant Bell waved the bag at the rusted shed. "Empty your rucksacks, gentlemen."

Everyone shed their rucksacks and flipped them over. The survival gear and MRE packages spilled to the ground.

Everyone except Melissa.

"Something wrong, Stone?" Sergeant Bell flipped his rucksack right side up.

"What are we doing?" She stared at the rest of the unit as they carried their empty rucksacks into the rusted shed.

"Investing in our retirement." Hooch winked at her.

"Do we have a problem, Stone?" Bell walked up to her.

She snapped her head back to look at Sergeant Bell.

"No, sir." She dropped her rucksack and flipped it over.

Bell turned with a smile and disappeared into the heroin lab. She looked at the spilled contents of her rucksack. She spotted the compass and her map. If she left now, she could reach the NATO supply station in less than a day. She had to report what this Delta Unit was doing out here without supervision.

She dropped and refilled her rucksack with its original contents. She looked up. Everyone was still in the shed. She turned and ran top speed out of the small clearing. She hit the tree line and knew she had to run faster.

"Stone!"

She didn't know their voices enough to know who had yelled after her, but she refused to stop running.

She ran just under her top speed for half an hour. She kept in a straight line and didn't veer from her course until she hit a river. She ran two feet into the water's edge and headed up the river, away from the NATO station. The unit would easily follow her ramrod straight trail to the river. Once there, they would assume she headed down the river to get to the NATO supply station and report them.

She decided to take a long approach and wait a couple of days before she approached the supply station. The unit would already have left by then. Sergeant Bell would report her as a deserter. She would just have to deal with that.

She crossed the river and headed south again. By nightfall, she thought she heard voices. She crouched and walked slowly towards the sounds of human activity. She stopped at the edge of the tree line and looked at a large encampment filled with children playing soccer, or football as they called it here in Colombia. Many girls huddled around the fire, cutting vegetables into a large pot.

Every one of them was dressed in fatigues. A few adults walked around with Kalashnikov AK-47 assault rifles slung around their backs. She had stumbled onto a guerrilla training camp. She backed slowly into the dense jungle and kept moving south towards the NATO station.

She took short naps during her journey to limit the amount of time she spent in one location. By the time the sun peeked over the mountains, she knew she was close. She crossed the deeply rutted road that gave supply trucks access to the NATO station. She circled the station and watched for over an hour. She hadn't seen anyone come in or out during the entire hour.

Something was wrong.

A truck rumbled down the rutted path that led from the airport ten miles away. She circled back to the front where she could see who came out to greet the truck.

The front door opened and a lone NATO worker walked out slowly. He glanced behind him a couple of times before he approached the truck. The worker motioned for the driver to follow him inside.

As the driver reached the door, a man in green fatigues and a mask grabbed him inside the door just as it shut. The guerrillas must have attacked after Sergeant Bell and his men left. There wouldn't be another scheduled U.S. Military team here for another four weeks.

She had no choice. She had to rescue the NATO

workers alone. She ran to the side of the truck. She picked up a large rock and shattered the side mirror. She waited to see if anyone else had heard her. She picked up one of the larger pieces of broken mirror, shuffled silently to the side of the main building, and lifted the mirror to look inside.

She saw the NATO workers tied up and guarded by Hooch.

Bell did not intend to let her tell anyone what she had witnessed. He had taken over the NATO station posed as local guerrillas. This changed the situation. She couldn't barge in and shoot without discretion. Bell could have already reported her as AWOL. Any prosecutor would prove she snapped under the unique pressures brought on by jungle warfare and killed her entire unit.

She retreated away from the station. She would have to find another way. Halfway through the open ground Hooch came to the window and looked out. His eyes locked with her's. A wicked smile spread on his face as he shouted something and turned away from the window.

She abandoned stealth and ran full speed for the jungle. Behind her, the window shattered and Hooch fired the AK-47 at her. She hit the ground and rolled sideways. She fired wildly at the window. It forced Hooch to search for cover. She was on her feet and running again.

The front door slammed open, and the rest of her unit spilled out of the NATO building. They fired at her as she dove into the forest. The 7.62mm rounds shredded the forest all around her. She knew if she stayed there, they would quickly surround her and kill her. She shed her rucksack and M4A1.

She jumped up, despite the ballistics screaming around her, and ran deeper into the jungle. Freshly fired rounds ripped at the edges of her uniform and grazed her skin.

She kept running.

The unit pursued her into the dense vegetation. She was feeling weak from the loss of blood. Several times a round would pound into the body armor on her back and she went down. Each time it took her longer to roll back to her feet and keep running. She wanted to make a stand, but she knew that it would be her last. Her only chance of survival was to keep running.

She halted abruptly at the edge of a cliff. The ground dropped sharply, a hundred feet into the jungle below. She spun around as Bell emerged from the jungle. He was breathing as hard as she was.

"I won't tell anyone what I saw," she heaved out between breaths.

"That's right, you won't." Bell fired a single round to her chest.

The round slammed into her with fourteen hundred pounds of force and propelled her backwards over the edge.

When she woke up, all she could see was the dirt as it pressed into her face. She tried to move. Her body refused to respond. The jungle became quiet all around her, and she felt the presence of others approaching. She expected to see Bell and the rest of the unit. They had climbed down the cliff to finish the job.

The boots that came into view were too small for an adult. She strained to look up. Several children in green fatigues gathered around her.

She closed her eyes and passed out again.

Her eyes fluttered open. The sun shone brightly through the canopy of the jungle. She swayed back and forth on her back. She heard the grunts of several young voices as they carried her through the overgrown jungle.

The sun blinded her as they hit a clearing. She shut her eyes quickly and fell asleep again.

She woke up in a bed this time. She felt no pain. In fact, she felt better than good. She tried to sit up when a woman leaned into her vision and stopped her.

"Don't try to move." The woman pressed Melissa's shoulders back onto the pillow. "You have been through a lot and need to rest."

Melissa took her advice and settled back down. She opened her mouth to ask a question and made a low croaking sound instead.

"Drink this." The woman lifted a glass of water to Melissa's lips.

She slurped at the glass and spilled more than she got into her mouth. She had never been so thirsty before in her life.

"That's a side-effect of the medication." The woman refilled the glass. She held it to her lips again.

She took greater care to drink the contents than she had the last time. Her throat felt better, and she attempted to speak again.

"Where am I?"

"Safe. You need to rest now." The woman twisted a knob attached to a tube in her arm.

"What...what..."

She couldn't finish her question. The room spun around her, and she fell into a drug-induced sleep.

Melissa woke up and looked around. It was pitch black all around her. She opened and closed her eyes several times but still couldn't see anything. Her mouth was even dryer than the last time. A faint light approached, and the woman from earlier stepped into the tent holding a gas lamp.

"Thought you might be awake again." The woman set the lamp down on a table in the middle of the tent. "My name is Gina. How are you feeling?"

She sat up slowly and tried to swallow. Gina poured another glass of water and held it to her lips. She drank the entire glass without spilling.

"Where am I?"

"You are a guest of the Fuerzas Armadas Revolucionarias de Colombia."

"The FARC?"

"At least for now." Gina refilled the glass and handed it to her. "We will get you strong enough to travel and then trade you back to the Americans for money and weapons."

"They won't take me back." She held the glass without drinking.

"Don't be foolish. The insignia on your shoulder is for the 1st Special Forces Operational Detachment-Delta. You are a Delta Force warrior. They will pay a king's ransom to get you back. Your capture has brought prestige to the commander of our little group in the eyes of Tirofijo."

She flinched, not from the pain but from what Gina had just said. Tirofijo was the nickname of Manuel Marulanda Velez. He was the legendary mastermind of the

Revolutionary Armed Forces of Colombia, the FARC. He had controlled the guerrilla movement for the past forty years and would use her as proof that the United States interfered in their struggle to free the Colombian people from a corrupt democratic government.

Her capture would become public knowledge.

Sergeant Bell would convince his superiors to allow him the opportunity to stage a rescue. They would agree with the understanding that she might not survive the rescue attempt. She knew that if Bell's unit found her, she would never leave the jungle alive.

"Gina, you have to help me." She sat up as straight as her aching body would allow. "The people who did this to me, they killed your people to take their drugs for themselves. I tried to stop them."

"Why should I believe you?" Gina came over and took the empty glass from her. "Your wounds are consistent with the AK-47's we use. It looks more like you came across one of our patrols."

"My unit dressed as guerrillas and came after me with AK-47's so that they could blame you for my death."

"You lie very well." Gina picked up the lamp and left the tent.

The light faded into the distance, but not before she noticed the two young boys stationed to guard her tent. She was in no condition to run even if she wanted to. She slid back down and stared into the darkness of the tent.

Gina did not return that night. Nor the next night.

Melissa's wounds were tended to with expert skill, and she grew stronger every day. For the next six months, she formed fragile friendships with some of the boys who guarded her tent.

When she was strong enough to move around with the help of crutches, she asked Alex if she could walk around outside the tent. He was no more than fifteen years old, and he like her. He convinced the camp commander that she would be under constant guard outside her tent. And there was nothing she could do anyway. The commander agreed since it was the only way to stop him from pestering him.

She was watched more than she was guarded when she made her daily walk around the camp. Everyone wanted to see the American warrior. Eventually, she was able to discard the crutches and use a cane to lean on for support. Alex, whether he was on duty or not, was there each morning for her walk.

"So where were we?" She hefted herself off the bed with the cane.

"JR was plotting to put Sue Ellen back in the…in the…"

"The sanitarium."

"Right, the house for insane people."

She stepped out into the warm sun. She squinted while her eyes adjusted. She leaned heavily on the cane. She no longer needed it for support and had been quietly exercising late at night in her tent, but as long as she was still perceived as weak, she could continue her walks around the encampment.

She had counted less than twenty guerrillas permanently stationed at this camp. She heard the training of young new recruits taking place on the other side of the Commander's tent. She stopped her play-by-play of the popular eighties television show Dallas.

"Do you think I could see your training grounds for a change?" She grunted as she shifted her weight on the cane to show Alex how much she was still in pain.

"I don't think so, Melissa." He turned and saw the commander step out of his tent. "Stay right here."

He ran over to the Commander and explained her request to him. The Commander walked over to where she leaned against a tree. She hoped she looked helpless.

"Alex tells me you want to see our training grounds."

"I was just curious…"

The Commander kicked the cane out from under her. She fell to the ground and looked up at the commander.

"If you want to see it that bad, walk over without your crutch." He picked up her cane and walked off.

Alex helped her to her feet. She leaned on him.

By the time they had made it to her tent, she had worked Alex's knife from its sheath and taken it from him without him noticing. She plopped onto the bed and stuffed the knife under her pillow.

She rolled over and lay on the bed panting.

"Do you need anything?" Alex looked very concerned.

"No, I just need to rest. I'll be all right."

"I have to go." He slipped quickly out of the tent.

She removed the knife from the pillow and looked around the tent. She had to hide it somewhere where it couldn't be found.

That night before dinner the Commander stepped into the tent with Alex and two muscular men.

"Search her."

"I'm sure I dropped it in the jungle." He had a bruise forming on the side of his face.

The men tore at her clothes violently until she stood naked before them. They never found what they were looking for.

"Take everything from her tent." The Commander stepped outside as his men removed and tore apart everything in the tent. They found nothing. He looked at her sitting in the corner of the tent. She refused to hide her nakedness but looked away. She didn't want to challenge him just yet.

"She does not eat tonight." He stepped from the tent into the growing darkness.

Alex looked at her and shook his head. He wanted her to know that this was not his fault. She smiled at him. That seemed to calm him down.

"I'll get her some new clothes." He left quickly.

The two guards stared at her naked body. She could feel their eyes enjoying her.

Alex returned quickly with green fatigues. He handed them to her and leaned in close.

"There is a piece of bread in the pocket."

She smiled and took the clothes. He looked at the two large men and ran from the tent. She kept smiling and looked at both men. She tossed the clothes aside.

"Who's first?"

The men exchanged glances and smiled big. The one on her left stepped out of the tent while the other one reached down to unbuckle his belt. He unzipped his pants and looked up as she slammed a fist into the side of his head.

She jumped to the door as the other guard rushed back in. He quickly fell on top of the other unconscious guerrilla.

She quickly dressed in the green fatigues. She crouched near the far corner of the tent, pulled at the edge and dug into the dirt. She extracted the knife from its hiding spot and gripped it in her hand. She bent down and checked the two guerrillas. They would be out for at least an hour. What needed to be done wouldn't take that long.

She peeked out of the tent. The camp was empty as everyone was at the dining hall, a large tent where everyone at the camp gathered for dinner.

Everyone except her.

She looked across at the Commander's tent. A light shone inside, and the shadow on the side revealed that he was alone.

She stepped out of the tent. She wished she had a hat to hide her sandy blonde hair. She moved quickly and walked as if she belonged in the camp, hoping someone wouldn't look too closely at her.

She walked right into the Commander's tent and gripped the knife harder. His back was to the door as he folded a clean uniform. She silently glided up behind him in a crouch and slammed a tight fist into the back of his thigh.

The Commander's leg buckled from the pressure-point strike, and he fell down at her feet. She wrapped an arm around his neck and pressed the knife into his cheek.

"I don't want to hurt you." Blood welled up at the tip of the blade as she pressed the knife into his skin. "I just want to talk. Can we do that?"

The Commander didn't say a word.

"Okay. I'll go first." She moved the knife away from his skin. "The United States Government thinks that I am dead. Before that, they thought I was a traitor. I can never go back. Do you understand me? My commanding officer killed your people and stole their drugs. I was going to report him, and he tried to kill me. If I go back now, he would have already covered his tracks. I would be convicted as a deserter and a traitor and thrown in a military prison for the rest of my life. You understand my reluctance to let Tirofijo trade me to the U.S. Government. I would rather die first."

"So what happens now?" The Commander shifted his weight.

She kicked his foot back outward and put him off balance again.

"How about you let me go."

"You must let me go first."

She rolled the Commander over on his stomach and stood up. She drove the knife deep into the table by the door. He rolled into a sitting position and rubbed his leg.

"Where did you learn to disable a man so quickly?"

"Part of my training with special forces."

"If I grant you your freedom, would you stay long enough to train my warriors with your special skills?"

She looked for a sign that this was a trick. She saw none.

"I will bring special forces skills to your training if you teach me how to exact revenge on those who tried to kill me."

"We are all about vengeance here at the Fuerzas Armadas Revolucionarias de Colombia." He stood up.

"Come; join me at my table for dinner."

She expected him to lunge for her at any moment. Instead he walked past her and out of the tent.

She stepped out of the Commander's tent and saw that he was halfway to the dining hall. He stopped at the entrance, turned around and motioned for her to join him. She walked barefoot across the camp to the dining tent. He stepped inside and she followed right behind.

Silence spread throughout the entire dining hall as everyone became aware that she had walked in behind the Commander. All eyes watched her as she followed him to his table. He slid a folding chair out for her to sit right next to him.

She settled into the metal chair.

"I'm afraid we don't have a menu, it's whatever the cook has prepared for the day." He watched as a plate was set before him. "Which is the same thing he has prepared every day. I hope you like guanaco."

She had seen the llama-like creature roaming the higher plains in the mountain regions, but never this far in the jungle.

"I think it's the only thing the cook knows." He picked up a fork and dug in.

Another plate was placed before her. It didn't matter what it was. It was a hundred times better than the scraps tossed at her for the past six months.

For two years Melissa trained the FARC recruits the best skills that the United States Special Forces had to offer. In return, she was taught the tricks of jungle warfare.

Every day her vengeance was fed raw hatred until it

overflowed and changed her very spirit.

She looked across the yard of new recruits doing pushups and saw Alex point her out to a woman. The woman came closer, and Melissa recognized her. When they first met, she had no idea who she was. Last year she heard that the woman had been promoted because of her actions against the Colombian government.

She rolled the chart that outlined several pressure points used in hand-to-hand combat and saluted the woman that approached.

"Commander Gina."

"You are looking much better than the last time I saw you."

"I never got the chance to thank you…"

"What you are doing here for my brothers and sisters is more thanks than I could have asked for." Gina looked around at the recruits exercising and training harder than she had ever seen before.

"I understand that you have been undergoing training yourself."

"There are some people that need to be taught a lesson."

"And by lesson, you mean kill?"

"They turned on their government. For that they are traitors. If it weren't for you, I would be dead. For that, they must die."

"Then I have something that might be of interest to you."

She took the folded paper that Gina offered to her. She opened it and saw a picture of Hooch. He was being commended for his actions as a fireman in a small town.

She looked up at Gina.

"Thank you." She felt a tear run down her cheek. She knew that her time in the jungles of South America had served its purpose. She was stronger in her new life, and she finally had an outlet for the rage that had built slowly inside of her.

"Promise me one thing. When you are done, you will return to cleanse yourself." Gina turned and walked away.

She confirmed the promise quietly to herself.

Five years later she had all but forgotten her promise.

She was far too focused on removing scum from the face of the earth. And today, one of the scummiest was under FBI protection in the very same hotel she had been watching for several days.

Her mercenary training in the jungle had prepared her for a situation just like this. Whether the jungle was made of dirt and trees or cement and metal, nothing would keep her from her target.

The elevator door chimed and opened. She let out two breaths and her whole demeanor changed instantly from predator to prey. She grabbed the several pieces of luggage and made a show of struggling out of the elevator, dropping and picking up different pieces as she tried to exit before the doors closed.

The FBI agent standing in the hallway just outside the doors spun around and watched her struggle for the briefest of moments before speaking in his well-trained authoritative voice.

"Excuse me, ma'am. This floor is restricted."

She looked up from her struggle and dropped half the

luggage.

"What?"

The FBI agent motioned back and forth.

"This entire floor is reserved."

She looked at him as if he had told her she was walking around naked. She let several emotions pass on her face to hide the one she actually felt. She looked at the FBI agent with innocent eyes. "I think I'm on this floor."

"I'm afraid that's not possible."

She dropped another piece of luggage as she gave the impression she was lost in thought of what to do next.

Her eyes lit up suddenly. "Let me check my key."

She dropped the rest of the luggage and felt her dress before realizing she had no pockets in the flowing sundress.

"Oh, god, I left the key at the front desk. It has been such a bad day for me."

"I can call someone to help you."

She looked at the FBI agent for a moment before she responded by looking down at the scattered luggage and grabbing them one at a time.

"That's okay, I can do it."

She struggled with the luggage and kept dropping one while she tried to pick up another one just as that one fell. After several attempts, she dropped her shoulders and looked at the FBI agent, a pleading look on her face.

"Can I leave these here while I go back to the front desk?"

The FBI agent didn't even look around, a bad sign that he had already made the decision before she even asked.

"I'm afraid not."

She pasted the warmest smile she could on her face.

"I promise to come right back with a bellboy."

The FBI agent's back locked up straight. A definite bad sign.

"I'm not authorized to allow that."

She gave the FBI agent her sweetest smile, but the neutral stare he returned told her everything she needed to know. She grumbled to herself, not so much an act as her actions before, as she tried to gather the luggage again. Her mind worked in overdrive as she tried to formulate her next move when her over-emphasized struggle finally struck a chord with the agent, and he showed that he was human after all.

"Ma'am, you can leave it right here by the elevator, but you have to come right back for it."

She let the luggage drop back to the carpeted floor, and the relief she felt was very real. She had finally gotten through to him, and she could proceed as originally planned.

"Thank you so much, I'll be right back, I promise."

She gathered the luggage together and lined it up on the side of the hallway. She entered the elevator and waved to the FBI agent as the doors closed.

The elevator doors on the other side of the hallway chimed, and FBI Agent Daniels turned his attention away from the woman who had not been blessed with the best intelligence, but had been compensated with sensational looks, and back to his primary job at hand.

The elevator doors slid open and the tranquility of the

hallway was instantly transformed into an elaborate ballet of controlled chaos. Several FBI agents spilled out of the cramped elevator and formed a protective shield around Horace Logan.

They walked as one as they led Horace to one of the doors. They opened it, and he walked in without saying a word to any of them. As soon as he was safely locked away, the remaining agents split up and took the rooms on either side.

Agent Daniels was once again alone with his thoughts in the hallway. Alone except for the luggage.

The elevator chimed, and a luggage cart rumbled noisily out before the doors had even finished opening. The woman exited right behind the bellman and pointed at the luggage lined up along the wall. "They're all right there."

She turned her attention back to him and smiled.

"You were right; this was the wrong floor, I'm sorry to have caused you any trouble."

Agent Daniels gave her the first smile of the night.

"It was no trouble, ma'am."

Her smiled grew even wider. "I can't thank you enough for watching my luggage."

For the briefest of moments, Agent Daniels was interacting with someone who was not out to kill him or his charge. It was a refreshing moment that he would think about and savor for as long as he could. "You're welcome."

The bellboy finished loading up the cart and pushed it back into the waiting elevator. The woman paused and batted her eyes at him as she gave him the most enticing smile. Yep, he would be cherishing this moment for a long time.

The doors whispered shut, and the moment was gone forever. It would be a long time before he would share a moment with someone of the fairer sex again. He closed his eyes and committed her face to memory. And her long jet-black hair. And those long eyelashes that guarded her beautiful brown eyes.

In the elevator, she turned to the bellboy and handed him a valet parking ticket.

"Can you take these out to my car?"

"Of course, ma'am."

"I need to use the restroom before my long trip."

"Good idea, ma'am."

She grabbed the smaller makeup case and looked at the bellboy. "The curse of having to look beautiful all the time. You have to lug this heavy thing around everywhere you go."

The bellboy looked like he wanted to say something, then just smiled and looked at the numbers denoting the current floor of the elevator.

The display showed the digital representation of the letter L right before the doors opened with a faint whooshing sound. She dashed out and headed for the restroom, makeup kit in hand.

Once inside a stall, she opened the makeup case and removed a tiny HD camcorder and a piece of gum. She unwrapped the gum, stuck it in her mouth before she flipped open the viewing screen, and hit the rewind button on the camcorder. After a moment she hit the play button.

She had positioned the makeup case perfectly and had a complete view of the entire hallway. She hit the fast-forward button and watched time speed up. In rapid motion she watched the elevator open and several FBI agents form a ring around Horace Logan. The man she had once known as Hooch.

While she watched the tape, she removed two black gloves from the makeup case and put them on. As soon as Hooch entered his room, she paused the video and counted the number of doors between his and the elevator. She shut the viewer on the camcorder, dropped it into the garbage can, and grabbed the makeup case as she made her way back to the bank of elevators in the lobby.

She got off on the top floor. These rooms were always suites and for the extra thousand dollars a night provided the occupant with a balcony, something she was in desperate need of right about now.

She counted silently to herself each hotel room door as she passed it. She stopped at the correct door and looked up and down the hallway. Another benefit of the expensive rooms at the top of every hotel was the lack of traffic. Very few of the rooms were occupied at any given time, and that meant fewer people coming or going.

She spat the gum out of her mouth into her hand and stuck it on the peephole of the door right before she rapped lightly.

Worst-case scenario, the room was empty and she would have to pick the lock. That would mean time she would have to spend in the hallway exposed. She knocked again, and this time heard the faint voice from the other side.

"Who is it?"

Tonight, luck was on her side. The room was occupied, and she would get whomever it was to open the door with a minimum of noise. Despite the possible lack of neighbors, it was better to be safe than sorry.

"Turndown service," she replied and then held her breath and waited. She had no idea if the room already had been serviced or not, but it was a better chance at getting the door open than a phony room service call. Most people would yell through the door that they didn't order room service. But if you were the maid knocking? Well, everyone always needed a couple extra towels.

She heard the deadbolt swing back and watched the handle turn. She took two steps backwards and dug the ball of her foot into the carpet. As soon as the door moved slightly inward, she lunged at it with all her strength.

The force knocked the man who had opened the door backwards, and he landed hard on the burgundy-carpeted floor. Before he could recover from the shock of being knocked down, she whacked him on the side of the head with her heavy makeup case. He was down and out for the count.

A quick glance into the room showed that, thankfully, he was alone.

She turned around and quietly shut the door and swung the deadbolt back into place. She spun around, removed the black wig, and shook her golden blonde hair out. She stepped into the bathroom, pulled the false eyelashes off, and quickly removed the contact lenses that had hidden her startling blue eyes from the FBI agent.

Back in the room, she opened her makeup case and removed several metal tubes. She assembled the pieces with expert hands as she walked out to the balcony. She clamped the assembled unit onto the edge of the balcony and inspected her work. She unspooled the cable from the reel and switched on the unit.

With a fluid motion, she pulled off her flowing dress to reveal the skintight catsuit underneath, complete with repelling harness. Out of the makeup kit came a wool cap that once again hid her golden hair.

She connected the hook on the end of the cable to her harness and removed the wireless remote from the winch assembly. She punched buttons on the remote, and the display showed "40 feet range controlled."

She tugged at her harness and was satisfied. She climbed over the edge of the railing with the remote in one hand and dropped off the edge of the balcony.

She heard the winch motor whine as it let out the cable that lowered her in a quick, but controlled, descent towards the window of Hooch's room.

She hit the button on her remote and stopped just above the window. She hung upside down and peered into the window.

Hooch sat on the bed in a bathrobe and flipped through the channels on the TV in his room. He shut off the TV, tossed the remote onto the bed, and wandered into the bathroom.

She removed a suction cup, with built-in handle, from the vest pocket of her catsuit and used it to slide the window open slowly.

Once the window was fully open, she took the remote control and punched a sequence on the keypad. The display on the remote changed from "40 feet range controlled" to "43 feet range controlled" and the motor wound out more cable as she slowly maneuvered herself into the room.

Once inside, she unhooked herself from the cable.

A knock on the hotel room door stopped her in her tracks. He walked out of the bathroom facing away from her and towards the door. She ducked down behind the bed as he opened the door. An agent handed him a large flat box. "Your pizza."

He snatched the pizza from the agent's hands and slammed the door shut. He lifted the box cover and looked at the pizza for a moment before turning back towards the door.

"I said no anchovies!"

He tossed the pizza onto the dresser next to the TV and headed back into the bathroom.

She was back on her feet again and swiftly approached the bathroom door. She peeked into the bathroom and saw him sitting on the edge of the tub feeling the water as it filled.

She reached over to the hotel door and quietly swung the upper deadbolt over the hook bolted to the doorframe. She needed absolute privacy for what was she was about to do next.

She pulled a thin wire from her pocket, wound it around her gloved hands, and stood in the bathroom doorway.

He shut off the tub and turned around, his hands on the

ties of his robe, and froze.

She smiled. "Hello, Hooch."

He finally gained his composure and tried to smile.

"I thought you were dead."

She stopped smiling.

"Because you shot me in the back in Colombia?"

He held his hands up.

"That wasn't me, Melissa."

"Whether it was you who pulled the trigger or not, you are all equally responsible for what happened."

Realization spread across Hooch's face.

"You're the one who's been killing everyone from the unit?"

The smile slowly returned to the corners of her mouth.

"And you're next."

She lunged at him.

He reacted swiftly and twisted to the side, deflecting the cord she tried to wrap around his neck.

As he spun sideways, he whipped his legs around and tripped her, using her own momentum to propel her to the floor.

She hit the tile floor hard and rolled back into a standing position, not an easy task in the tiny hotel bathroom.

As soon as she was on her feet, he pulled a gun with a massive silencer from the pocket of his robe. Who knows how he had snuck that past his FBI handlers, but that didn't matter as much as keeping him from using it on her.

She kicked upward and the gun flew from his grasp before he had a chance to fire it. It clattered to the floor and slid under the toilet.

A swift kick with her other foot sent him backwards into the bathtub. She was immediately right on top of him and held him under the water.

He kicked wildly, his feet banging loudly on the wall. In an instant, someone was knocking at the hotel door.

She placed her knee on the back of Hooch's neck to keep him under while she waited for that first panicked gulp that would fill his lungs with water.

The banging on the door got louder, and finally the locked clicked and the door slammed open, only to be stopped short by the deadbolt.

"Mr. Logan, the deadbolt is on the door."

He suddenly shuddered and kicked even harder. She was almost done here.

"Mr. Logan, are you okay in there."

In that instant, he stopped struggling and became motionless. She held him for a few moments longer as more voices began yelling through the tiny opening of the hotel room door demanding that he answer.

She finally let go of him and retrieved the gun from under the toilet. Depending on how much more time the FBI would give him to answer meant she might need his gun to keep them back until she could escape.

She dashed out of the bathroom and into the room, but not before one of the FBI agents saw her through the partially opened door. "Someone's in there. Get this door open, now!"

Agents began taking turns slamming against the door while she hooked herself back up to the cable coming in through the window. A quick glance showed that the doorframe was starting to splinter and the FBI would flood into the room any second.

She aimed the silenced pistol above the doorframe and fired three shots.

Panicked voices erupted outside the room, but they no longer attempted to break the door down.

She looked out the window and calculated the distance to the grass in her head. She punched a few buttons until the display on the remote said "150 feet range free-fall."

It was quiet in the hallway, which could only mean they were planning to come in hard and fast. It was the psychological calm before the storm that always preceded invasive tactics. She walked calmly to the center of the hotel room, and as soon as she heard several loud feet charging at the weakened door from the hallway, she ran and launched herself head first in a swan dive right out the hotel window.

She arced out over the front parking lot of the hotel. The cable unspooled quickly and then suddenly her remote emitted an unexpected beep.

The cable jerked to a sudden stop and swung her hard into the side of the hotel, fifteen feet off the ground. She hit the large windows of the second floor and a spider web of shattered glass formed around her, but the window didn't break completely.

She glanced at the remote and saw only the words "Error" flashing on the display. Her luck was running out.

She looked up. The FBI agent she had talked to in the hallway poked his out the window. He looked up, noticed the cable was empty and then followed it down with his eyes to look right at her.

She pointed Hooch's silenced pistol up and fired, the windowpane sparking as the bullet impacted near his head. He ducked back into the window and never came back out. It didn't matter, she wasn't shooting at him. It took two more shots to hit the cable.

She fell unceremoniously into the bushes on the side of the hotel and stood up to shake the dirt off her catsuit.

But instead of removing the dirt, she removed the catsuit in a fluid motion to reveal the red evening dress curled up inside.

Two shakes and the dress fell smoothly down to cover the fact she wasn't wearing high heels. She dumped the catsuit and the wool cap into the bushes and walked right for the front door of the hotel.

She reached the hotel's revolving door the same time several FBI agents crowded into the other side. She was hurried around inside the door and nearly collided with another FBI agent as she entered the lobby. She sidestepped the agent as he rushed past her without even a second glance.

She watched them rush outside, guns drawn, and then continued through the lobby to the restaurant.

Within moments, she saw a man who was looking expectantly at her. He had probably given this same look to every woman who had entered the restaurant alone. And this was exactly the person she was hoping to find in a hotel restaurant.

A hotel restaurant was the best place to arrange to meet someone for the first time. It gave you a chance to check them out first and then stand them up if you didn't like what you saw.

She suppressed the urge to frown and instead smiled at the slightly pudgy man with oversized frames for his glasses and headed in his direction. He stood up as she approached. "Rebecca?"

So that was going to be her name for the rest of the night. It wasn't the best name for her, but she had been called far worse names in the past.

She looked at the half-eaten appetizer then back at him apologetically. "Sorry to have kept you waiting, I got hung up at work."

Chapter 52

The walkway lamp closest to the bench flickered and went out. Melissa blinked in the sudden darkness. She had been lost in her own world of self-doubt and self-pity. She looked around and saw that the park was now deserted. She hadn't expected to be away from the warehouse this long. Nick wouldn't come looking for her until the morning, so she still had time to figure out a way back in.

She waited until her eyes adjusted to the darkness. She was glad she let herself relive what had started her on the current path she walked. When one man was given ultimate power over life and death of others, he became extremely dangerous.

He was doing the same thing. He had formed a small group to take matters into his own hands. Would this power corrupt him? She would have to keep an eye on him and watch to make sure that didn't happen. When this was over, she would look in the mirror and make sure she hadn't changed.

General Archon crouched in the bushes. He had ordered his men to take Melissa as soon as she left the park. He had expected them to have her waiting for him when he arrived. When he arrived, they told him that she was still sitting on the same park bench and hadn't moved in all that time.

He was glad to have put a watch team on as many contacts she had on the East Coast. It had strained his private resources to cover such a large area, but it had paid off.

What was she waiting for? Did she know he was coming?

He sent his men outward two blocks around the park on counter-surveillance. He sat in the bushes and watched her as he waited for each member of his team to report back. If someone else were with her, he would know soon enough.

One by one, he called each team member and requested his report. Each called in the "all clear."

He called to the final team member.

And waited for this last man to respond.

Nick held the gun in one hand. He lifted the walkie-talkie to the guard's mouth, pushed the talk button and motioned with the gun for him to speak.

"Alpha one, this is beta four," the guard reported. "Everything is clear from the south end."

He released the talk button and slammed the butt of his gun across the guards head. The guard crumpled at his feet.

"All units to active beta," replied General Archon.

He wasn't sure what she was up to when he watched as she clung to the windowsill and then dropped down out of sight. He was glad that he hadn't relied solely on the tracking devices in the jacket or the shoes. He had also set up a camera system to watch the window and the door of her room.

As he followed her through the streets of New York, his GPS tracker showed that she was still at the warehouse. When she hailed the taxi a couple of blocks from the warehouse, he thought he had lost her. But then he knew exactly what she was doing. Despite his reluctance, she was trying to find someone to help them. It didn't take long to find her.

It was then he noticed the black van with the driver pointing binoculars in her direction. He recognized him as one of the guards from the New York building. He no longer needed to worry about how he was going to get to General Archon. The General would be coming to him.

General Archon switched his walkie-talkie to channel four. The guard to the south reported that he had been compromised. Instead of giving the "all clear," he had reported that everything was clear, which meant that he had been forced to give a false report. This also meant that this guard had been captured, bringing his total assets down to four, including himself.

He immediately ordered his team to switch channels. They all carried ten-channel walkie-talkies. If he said any code from alpha to epsilon, they would double the number it represented and switch to that channel.

He looked at her sitting on the bench. If she knew what was happening out in the park all around her, she sure didn't reveal any of this in her body language. She appeared to be lost in her own thoughts and completely unaware of the drama unfolding around her.

He couldn't let her control the situation again. He had to do something about who was with her in the park. He fingered the talk button on his walkie-talkie.

"All units," he began. "We have opposition coming in from the south. Unit four is out. Units one and two, stay with the target. Move when she moves. Take her at the first opportunity. Unit three, meet me at the southeast corner, we are going to confront the opposition, strength unknown."

He dropped back into the bushes away from her.

After hours of thought, she had concluded that she needed – no, she was destined to help Nick stop the assassination plot on the President of the United States. It was what she had to do to atone for the sins of her past. She would learn to trust herself. And trust Nick. They were, after all, on the same side. As long as she continued to trust him, they would accomplish their objective and save the President.

He had helped her on her previous personal mission to destroy The Council. He proved his loyalty to the United States back then.

Out in the darkness she thought she saw movement amongst the shadows to her left. She smiled to herself. Even she could still get spooked in a dark and empty park late at night. She almost stood up from the bench when the dark shape shifted and moved in a different direction than it should have.

She froze and strained through the inky black darkness to see if the shape would move again. Her senses were on overdrive. In the darkened conditions, her hearing compensated and alerted her to every sound around her.

A leaf cracked on her right. This almost insignificant sound spoke volumes to someone trained as she had been trained. This sound meant that the shadow on her left was not alone. She didn't take her eyes off the shadow to her left while she focused hard on the sound to her right. Leaves scrapped the ground as if pushed by the wind. Yet there was no wind in the park.

She fought the natural impulse to look to her right and continued to watch the shadow on her left. The lamp that had plunged the bench into darkness flickered back on and flooded the area in its warm glow. Her eyes adjusted to the increased brightness, and she completely lost the shadow to her left. But as her eyes settled to the current level of brightness, she watched as the shadow of whoever was on her right sway slightly.

The walkway lamps were five feet high and about twenty feet away. Her stalker would be crouched. Since the shadow crossed in front of her by a little under two feet, whoever was approaching would be about six feet away to her right.

Knowledge was power, and she knew they were there.

She sat still on the bench. She would have to get up first to mount any attack, and she hadn't reacted when she first saw the shadow move to her left.

She tensed and relaxed her muscles in anticipation of the quick reaction that was inevitable. She would need to move fast if she expected to get the attacker on her right without being shot by the one on her left. She had survived much worse than this many times before, but that didn't make it easier each time.

Nick rolled the unconscious guard into the bushes and out of sight. The walkie-talkie had been silent since the guard reported in. The guard must have spoken some code word and warned General Archon. The General obviously ordered a frequency change. He switched the walkie-talkie to each frequency and listened.

He found no traffic and tossed the walkie-talkie into the bushes with the guard. He headed south out of the park. If General Archon suspected that he was there, then he wanted to be somewhere else.

He traveled two blocks and swung around to enter the park from the east. He had to get to her before Archon did. If he was right, then Archon had broken up his team to deal with her and the unknown attacker from the south. He had only counted five darkened figures leave the black van. He had taken out one of them. The General would want to maximize his odds and would send two after her and two to investigate the south gate.

He slipped across the street between the streetlights and entered the park parallel to the bench. He could barely see her. She was still sitting on the bench. He approached the bench from the darkest area possible. The light flickered back to life and he froze. A few more feet and he would have bumped into the black-clad figure crouched in front of him.

General Archon squinted into the darkness. He couldn't see anyone. This was a problem. He ordered his other guard to cover while he checked the area. He quickly found the unconscious guard in the bushes. He scanned the area around him and listened intently to every sound. There was no movement and no sound that he didn't expect to hear on a cold autumn night in the park.

He noticed the walkie-talkie lying next to his unconscious guard. Whoever was here was no longer in the south end of the park, and he had made a big mistake by breaking up his team.

He lifted his walkie-talkie to warn his team and then remembered his order of radio silence. They would not turn their walkie-talkies back on until the operation was complete.

He looked at the unconscious guard and then back at his partner.

"Get Wallace back to the van and turn on your walkie-talkie. I will need you to bring the van quickly into the park once we have Melissa."

"Yes, sir." The guard reached down and struggled with the dead weight of the unconscious Wallace.

Melissa sat still as her mind whirled a million miles a second. If she reached for her P226 X-Five, the shape on her left would shoot her. If she dove under the bench for protection, the noise on her right could easily get to her. Then she noticed the second shadow creeping up to meet the first shadow. She had to move before she was completely outnumbered.

She leaned forward in a stretch. She brought her arms

back and tugged the X-Five from its holster. In a single fluid movement she swung it out and lay prone across the bench. A single shot took out the light closest to the bench, and she rolled to the ground just before the back of the bench splintered into wood chips.

She rolled under the bench and turned to face the shape on the left. She saw the tiny flashes as more rounds sought her out. She aimed the X-Five and shot straight at the flashes. The flashes stopped and were followed by a loud thud. She had made contact with her target.

She swung her gun around to the noise on her right. In the semi-darkness she could see two shapes. And one was standing over another lying on the ground. The standing shape crouched and turned to face her.

"It's Nick. Don't shoot."

"Nick? What the hell…"

"Shhhh!" Nick cut her off. "General Archon's out there."

General Archon paused as he heard bullets impact wood. That meant his man had no choice but to fire on her. He listened for the all clear on his walkie-talkie. After thirty seconds he still only heard static.

He pushed the talk button to reach out to anyone on his team. He changed his mind and released the button.

He needed a much bigger team if he hoped to go after her, and whoever was helping her. He decided that this operation was over and headed for the van. He would send in a cleanup crew to collect the others before the sun came up.

He was constantly misjudging her abilities and resources. It would not happen again.

He studied the van for a few minutes before approaching it. He could see his guard in the driver's seat waiting for him, still wearing his mask.

He climbed into the back of the van, sat down next to the unconscious guard, and tugged the door closed.

"Let's go. And for god's sake, take off that mask. We don't want the police pulling us over."

The driver pulled off the mask and let her long sandy blonde hair fall over her shoulders. The unconscious guard sat up and pulled his own mask off.

"Hello, General," Nick said as he plucked the MP5SD from his grip.

Nick pulled a hood over General Archon's head. The zip ties the General's team had brought along to use on Melissa now bound Archon's hands and feet. Nick climbed backwards out of the van and motioned for her to follow him.

She stepped out of the van and went around to where he was looking in the side door at the General.

He slid the door closed and walked out of hearing range of the van.

"Take him back to the warehouse and don't pay attention to anything he tells you."

"Don't worry." She tenderly touched her nose. "The lines have been drawn very clearly."

He smiled and headed off into the darkness.

She climbed into the driver's seat and gripped the steering wheel. She sat motionless and waited. She didn't know how he had managed to track her, but she was glad he had. If she had managed to evade him tonight, she would be the one tied up in the back of the van instead of General Archon. It took everything she had to not kill him right there and then. Only the promise to her son stayed her hand. She watched him drive by before she started the van and pulled away from the park.

Chapter 53

Melissa pulled the van into the warehouse. Nick had arrived a few minutes earlier and held the large metal door open for her. He closed it behind her and locked it. She pulled around the Ford E-350, rolled the General's van to a stop along the side wall of the warehouse, and shut off the motor.

He yanked the sliding van door open and hauled General Archon out of the van and onto the cold dusty floor of the warehouse. He bent in close to the General.

"You are going to tell me everything I want to know. First, we need to make sure that you aren't tagged. I don't want any surprise visits."

He pulled the General across the floor over to a workbench set up just under the second floor offices. She saw the window she had escaped out of on the display. He wrestled Archon into a chair and sat him up. He pulled a wand controller with a loop antennae attached to it from the workbench and waved it all around the General.

He tapped a sequence on the keyboard and referred to the display. He noticed several dots form on the display and smiled. He set the wand down and sat down on his own chair across from the General. He leaned forward and whipped the black cover from General Archon's head. The General blinked in the sudden light. He noticed him sitting right in front of him, and their eyes locked.

He smiled at the General. "I am afraid that I am going to have to ask you for your clothes."

He stood up and walked over to her. General Archon slowly turned his head as he watched his every movement.

He stopped in front of her, his back to the General. "I'll understand if you don't want to stay for this."

She looked over his shoulder at the General. Her eyes met with the General's.

She looked back at him. "I'll stay."

She stared at the General. It didn't surprise her that no emotion showed on his face.

He turned back around to face General Archon.

"Imagine that, General. She wants to stay to watch your humiliation. Make no mistake, you are my prisoner of war, and I will do whatever I see fit."

She grabbed his arm and turned him back to face her.

"What do you mean 'prisoner of war'?"

"Don't worry. It's all part of the psychological effect. It makes him think that I am treating him as the enemy and not a fellow American citizen. It lessens his rights and increases my authority. We need to get those trackers off him and out of here before my warehouse is discovered. You'll have to drive the clothes and dump them in the river…"

"I'm staying here," she cut him off.

"His clothes will lead his men here. Someone has to take them away, and I need to stay here. You are the only other choice."

"Can you cut the tracking devices out of the clothes?"

"Yes." He eyed her with an angle of his head.

She pulled her cell phone out of her pocket and dialed 411.

"I would like the number to the fastest taxi service in New York." The operator connected her, and she ordered the taxi. He promised to be there in less than five minutes."

She closed her cell phone.

"Give them to me, and I'll make sure that whoever is following the General will never find him here."

He smiled.

"I'll need to cut the zip ties in order to get his clothes off. I'm going to Denny's room and see if I can find some clothes that might fit the General. It's too cold in here to leave him naked. I want him to be warm for now. It gives me one more thing to take away during the interrogation."

He walked up the stairs and into Denny's old room.

She looked at the General. He sat there and looked at the floor. He returned with a pile of clothes and walked up to the General.

"I'm going to cut your restraints."

She drew her SIG-Sauer P226 X-Five from the holster and tightened the silencer for dramatic effect. The General looked from her back to Nick and shook his head in defeat.

Nick pulled the KA-BAR from its sheath above his left boot and sliced through the plastic zip ties like they were paper. He placed the knife on the table several feet from the General.

She aimed right at General Archon while Nick demanded he undress to complete nakedness. Nick pushed the General back down. The General's naked butt slapped the chair. Nick used the wand again to locate each tracker and cut them out of the clothes and the soles of both of the General's boots. He passed the wand over the pile of clothes and was satisfied that he hadn't missed any.

He brought the small tracking devices over to her. She pocketed them in her jacket.

Nick tossed the new clothes to General Archon.

"Put these on."

A honk outside signaled the taxi had arrived.

She left out the side door by the alley and crossed the street half a block down from the taxi. She walked past him and noticed he was looking at the warehouse door. He honked again.

She turned back onto the street and ran down the middle of the street right in view of the taxi headlights. She wanted to make sure he saw her running up the street to get to the taxi. She stepped onto the sidewalk right in front of the warehouse, opened the taxi door, and slid in.

"What the hell are you doing way over here?"

"This is the address dispatch gave me." The driver was immediately defensive.

"Well, they were wrong." She slammed the door a little too hard rocking the taxi.

"Where ya headed?"

She sniffed the air in the taxi.

"What is that smell?"

"I don't smell anything."

"Dammit," she barked. "Do all the frickin' taxis in New York smell like this?"

She bent down and made loud sniffing noises. She tucked her hand deep in the slot between the seat and the floor and deposited the tiny transmitters. She sat up quickly and opened the door to the taxi.

"Never mind, I'll walk."

She stepped out of the taxi. She had barely shut the door when the driver roared off with a squeal of the tires.

She waited until the taxi turned a corner and was out of sight. She went around the back of the warehouse and entered through the side door. The General had just finishing dressing while Nick held the MP5SD trained on him. Nick stood back several feet to give himself enough time to take the General down should he have any ideas of charging him.

She walked up next to Nick.

"Anyone following the General will be bar hopping and stopping at cheap motels."

"I'm glad you're on my side. We need to get him in Denny's old room. Anyone passing by won't hear his screams from there."

"Nick." She placed a hand on his arm. "Let me do the interrogation."

He looked at her, and his eyes bore right into her soul. He shook his head. "I can't leave you in a room with him alone. He is a direct threat to you and your family. I let you in there alone, and you're liable to kill him before we even get his name, rank and serial number."

"Then let me be in the room with you. I'll stay back and won't…"

He turned away. "I don't think it's a…"

She yanked him back by his arm to face her. "You brought me into this. I am with you all the way. All the way. Let me be in there with you. I might notice something you missed."

He softly removed her grip from his arm.

"I will get what I need from him, but I can't do it with you looking over my shoulder. I must have complete control over everything in that room if I am going to crack him. You would change the dynamics in that room too much. I am sorry. You can't go in with me."

He walked away from her and over to General Archon.

"Get up," he ordered.

She watched them climb the stairs. General Archon looked down at her as he climbed each step. She could see in his posture and his eyes that he was convinced these were the last steps he would ever take in his life.

She could hear the muffled shouts as soon as the door closed. Nick was no doubt starting the treatment. General Archon was a strong man, and despite Nick's confidence, this could take some time. She poked around the warehouse and saw a computer running with the screen turned off.

She sat down and turned the screen on. A view of a password screen faded into view. This was not any type of password screen she had ever seen before. It had several colors and shapes that needed to be matched like a puzzle to allow access.

She listened to the violence taking place above her. Archon was the only one who knew the answer to this puzzle.

The answer that would give Nick access to Digital Storm.

Chapter 54

Hartford forced the delivery van up the deeply rutted dirt road. This far from civilization, the only light came from the headlights which only gave a moment's warning that the road twisted in the opposite direction from only a moment ago.

The twisty road lead them deeper into the woods to the house Melissa had bought on the Tug Hill Plateau, a 2100 square mile remote region of New York State located between Lake Ontario and the Adirondacks. Tug Hill's most notable characteristic was its relative lack of people, and Nick agreed that this was the best place to hide her family and the Vice President until they had managed to capture General Archon and force him to tell them where Hartford's daughter was. Nick gave him his personal guarantee that he would bring his daughter safely to him no matter what.

The delivery van was not designed to go off road, and despite the six-foot-wide space between the trees that defined the road, this was as much off road as the van could handle. Billy, Melissa's son, leaned forward again and watched him struggle to keep the van on the road.

The trees suddenly gave way and the headlights pierced the darkness to reveal a cabin at the far end of the clearing. Everyone breathed a sigh of relief as their perilous journey had come to an end and they could finally rest for the night.

Chapter 55

Melissa wandered aimlessly around the warehouse. She glanced up at the window and saw the first hint of morning. Nick had been with the General all night. He came out of the room about once an hour to drink water and wash his face.

The door opened and he walked out again. He was looking more exhausted than she had ever seen him before, and his clothes were drenched in sweat and blood. He walked down the steel steps, plopped down in the chair and swiveled back and forth. She approached cautiously.

"Any luck?"

He looked wearily up at her. He shook his head no.

"You need to rest."

"Can't rest now. He's almost broken."

"Let me go."

"Not necessary."

"Haven't you heard of good cop, bad cop?"

He looked at her, a smile formed on the edges of his mouth.

"That only works in the movies."

"I go in there and pretend to be his friend. I make him think that I disagree with what you are doing, that I am on his side. He will tell me anything."

He stretched his arms over his head. "I guess I could use the break."

"So I go up there and ask him what he knows..."

"Not yet," he cut her off. "First we need the password to

Digital Storm. In order for us to determine if he is telling us the truth, I need to verify any information he provides against what is stored in the DS archives. It's the only way we can be sure that he tells us everything."

She looked up at the room. For the past six hours, General Archon had refused to give him the password to the archives. He had predicted this. She looked back at him.

"How critical is this password?"

"It means the difference between success and failure."

"I'll get it."

"Good luck. He's not really much of a talker."

She started for the stairs.

He grabbed her arm. "Give me your gun."

She stopped and turned back to him.

"What?"

"I don't want you making a mistake we will all regret."

"I won't kill him."

"I can't take that chance." He held out his hand.

She pulled the X-Five from its holster and handed it to him. Maybe he was right.

She walked slowly up the stairs and didn't know what to expect when she opened the door.

She stepped inside and closed the door behind her. General Archon's face was swollen to the point that she could barely recognize him. There was blood everywhere. He heard her enter the room and looked up with his left eye, the only eye he could currently see out of. She moved in close and sat opposite him in her own chair.

"He is going to kill you."

He stared at her across the empty space between them.

"I know. He's also going to kill you."

His voice was altered from the injuries, and the sound was muffled. She almost couldn't understand him as he continued.

"All he wants is the password. Once he has that, he will kill me. And he will kill you."

"He's had plenty of opportunity to kill me. Why wait?"

He tried to laugh. It built up slowly as a gargling sound in his throat before it quickly morphed into a coughing spree as blood sprayed from his mouth. He turned his head so that none of the blood hit her. When he calmed down from the spasm, he turned to look at her.

"He is using you. Once he has the password, he will kill both of us."

"Then give me the password and we'll see."

He shook his head. "He will kill me as soon as he has it."

"You don't know that."

"Yes, I do."

Nick stared at the computer screen. The cursor hovered over multiple shapes waiting for a selection. He glanced up at the door Melissa had entered almost an hour ago. He wished he had set up a camera to monitor that room, but he never expected the General would have held out this long.

He would give her a few more minutes before he went back up there.

The door opened above and she stepped out. She closed the door and walked slowly down the steps. She walked over to him sitting at the display waiting to enter in the password.

She looked him right in the eyes. "I got it."

He jerked his head back slightly in surprise. His mouth opened to speak, then closed again. She pushed him lightly aside and took the mouse under her palm. She clicked a series of shapes and moved them around like puzzle pieces.

The screen flashed and was immediately replaced by the Digital Storm search window. The cursor blinked as it patiently waited for an entry. He looked over her shoulder, and she felt him breathe a sigh of relief.

She exited out of Digital Storm before he could say anything else.

He stopped short. "Why did you do that?"

"The General doesn't think that you'll let him live once you have the password."

He looked amused. "And he made you promise to keep it from me until he was safely away?"

She still didn't smile. "Something like that, yes."

"Then it's time to release the General from his prison."

She wanted to smile but couldn't. She knew she had just made another wrong choice. He was doing everything he said he would. She silently berated herself for letting the General get to her and doubt him.

She entered the room moments after Nick and looked at the General. She was about to tell Nick what she had done when suddenly her P226 X-Five was in his hand and he shot General Archon three times in the chest.

The General tipped backwards from the force of the impact and fell over. Nick turned to face her with the gun raised and pointed it right at her.

She was stunned into silence.

General Archon had been right the entire time.

"He outlived his usefulness," he said as he kept the X-Five pointed at her head. "And so have you."

Chapter 56

"He gave me the code," Melissa reminded him quickly. "But I didn't give it to you and I backed out of the database. You'll need it again."

Nick smiled and held the gun steady.

"I had a screen recorder running on the system since before you came out of the room. You already gave me the code."

She lifted the chair sitting next to her with one foot and kicked it right at him. He fired but the chair took the bullet before slamming full force into him. He stumbled back long enough for her to roll out the door. She pounded her fists on the metal floor of the landing, softening her strikes with each successive blow. She hoped it sounded like her running down the stairs.

It worked because he darted out of the room and aimed for the bottom of the stairs. He realized his mistake and swung around just as she kicked out and slammed him in the chest.

The force of her kick sent him somersaulting backwards over the railing and down to the cement floor below. She looked over the landing. He lay on the floor below and didn't move. She watched him for an entire minute. He still didn't move. She couldn't risk that he was dead and had to tie him up in case he recovered. She looked around the warehouse for something to tie up Nick with. Then remembered the only rope in the warehouse was being used to tie General Archon to his chair.

She ran into the room and lifted General Archon's chair to sit him up. She pulled his shirt up past his head and stared at the three mushroomed bullets embedded in the bulletproof vest.

He had promised to provide her with the working password, but only if she would take a chance that he was right. It had taken her twenty minutes to decide. She had pulled one of Denny's old bulletproof vests from the closet and put it on him.

She inspected him. His breathing was shallow but his pulse was strong. He was unconscious from the impact of the bullets and falling backwards, but he would live if treated quickly. Right now she needed the rope. She tugged at the ropes and he pitched forward with a moan.

"It's okay. I'm going to get you some help."

She pulled the ropes away and eased him to the floor to rest while she went downstairs to tie Nick up and call an ambulance.

She had just stepped out of the room onto the landing when a searing hot bullet tore into her shoulder, spinning her off balance.

Nick had aimed for her head but the fall had made him slightly dizzy. The force of the impact spun her back into the room, and she disappeared from sight. There were no weapons in that room, and he still held her precious X-Five trained at the door to see if she was coming back out.

He didn't hear any movement upstairs. Maybe he had killed her with that shot. He wasn't going to make the same mistake she had. He stood up and made his way to the stairs. He was still dizzy, but he had to make sure.

He climbed up the stairs and managed to make it to the top without falling over the railing. He shook the cobwebs that formed in his vision. He looked at the door. It was closed. But it wasn't closed when he started up the stairs.

He wasn't in any condition for hand-to-hand combat, so he slowly moved back down the stairs. He didn't think she was ready for a fight either, but he had things to do, and he couldn't waste any more time on her. As long as she thought he was out here with her gun, she would stay in that room.

He stumbled over to the computer and saved the video screen capture along with the IP of his remote connection to a DVD. He could now access Digital Storm from any computer with internet access.

He fired the X-Five into the computer and watched as it ignited into flames. Moments later the wood table also caught fire.

He kicked over two barrels of kerosene and watched the liquid spread across the floor.

Melissa landed hard on the same shoulder that had just been shot. She almost passed out from the pain. She checked the wound and was pleased to discover that the bullet had gone completely through.

She bit down hard on her jacket to silence her cries as she wrapped a t-shirt around her shoulder to control the bleeding. She heard Nick step onto the first metal stair. She crawled across the floor and silently shut the door. He would have to open it before coming in. She didn't know what she would do with that extra two seconds, but it was better than nothing.

General Archon had gone unconscious again, but his chest rose and fell in shallow breaths. She instinctively ducked at the sound of gunfire from downstairs. She waited but didn't hear anything else. He moaned. He was awake again. She ran over to him.

"General Archon. Can you hear me?"

The General's head lolled around and he looked up at her. The only eye he could still see out of searched the room and stopped on her.

"You were right," she stammered. "I was…"

He forced himself to sit straight up and spoke. His words came out garbled.

"What? I can't understand you."

He looked around him and back at her. He took several breaths and strained to speak again.

"We have to stop him."

She laughed aloud. "Look at us."

He struggled to stand. She grabbed him and winced from her own pain.

"We have to," he grunted out between pained breaths. "I noticed a Mistral missing from its case."

"A what?"

"It's a surface-to-air missile. It can be launched from a man-portable unit. That missile has a reported success rate of ninety-two percent. It will hit whatever it's fired at."

"You think he's going to shoot down the President's

plane?"

"At this point I think he will do whatever it takes."

"Can you warn the President?"

"I just need a phone."

She looked around. There were no phones in this room.

"There's a phone…" She stopped talking and froze.

She smelled something.

She sniffed again.

She smelled smoke.

Chapter 57

The smoke could be Nick forcing her to open the door, but Melissa had no choice.

If this were a trick, he would kill her as soon as she opened the door. Then he would kill General Archon. But if it were a real fire and they stayed closed up in that room, they would be dead from smoke inhalation long before the fire even reached them.

She risked a peek outside. Nothing happened. She opened the door wider and looked around. The smoke was coming from the desk and the computer just below the office. She saw the wet floor and the empty barrels of kerosene. She ran back and grabbed the General.

"We have to get out of here now!"

He didn't question her and let her help him to the door. They limped down the stairs, both in immense pain. The fire was still confined to the desk, but it wouldn't stay that way for much longer. She leaned him on the Ford E-350 van and peeked inside. The keys were still in the ignition, right where she left them. They were actually catching a break. She looked at the lock on the warehouse door.

"Come on, General," she said as she opened the side passenger door. She twisted him into the seat. She slammed the door closed and hopped into the driver's seat. She buckled herself in and leaned over to buckle him in.

"Hold tight, General, this is going to be a bumpy ride."

She glanced out the side window. The air above the kerosene started to smolder. She twisted the key and the

Triton V10 engine roared to life once again. She glanced out the side mirrors at the warehouse door. It looked very solid.

The kerosene ignited in a blinding flash.

The kerosene-fed wave of fire sped towards the Ford E-350 van. She shifted into reverse and smashed down on the accelerator. All ten cylinders responded as the van shot backwards just as the flames licked past on their way to the armory. She prayed that the Super Duty van was stronger than the metal warehouse door.

The van slammed into the metal door and came to a dead stop. Every tinted window along the sides and back shattered inward as the van's frame compressed slightly from the impact. The warehouse door bent outward, but hadn't broken.

She needed more speed. She shifted into forward and drove right through the wall of flames to the far side of the warehouse.

Plastic cases in the armory started to melt from the intense heat. She ground the gears into reverse and pushed the pedal flat against the floorboard. The van's tires squealed for a moment before gaining traction. The van launched itself straight at the warehouse door. She saw several boxes collapse in the flames as she roared past the armory.

The van connected with the metal door.

The shrill sound of metal against metal filled her ears as the warehouse door buckled under the tremendous force. The warehouse door sheared free of the rails and ripped apart like tinfoil allowing the van to bounce unhindered into the street.

The back bumper crumpled downward and tore into both rear tires. The tires shredded and the metal rims ground into the pavement shooting sparks into the air all around the van as it continued across the street under its own momentum. The Ford E-350 Super Duty XL Wagon slammed into the far curb across the street and jolted to a stop.

The heat in the warehouse reached critical mass, and several thousand rounds of ammunition triggered simultaneously. Hundreds of pinholes formed in the walls of the warehouse. She reached over, unbuckled him, and tossed him forward as she hunched down behind the dashboard. Bullets pelted the windows and unarmored steel of the van. They shattered the front window and pierced the thin metal of the van but never obtained the velocity to pass through the engine block of the 6.8L Triton V10.

Once the hail of bullets subsided, she forced open her door. It creaked with displeasure but opened all the way.

She pulled at him. He moaned but was still alive.

"Can you walk?"

"You lead, I'll follow," he said from the floorboard of the van.

She pushed on the passenger side door, and it opened only half way. The frame of the van had bent, and the door wouldn't fully open. She pulled him out of the van through the half-opened door and gritted through the pain.

They hobbled down the street away from the warehouse. They couldn't be anywhere near the warehouse fire when the police arrived. They had to warn the President, and trying to explain this to the police would only delay them.

They reached the end of the block, and she paused to see which way to go. The heat of the fire and damage from the bullets set off a hand grenade. Within milliseconds of that explosion, everything else in the armory exploded. The shockwave blew out windows for three city blocks and knocked them to the ground.

She sat up and saw the black cloud rise from where the warehouse used to be. Her ears rang with a high-pitched whine. She rolled him onto his back. The blast had been too much for him, and he was unconscious again.

People filed out from the buildings on both sides of the street in a panic. She saw a woman holding a cell phone. She grimaced as she stood up and stumbled over to the woman.

"Call 9-1-1. My friend is hurt." She pointed to General Archon on the sidewalk.

The woman looked at her. She was still slightly bruised and swollen, and blood seeped from her arm. Melissa grabbed the cell phone from the woman and dialed the number herself.

"9-1-1, please state your emergency," the unemotional voice spoke into her ear.

"Send an ambulance to one block east of the explosion."

"What explosion?"

"Don't worry, you'll find out soon enough."

She hung up the cell phone and handed the phone back to the woman.

"Thanks."

More people spilled out onto the streets and sirens could be heard in the distance. She bent down over him and then looked into the growing crowd.

She pointed at specific individuals. "You," she commanded, "get some water in case he wakes up before the ambulance gets here. You, put your jacket under his head. Everyone else, back up and give him some space."

She leaned down to the unconscious General.

"Someone's coming for you."

She stood up. A wave of dizziness overcame her, and she wobbled. A couple of the people standing the closest to her reached out to steady her.

She grabbed the man next to her and leaned heavily on his arm even as she tried to reassure him that she was fine.

She regained her balance, let go of the helpful bystander and stepped backwards away from General Archon. She couldn't be here when the police showed up. She had to stop Nick, and the only person capable of helping her lay unconscious at her feet.

Explosions pounded from the building next to Nick's warehouse. Everyone jumped and looked as the second building became engulfed in flames of its own.

With everyone distracted, she limped into the crowd and hobbled quickly around the corner to disappear deeper into the city.

268   INHERIT THE THRONE

Chapter 58

Wilkes woke precisely at six thirty in the morning. He kicked dirt onto the still smoldering ashes of the fire. Ten minutes later, he mounted the ATV with Samantha gripping him tightly and headed straight for the location marked on his map. He needed to get there, set up the equipment and get back to Tug Hill for the final phase of the operation.

He was glad for this opportunity to prove himself. He wanted to make the United States a country of true power, not remembered power. He joined the United States Marine Corps right out of high school. His aptitude for violence and his high tolerance of pain promoted him to the Marine Special Operations Command Force Recon quickly.

He spent the next twelve years on secret missions in other countries. The actions of his unit were never publicized. During that time he saw the United States through the eyes of the rest of the world. The United States was viewed as a bully, not the political, economic and military powerhouse that the Marines had indoctrinated into him. The United States was big and used its weight to push the rest of the world around, but it held no real power. The only reason anyone really feared the U.S. was its immense nuclear arsenal.

He felt that the rest of the world should respect the United States. Instead all he found was hatred, disdain and indifference. To make matters worse, when the latest President took office, he reduced the spending on the military. His unit was disbanded and fewer overseas operations were being authorized.

With the rise in terrorism, the operations of his unit were no longer secret. In fact, they were headlined on CNN. The current administration felt that a softer touch needed to be presented. The secret wars were over and the secret warriors were removed from active duty.

After September 11, 2001, open war was declared on terrorism, and the small operations that he thrived on were replaced with large-scale military action. News crews accompanied every unit to show the humanity of the fighting and made heroes out of children. This new breed of television warriors quickly became ineffective. With the whole world watching over their shoulders, they could not get the job done properly. Every terrorist leader watched CNN like it was his own personal counter-intelligence system.

He pushed his commander for a secret unit to cripple the al-Qaeda network better and faster than the television warriors could. The commander denied his request and, in a blind stimulant-fueled rage, Wilkes crippled him. After the court martial and dishonorable discharge, he had nowhere to turn. He never had any experience living outside the military and, with the dishonorable discharge hanging around his neck like a neon warning sign, it made finding work impossible.

For over a year he lived in cheap motels and worked illegally at construction sites. He was at the bottom, and the only reason he didn't take a gun to his head was he couldn't afford the gun. Two years ago, someone who called herself Hannah approached him. While they had never met in person, she had informed him that his help would be useful in bringing the United States back to its rightful place as the leader of the free world.

He immediately offered his services, and his allegiance.

He never once looked back except to reflect on his good fortune, and when he was informed about his part in the assassination of the President and Vice President, he quickly accepted. These two people were the reason he had been kicked out of the Marines. They didn't deserve to run this country.

And when he had proven himself, Hannah would have no choice but to congratulate him personally.

Chapter 59

Wilkes arrived at the drop site marked on his map. He cut the engine to the ATV and looked around. Somewhere close by was the package.

He stood quietly and listened. A quick look at his prisoner stopped the whimpering. In the resulting silence, he could barely make out the faint beeping sound. But it was there. He glanced in the direction of the sound and saw the parachute tangled in a tree. This was the spot. He glanced around to see if he could see the other two parachutes. Maybe they had been caught up in trees as well. He spent a few moments scanning the treetops in a wide sweeping arc. He didn't see anything and would have to go looking around on foot.

He had untied his captive's feet so she could ride on the back of the ATV. Now that they were at their destination, it was time to tie her up again. He turned towards her with a devilish grin that turned to pure hatred. She was gone.

He jumped onto the ATV and looked around him. He saw her as she leaped over a fallen branch and disappeared into a deep river bed.

Samantha slid down the wet dirt and landed feet first into the creek. She ran full speed but stumbled often. Her hands were bound and kept her balance more than a little off. She ran without knowing where to go except away. In her entire life she had never been involved in her father's career, and this was not how she wanted to start. She knew the minute she was grabbed and not robbed or raped that this was not about her. She was being used as a pawn in a deadly game that had to involve her father. She did not blame him and was now doing her best to not play the part of damsel in distress.

The man with the military tattoos had not yelled after her. That meant that either he had missed her escape or he was right behind her. She ran through the center of the creek. She knew it would hide her trail and improve her chances of escape.

Escape to where? It had taken them more than a day to get out here. And that was on the ATV. She stopped. She had to stop running away from the ATV. It was her only real chance. She ran up out of the creek, leaned against a tree, and tried to catch her breath. She had to make it back to the ATV before the tattooed man.

Then she heard the splashing through the creek.

Wilkes had trailed her easily. She thought that the creek would obscure the trail she left behind. What she didn't know was that only worked on dogs who followed by smell. He could easily see the recently loosened gravel and trail of floating dirt from every step she took in the water.

And right there she had run up out of the river.

Samantha crouched and slid around the tree. She saw "tattoo" following the river and then stop. He looked at the edge where she had left the river. Then his head snapped, and he looked right at her. She dove back out of sight. She fought the impulse to run. He was faster, and she could never outpace him. She had to hide and wait him out. She crept as low to the ground as possible and crawled into a thick bush. She didn't care what creatures might be living inside that bush. She only wanted to avoid the creature that was coming up the side of the creek bank.

Wilkes thought he saw movement up behind the large tree to the right. He decided to follow the trail his running captive had made and saw that it led him right to the tree. He inspected the ground and saw the markings of someone crawling into the bush about ten feet from the tree. He stood up and looked around. It would be too hard to follow into the bush.

Samantha held her breath as "tattoo" looked at the bush she was hiding in. Then he stood and looked all around him. Was it possible she had evaded him? He looked up the hill and broke into a full run. She didn't let her breath out for another minute. Then she relaxed and placed her head on the soft dirt and waited. She didn't move for what she thought was an hour. By now "tattoo" would be long gone. It was time to make her way back to the ATV. She slid quietly out of the bush and stood up. She used her bound hands to dust off the dirt from her clothes. She thought she heard something and looked up in time to see the blur of a person slam into her and knock her to the ground.

It took Wilkes only fifteen minutes to find the two remaining hardened cases even though they had landed less than a hundred feet from the first. He cursed repeatedly as he dragged the three cases to a clearing. He had wasted a lot of time chasing after Samantha, time he didn't have.

He had wanted to end his trouble right there by the creek, but his employer had been specific about keeping her alive.

He unclipped the latches on the first case and lifted the cover. He pulled the metal parts from each case and began to assemble the remote launcher. Soon it would be ready to deploy the surface-to-air missile that would destroy the U.S. Marine Corps Sikorsky VH-3D helicopter, call sign Marine One.

The call sign of any helicopter that actively carried the President of the United States.

Chapter 60

Wilkes peered at the house through the binoculars. He checked the GPS display again. Hannah had provided this exact spot last night. Occasionally someone would walk past the window, and he jotted down how many different occupants he saw. According to his rough count, Melissa's entire family was present along with Representative Hartford and the Vice President.

His cell phone vibrated in his pocket. Despite the rugged and isolated appearance of Tug Hill, it still boasted electricity, indoor plumbing, and cell phone towers in some of the more populated areas. The cell phone signal was weak on this side of the house, but he lost it completely when he ventured to the other side of the house.

He returned to this spot for both the easy view into the kitchen and the fact that he could still receive the call he waited for. And this could be it.

He placed the binoculars next to him on the ground and pulled the cell phone from the breast pocket of his BDUs. He hit the little green button and placed the phone to his ear.

"Yeah."

"Where are you?" The voice was faint, but he would recognize Hannah anywhere.

"I'm outside the house now."

"I'm en route. Can you handle the next part until I get there?"

His heart rate shot way up. Hannah was coming here!

He was finally going to meet her in person, and then she would be able to see firsthand how valuable he was to her. He smoothed the tremor of excitement in his voice as he spoke. "What is your ETA?

"I'm still four hours away. Move in at two hours. I want them very afraid by the time I get there."

"Yes, ma'am," he responded as the phone went dead. It had struggled so hard to maintain the weak signal that the battery drained quickly. He hoped that Hannah would understand that he hadn't hung up on her intentionally.

He pocketed the phone and heard an engine start. He lifted the binoculars and saw that the wife and child were taking the delivery van. He guessed that they were heading out to re-supply the kitchen for their unexpected vacation.

He waited until he couldn't hear the van before he approached the house. There were only three people inside. He knew he had to strike while he had the advantage. The nearest town with a decent store was fifteen miles away. He had plenty of time before they returned. And when they did, he would be ready.

Chapter 61

Melissa had walked for two hours in search of a phone. Each time she came across a payphone something was wrong with it. At first, the cords had been cut or the handset was missing. Later, as she reached the better part of downtown, if there was such a place, the phones were less vandalized but in desperate need of repair.

She finally found a phone that actually worked. She didn't have any change, or any money for that matter. She dialed the operator to make a collect call. Her first call would not be to the President. She needed to talk with Hartford and make sure that he had taken her family to safety.

She spoke her name after the beep and waited in silence while the computerized operator called the number she had provided and requested authorization for the collect call.

The phone clicked a couple more times, and she heard the familiar voice come on the line.

"Melissa?"

Her lips quivered and her hands shook. A tear formed in the corners of her eyes. Even though she knew he would be at the house, she wasn't prepared to talk to him just yet.

"Melissa?" the voice repeated.

"Hey, Drew." Her voice shook from both nerves and stress. She had endured so much, but this was something she could never prepare for.

"Thank god you're okay. Representative Hartford told us everything. We've been worried about you."

She was too engrossed in the call to notice the black van pull to a stop across the street.

"Is everyone okay there?"

"Yeah. This is a pretty out of the way place. I don't think anyone will find us here."

"How's Billy?"

"He's doing great. He went with Rebecca to the store for some more food. Do you have any idea how much longer we will need to be here?"

"I don't know. But I will let you know when it's safe. Until then, hold tight. Can I speak to Hartford?"

"Sure. It's good to hear your voice again. When this is over, I'd really like it if you came over for dinner. Billy misses you and Rebecca is great. You will like her a lot. You two have a lot in common."

"I promise," she lied. "But right now I need to speak to Hartford. Please."

"Of course."

She could hear him calling for Hartford in the background. She listened to the soft background noises. She wished Andrew would come back on the phone, but then again, wished he wouldn't.

Chapter 62

Wilkes ran up to the house on the side with the small bathroom window. Getting in would be easy. Houses in remote areas rarely had the same security measures as those in the city or urban neighborhoods. He moved around to the front of the house. His best option was to make a sudden entrance right through the front door. The phone rang, and he froze.

He shuffled noiselessly around to the side of the house until he heard someone talking.

He stood from his crouching position and peered in the window. A full-length mirror provided a clear view of the back of the husband. He stood talking quietly on the phone. He couldn't hear what was being said but it didn't matter.

He waited and watched. The moment the man hung up and left the room, he sprinted around to the front of the house. The element of surprise was to his advantage. He ran full speed and slammed his massive body into the door.

The doorframe groaned and splintered under the sudden strain. He bounced off the door and stumbled back. The expensive deadbolt had kept the door in place. He drew his GLOCK 21 pistol and fired point blank at the deadbolt.

The lock exploded inward from the destructive power unleashed by the .45 round. He kicked the door open. Hartford was at the end of the hall. Wilkes quickly decided to try the voice of authority for compliance.

"Freeze! FBI."

Hartford froze.

Wilkes was surprised it had worked so effortlessly.

"Get on the ground. Hands in the air where I can see them."

Hartford knelt in the hallway with his hands above his head. Wilkes approached cautiously and saw a flash out of the corner of his eye. Someone slammed into him from the bedroom, and the gun went off. The shot shattered a large picture hanging in the hallway. He hit the far wall of the hallway hard. He kicked the feet out from under his attacker and forced them both to the ground.

The attacker tried to roll out of his grasp. Wilkes was ready and used the momentum to maintain control. He spun the attacker around and slammed his head into the wall. Knocked out, the attacker slumped to the floor. He got to his feet quickly and was ready to chase down Hartford. He was surprised to see William Hartford had not moved from his kneeling position in the hallway.

Wilkes looked down at the unconscious form and saw that it was the husband. He had been surprisingly brave attacking what he thought could very well have been an FBI agent. He walked over to Hartford.

"Put your hands behind your head."

Hartford did as he was told, and he pulled the zip ties from his pocket and quickly secured William Hartford. Only then did Hartford attempt to speak.

"Do you know who I am?"

Wilkes leaned in close as he tightened the zip ties.

"I know exactly who you are, Speaker."

Hartford's eyes widened.

"You're not with the FBI, are you?"

"And you're not as dumb as you look."

Wilkes walked over and secured the husband's feet and hands with zip ties. He hefted him over his shoulder. The closet would be the best place to store him until he needed him. He carried Andrew into the bedroom. He dropped him into the closet and shut the door. He pushed the heavy dresser in front of the closet door. If he woke up, that would slow him down enough for him to get to him before he escaped. He turned around and froze. He was wrong about the phone being hung up by the husband. The receiver was sitting on the table lying on its side. He walked over and lifted the receiver to his ear.

"Andrew? Hartford?"

He quickly hung up the phone and spun around to look down the hallway at Hartford. He checked his watch. It would still be at least another three and a half hours before Nick arrived.

He dumped Hartford into the bathtub. The ceramic surface would make it difficult, but not impossible, for Hartford to sit up or even stand, despite his being bound so tightly. It would be necessary to give Hartford a reason to stay put.

He stepped out of the house and walked around the back to the ATV. Samantha was slung over the front handlebars and tied down like a slaughtered deer. A quick family reunion would ensure both of their cooperation.

Chapter 63

Melissa heard the thump followed by a gunshot and shouting. She thought she had heard someone announce himself as a federal agent followed by more shouting.

"Andrew!" she screamed into the phone.

A second gunshot was followed by the sound of breaking glass. She could hear furniture shoved around followed by a loud thud. Then she heard nothing.

"Andrew!"

There was no sound for the longest time, but she refused to hang up the phone. She thought she heard what sounded like the faint clunk of the receiver being lifted off the table.

"Andrew? Hartford?"

The line went dead. She stared at the phone in her hand in disbelief. The FBI would not have just hung up the phone.

Nick had her family. She had to get to them before he killed them.

The unmarked black van pulled quickly up behind her, and two men jumped out. One grabbed her while another yanked a black hood over her head as she was pulled into the van.

The van sped off before anyone even noticed.

Chapter 64

President Sparks watched out the window of the tiny guardhouse as the Sikorsky VH-3D helicopter, call sign Marine One, touched down on the empty parking lot of the Raven Rock Mountain Complex in Pennsylvania. First the Vice President's limousine was attacked. And now, his most trusted speechwriter tells him that the Vice President is actually alive, and all it takes is a signature to set him free. A signature the President was unwilling to give.

He had stayed away from the White House long enough. It was time to return and show the nation that he was not afraid to stand at his post in the Oval Office.

Michael O'Brien wanted to live. While stationed overseas, he had begun to gamble in the Asian casinos. He had won at first, and the bug bit him hard. He successfully hid his growing habit from his superiors and fellow soldiers. But he couldn't hide the quarter of a million dollar debt he had quickly accumulated from the people he owed it to.

He flipped switches on the console in front of him that slowed the mighty rotors of the Sikorsky VH-3D helicopter to a complete stop. He glanced out the side window of the co-pilot seat and watched as the President of the United States walked across the dirt roadway with his entourage.

This was the first time he would be on the flight crew for the President, thanks to a mysterious food poisoning incident that had taken out enough of the Marine Helicopter

Squadron One pilots, code-named "The Nighthawks," to put him into the co-pilot seat of this special flight. It would also be the last time he would be on the flight crew for the President. But at least his debt would be paid in full, and he would have more than enough to keep his habit fulfilled for several more years until he got good enough to consistently win on his own.

The man who approached him promised to not only cover his current debt but reward him greatly for a special mission that could very well save the President's life. This mission would require him to transfer into the Executive Flight Detachment of the Marines and be ready for when he was contacted again.

He told the man that any investigation into his personal life would reveal his addiction, and he would never be admitted into The Nighthawks. The man asked Michael that, if he could ensure he passed the Yankee White security clearance, would he be ready to do whatever was asked of him?

Michael flipped the switches on the panel in the reverse position and started the rotors spinning again. While the pilot was busy with his own panel switches, he slipped the hypodermic syringe from a side pocket and set it on the seat next to him, out of sight.

President Sparks watched the massive steel doors embedded in the side of the mountain recede from view as the VH-3D lifted off abruptly to join four other identical Sikorsky helicopters. They would constantly shift formation in the presidential shell game to deter any attempt at shooting down Marine One. He had become used to the sudden shifts in position and speed as the shell game continued uninterrupted until he safely touched down at his destination.

"Roger vector two."

This was the last thing the pilot said before the needle pierced his skin. By the time he looked down to see the needle stuck in his leg, the paralyzing agent had spread, and he couldn't yell out to warn anyone about what had just happened.

O'Brien grabbed the control stick as the pilot slumped down in his seat. He swung the VH-3D into the final position behind the other four helicopters. He twisted the stick again, and the Sikorsky dove sideways into a riverbed. It would be five minutes before the next formation shift.

Five minutes before anyone knew the President was no longer in the game.

Chapter 65

Melissa rode silently in the van. The black hood was effective in keeping her from knowing where they were headed. She had been through so much, and now Nick had her family. She no longer cared what happened to her. There was nothing one person could do to stop him now. It would take the resources of something much larger to even try.

A half hour later the van stopped. She could feel the close presence of one of her kidnappers. She thought about striking out. If there had been only one of them, she would have considered it. She knew two men had grabbed her. In her weakened condition, she knew she couldn't take them both. No one had said a word since she had been shoved into the van. For all she knew there could be more men in the van that she didn't know about. She decided to let them take her without a fight. They were most likely taking her to Nick so he could kill her in son in front of her before killing her.

"I'm going to take off the mask," the first kidnapper said. "Do you understand everything else?"

She nodded. The mask was pulled up, and she closed her eyes before the sunlight could blind her. The door slid open, and she was helped out onto the street right in front of Hamilton Park. She looked at the bench across the grass where Robert sat with one hand resting on his polished cane. She strode across the lawn and stood less than a foot in front of him.

He looked up at her. None of the frailty from the night before was evident. It was as if he had found a renewed sense of strength.

"General Archon sends you his gratitude for saving his life. I am also pleased that you didn't let Nick kill him."

"I thought you were out of the business."

He smiled. "No one ever really gets out."

"Why didn't you tell me that Nick was involved in all of this?"

"I wasn't sure that he was."

"Well, now it's too late."

"When you have been doing this as long as I have, you will find that it is never too late."

"Robert, why did you bring me here?"

"I just received word from a source inside the White House that the President left this morning on Marine One bound for Camp David. Half an hour ago, Marine One left formation, dropped below radar and ceased all radio transmissions. Everyone's in a panic and nobody knows where he is or where he might be going. I was hoping you might."

It was then that she understood what Nick had really wanted from her all along.

The only thing that she could provide.

He needed a safe place. A secluded place.

A place that could never be traced to him.

A place where the three most powerful positions in the United States government would all be together in one room.

She looked directly into Robert's powerful gaze.

"They're going to my house."

Chapter 66

"I bought property on the Tug Hill Plateau in the Adirondack Mountains. I had planned to retire there and stay out of everyone's way after I had finished what brought me back to the States in the first place. Nick knows about it. And it is very out of the way."

"Can we stop him?"

"When you say we, you really mean me?"

"I am afraid I cannot commit very many resources to this operation. Things beyond my control have tied my hands.

"There's no way, I can't get there in time."

"I can call in some favors and get you on a plane almost twice as fast as the helicopter the President's in. You can get there long before the President arrives."

"And what am I supposed to do once I get there? I can't take on Nick alone."

"I have someone who trained with the SEAL Six team. He will join you."

"And do what?"

"Do what he was trained to do. Follow orders. Your orders."

Melissa looked at Robert. She saw something in his eyes as he looked at her that she hadn't seen in a long time.

He had faith in her.

He believed she could stop Nick. Not because she was the superior warrior, but because of something far more personal. She had spent a quarter of her life getting vengeance on those who had betrayed her. And that list never seemed to get shorter.

"I can do it."

Chapter 67

Wilkes waited in the bushes for twenty minutes before he heard the van struggle its way up the dirt road that led to the house deep in the Tug Hill countryside. The mother, Rebecca, was driving cautiously. He could see from the dented and muddy fender that they had already had trouble and didn't want to get stuck again.

Before the van came to a complete stop, the boy, Billy, jumped out and ran towards the house.

"Billy." Rebecca shut off the engine and pulled the parking brake. "Come back here and help with the groceries."

"I have to go bad, mom. I'll be right back."

Billy disappeared inside.

He would find Hartford tied up in the bathtub very soon. He had to move quickly or he would lose control of the situation. Rebecca opened the back of the van and reached in. He soundlessly came up behind her.

Billy ran into the house and straight for the bathroom. He should have used the restroom at the gas station half an hour ago. Instead he bought a Pepsi. He was certain he was going to explode before they made it to the house. He had made his mother promise to stop killing people. This house in the middle of nowhere was the best way she could keep her promise.

He stood over the toilet and was glad for the instant

relief. He finished and zipped up. Just as he turned to leave he noticed something move in the bathtub. He jumped and let out a loud scream.

It was all happening again.

He ran to the front door and stopped as he looked outside. Someone held Rebecca from behind and was directing her into the house. He had big muscles, but all he focused on was the gun pointed right at him.

"Hey, kid."

He remembered what it felt like to stare down the barrel of a loaded weapon. His fear intensified. His mother was not around to save him this time. He had to act quickly if he wanted to get away. He couldn't leave his family behind. But no one would come to their rescue if he didn't get help.

He backed slowly into the house.

"That's a good boy." The man pushed his mother forward.

He knew that if he didn't do something, they would all die. He vaulted sideways through an open door into a bedroom.

Wilkes saw the boy jerk to the side and fired twice. Rebecca kicked him in the shins and drove her elbow into his ribs. He was better than she was at hand-to-hand combat and dodged the elbow after his shins were raked by her shoe. He swung the GLOCK around and Rebecca went down hard. Her shallow breathing told him she'd be out for a while.

Time enough for him to get the boy.

He ran into the house and entered the room. The room was empty but the window was open. He ran to the window and looked out into the forest. The boy was running as fast as he could through the forest away from the house.

If he got lucky, he might find one of the neighbor's homes. That would ruin the plan that Nick had spent so long developing. He was under orders not to kill anyone yet, but he also had an obligation to make sure that nothing would interrupt the plan. Not when they were this close.

The President was already on his way here, and Nick would arrive just before he did. They were so close to starting the second revolution this country desperately needed.

The boy continued to run deeper into the forest. He thought he could outrun him, and he was probably right.

He aimed the GLOCK and sighted on the boy as he ran.

"Outrun this."

He squeezed the trigger.

Billy felt the searing heat from the scorching hot bullet as it tore through the soft down of his jacket. He stumbled from the sudden overload of pain and went down hard onto the forest floor. He rolled over on his back and looked up at the crystal blue sky. The sun shone brightly through the thick forest.

It was at that moment that he wanted his mother to do something he made her promise to never do again.

He wanted somebody to die.

Just then that same somebody blocked the light right

above him and reached down to grab him. The pain was too much for him to endure, and his brain shut down just as easily as someone turning the lights out with a tiny switch.

Chapter 68

Melissa checked the straps on the parachute. When she first arrived at the airport and saw the Lockheed C-130 Hercules, she demanded to see the captain.

"The closest airport to my cabin is the Oneida County Airport. It's a municipal airport and the runway isn't long enough to land this thing. The only airport that can handle this is Syracuse International, and it's too far away. I'll never make it in time."

"Sorry, ma'am. This is the only plane available."

"I need something smaller. I have to get as close to the house as possible."

"We'll get you right on top of the house."

"What do you expect me to do? Jump?"

The pilot smiled.

She checked the straps again on the parachute.

She was strapped into the MC-5 Static Line Convertible Ram Air Parachute System and was briefed shortly after takeoff.

The oxygen tank sat next to her. The C-130 would climb to 25,000 feet, and she would jump out. A static line system would automatically deploy the parachute, and she could glide in as close as she wanted to the house without alerting anyone nearby that a plane had flown anywhere near the target area.

She looked over at the Navy SEAL who would be jumping with her. He had climbed onto the plane just before takeoff and wore his darkened helmet the entire flight. He was dressed in a black HALO outfit designed for the High Altitude Low Opening maneuvers that had become a popular method for dropping soldiers deep into enemy territory. He would deploy right after her and follow her down to any landing zone she picked.

She tried to engage him in conversation a couple of times. Each time his muffled voice told her that they would talk strategy once on the ground.

The pilot stepped into the back of the plane.

"We are over the drop zone now. Get ready." The pilot looked at her. "Are you nervous?"

"I made several jumps during basic training. None of them were even remotely like this."

"Don't worry," the Navy SEAL stepped up next to her. "It's just like riding a bicycle. It'll come back to you."

She looked outside as the ground rolled by slowly.

"Yeah, like riding a bicycle at 25,000 feet." She stepped out the back of the C-130 and into open space.

The parachute opened wide, and she felt the tug as she quickly transitioned into a controlled descent. 20,000 feet below her, she saw the whir of the rotor blades as Marine One slid beneath her on its way to her house. She expected to see a missile streak from deep within the Adirondack forest towards the helicopter at any moment. She watched the Sikorsky VH-3D helicopter skim along just above the tree line.

She looked up and saw the Navy SEAL hovering just above her. They both drifted slowly to the earth. Too slowly.

She swung around and waved up at him. She motioned

to the helicopter below. Then she made swooping motions with her hands.

He shook his head.

She reached into her back pocket and unsheathed the SOG SEAL Knife. Above her she could see him waving his arms wildly. He was helpless to stop her.

She reached up and gathered all the tethers that held her canopy. She bunched them and then swiftly severed each with the blade. She dropped like a rock and quickly reached terminal velocity. She was heading for the earth at a much faster pace. This is more like it, she thought.

She arched her back and spread her arms and legs to steer herself towards the house.

The Navy SEAL sliced his own tethers and fell away from his parachute. He closed his arms and legs to form his body into a straight arrow and gained on her as they rocketed towards the ground at 120 miles per hour.

Chapter 69

Hartford had heard the shot and panicked. For the next hour he sat in the tub as a wave of depression filled him. The door to the bathroom opened and Wilkes carried the still form of his daughter into the bathroom and dropped her on the floor still tied up.

The bastard had killed his daughter. He struggled against the ropes and mumbled at him through the gag.

Wilkes turned to him.

"Relax, pops. She's just knocked out. In case you're wondering, I shot the boy. I'm sorry to report he'll live."

He stopped struggling. What kind of monster could shoot a child? He knew he was looking at such a monster right in front of him. This filled him with ever-increasing fear. He wasn't going to survive this day.

"The President's here." Wilkes stood up and walked towards him. "Time to earn your pay."

Only then did he notice the approaching thrum of helicopter blades. Wilkes pulled him out of the tub.

"I am going to untie you. If you do or say anything that I don't approve of, you and your daughter will die slowly. Understand?"

He nodded his head.

Wilkes removed the gag and untied him. He smoothed out his wrinkled clothes and patted him on the shoulders.

"You look great. Just like the next President of the United States should look."

"What do you want me to do?"

"Tell him that you have someone he needs to meet and that she'll be here soon. Invite him inside for a cup of tea, if you wish."

He looked out the window and saw the trees sway under the powerful rotors of the President's helicopter. Wilkes pushed him forward, and they stepped out the front door. He shielded his eyes from the dust and small rocks kicked up by the Sikorsky VH-3D.

Wilkes turned his head away while Marine One kicked up dust as it touched down. He reached into his pocket and pushed the button to activate the remote launcher. The twin SAM missiles were programmed to seek out Marine One's flight signature within seconds and would destroy the helicopter upon takeoff.

Chapter 13

Fighting against the wind rushing up at her, Melissa pulled her arm around and checked the digital altimeter. The display ticked below two thousand feet so she pulled the cord on the reserve parachute. The parachute spilled from the compartment and expanded. She jerked from the force and swung back and forth as her descent slowed quickly. She picked a clearing less than a half mile from the house.

The reserve parachute was not as large as the first one, and she dropped in fast. She hit the ground and rolled. She stood just as the Navy SEAL hit the ground. Both parachutes fluttered to the ground as they each hit their release clamps.

She shed the parachuting gear and reached into the large pack on her back. She pulled the MP5SD out and snapped the thirty-round magazine into place. She turned to see the Navy SEAL had shed his gear and was now wearing a tactical mask. She couldn't work with someone unless she saw his face.

She walked up to him. "Take off your mask."

"If it's all the same to you, I'd like to keep it on." He bent down and dug through his pack.

"It's not all the same to me. If your mask gets ripped off during combat, I need to know who not to shoot."

"You won't shoot me."

"Then let's make sure."

He dropped his head and grasped the top of the tactical mask. He pulled it off and looked up at her with a smile.

She froze. It couldn't be.

"I can't be a hero unless I come to the maiden's rescue."

"But, you were..." She stopped talking and stared.

Denny pounded a fist on his chest. "Body armor. You don't point a grenade machine gun at somebody without protection."

"How..."

"General Archon's men grabbed me when they realized I wasn't dead. I was able to convince him that I was also trying to stop the assassination. Together we figured out it was Nick who had manipulated all of us."

He pulled his mask back on and stood up.

"Come on. We still have a President to save."

"Denny, I..."

"I know what you're going to say, and you don't have to. I decided it was better you thought I was dead. At least until this was all over."

"Better for who?"

"Better for both of us, I suppose," He looked around. "After this is over, we'll sit down and have a nice long chat. But right now we still have a job to do."

She smiled as their eyes locked on each other. Their relationship was about to take a whole new direction. And it was one she was much more comfortable with than when they had just been your average waitress and mechanic in small town America. There would be no more lies.

She broke their lingering gaze and turned away from him to dart into the forest on the quickest route to her house.

Chapter 70

The blades stopped spinning and a section on the side of the helicopter split open. It lowered, and two Secret Service agents hopped down the staircase built into the inside of the door. The sun reflected off the handcuffs that bound their hands together. They looked around and then both focused on Hartford and Wilkes standing by the front door of the house.

President Alan Sparks stepped out of the Sikorsky VH-3D helicopter and walked over to Hartford. He didn't offer to shake his hand, and Hartford could see that he was not happy.

"What's this all about, Bill?"

Before Hartford could think of anything to say, a dusty Cutlass Supreme roared up the dirt driveway and pulled up to the front of the house in a cloud of dust. Nick stepped out of the car and walked up to the small group.

"My apologies, Mr. President. I needed to ensure that we had absolute privacy for this meeting."

"What meeting? Do you realize that you have committed an act of treason?"

"When you hear what I have to say, you will see that I did what had to be done to keep you safe. Someone very close to you wants you dead."

"What the hell are you talking about?"

"Let's go inside, and I will tell you everything."

"I'm not going anywhere," President Sparks stood up to his full height of six foot eight.

"Wilkes, if you don't mind," Nick said calmly.

Wilkes reached out a meaty hand and grabbed the President roughly around the arm.

"Take your hands off me," the President spat. "I will have you both arrested."

"No, you won't," said Nick.

"Hartford, if you are in any way…" the President began.

"MR. PRESIDENT!" Nick shouted.

The President stopped talking and looked at him.

"Let's go inside and discuss this in a civilized manner. Please hold your judgment until after you hear me out."

Wilkes led the President into the house. Nick waved Hartford to follow. He looked back at Marine One as the co-pilot led the pilot out in handcuffs.

He walked over to the two Secret Service agents and the pilot as they stood in a line in front of the helicopter.

"Gentlemen. I apologize for the theatrics, but as soon as I have spoken with the President, you will be released from your shackles. You will be allowed to leave unharmed. I have no personal ill will towards the President. I only needed to speak with him privately. Your co-pilot will, of course, be staying behind with me. He completed his mission successfully, and I don't want to give the President any opportunity to make him suffer for his decision to do the right thing."

He spun on his heels and walked back to the house and up the front steps. Wilkes was waiting at the top of the steps. He blocked Nick's entrance into the house. "Where's Hannah?"

Nick cocked his head to the side. "She sends her regrets

that she was unable to make it in time. I will be sure to pass on to her how valuable you are to the organization."

Wilkes smiled and shifted to the side to let him into the house.

Melissa and Denny watched the scene unfold through their binoculars. He lowered his binoculars after Nick entered the house.

"What do you think," he asked. "Is he going to kill the President here?"

She scanned the area around the house.

"I don't think so. He has SAMs set up on a remote launcher somewhere in the Adirondacks. He will wait until the President has taken off again and then shoot him out of the sky."

"Why not shoot him down before they landed?"

"He had to make sure the President was on the helicopter. No doubt Nick activated the SAMs right when the chopper landed. They will launch as soon as the President leaves."

"What's the plan?" he asked.

She swept the binoculars around. They settled on the three prisoners and the Uzi-toting man who guarded them.

She lowered her binoculars and turned to him.

"Let's circle around and get Mr. Uzi. Once we have the Secret Service agents free, we will have Nick outnumbered."

She circled around and placed the Cutlass Supreme between her and the Uzi. He was right next to her a moment later. He pointed to a small grouping of trees.

"I can cover both the door and the helicopter from that spot."

She scanned all around her.

"You're right. It's the best place to create a cross fire if things get rough. I'm going to crawl right up to the edge of the Cutlass. I'll create a diversion and get the Uzi's attention. When he looks towards me, take him down."

"How long do you think Nick will stay inside?"

"I'm guessing that we don't have as much time as we want."

He nodded and turned away. She reached out and stopped him with a hand on his arm.

"Whatever happens, we keep the President, the Vice President and Hartford from getting on that helicopter."

"No matter what?"

"No matter what."

He slid from her grasp and disappeared into the trees.

Nick stepped into the room. His plan was almost complete. There had been a few hiccups along the way, but the true test of a great plan is how well it held up to setbacks. And despite a few, here he was in the middle of nowhere about to talk to the President of the United States.

"Mr. President, let me get straight to the point. I know who is behind the plot to kill you and the Vice President."

The President looked sharply at him.

"I staged the attack on the Vice President's motorcade to force the real person behind the assassination plot to action. And it worked. Unfortunately, he moved faster on the Vice

President than even I expected. I flushed him out, but at considerable personal cost. I'm afraid I no longer have the resources to continue this counter-campaign on my own. That is why I have decided to bring you into the loop, so to speak."

"If you know who is responsible for putting this country on the brink of anarchy," the President barked. "Then tell me."

"It is none other than your close personal friend and confidant, General Archon."

"I don't believe you."

"Oh, believe it, Mr. President."

"How does kidnapping me help you?"

"I'm afraid it was necessary. He has bugged every inch of your life. The White House, your cars, your planes, even your home. This was the only place that was safe from him and those who work for him."

"I have heard enough," the President stood up.

Wilkes stood reflexively and reached for his gun. He put a hand out and stopped him.

He turned back to face the President.

"Mr. President, you, the Vice President and the Speaker of the House are all free to leave. Nobody will stop you. But before you send someone to hunt me down, ask General Archon about Operation Omega Ascension."

The President moved in close and stared darkly into his eyes. "You and I will meet again."

President Sparks brushed past him and strode out the front door into the bright sun.

Melissa moved in closer and stopped a hundred feet from the house. She couldn't see the captives or their guard. The Oldsmobile Cutlass Supreme blocked her view entirely. She shuffled on her stomach and crawled right up to the Cutlass.

She ran her tongue across her lips and was ready to let out a soft whistle when she heard a noise that stopped her. The front door creaked open and President Sparks stopped abruptly at the base of the stairs when Mr. Uzi pointed the barrel at him.

Nick stepped out of the house and motioned to him to lower his weapon. Mr. Uzi nodded, then took out a tiny key and tossed it to the pilot.

From this distance, she couldn't hear what he said, but she made a good guess as the pilot unlocked the handcuffs of the Secret Service agents next to him.

Once the three prisoners were free, the man holding the Uzi motioned for them to get into Marine One. She watched them climb in and Mr. Uzi stepped away to halfway between the house and the helicopter.

President Alan Sparks looked at him one last time before he headed for Marine One without looking back.

She had to act fast.

She stood up and raised her MP5SD to take aim.

She tightened her finger on the trigger and bullets spat from the end of the barrel towards the President of the United States.

Chapter 71

Nick watched the most powerful man in the United States walk for the last time to Marine One and smiled. This had been way too easy.

Columns of dirt ripped into the ground all around the President's feet, and the President hit the ground covering his head. His man with the Uzi reacted quickly and started shooting at the figure that had popped up from behind the Cutlass. His hand swung back and forth puncturing tires, shattering glass and riddling the Cutlass with bullets. The Uzi clicked and the man reached for a second magazine.

The Uzi flew out of the man's grasp as he was torn to pieces by the responding hail of bullets.

He had been frozen in place with utter shock by what just happened. He quickly regained his senses and ducked into the house.

Wilkes was pressed against the wall of the hallway out of sight of any windows.

"Who's shooting?" Wilkes asked.

"It's Melissa," Nick spat. "It has to be her."

"Do you think she's alone?"

"I doubt it. But we can't take that chance."

Nick formulated a new plan quickly. He knew what he had to do. It wasn't what he wanted, but he had to live to fight another day.

Melissa crouched as she approached the house. She

reloaded the MP5SD with a fresh magazine and pulled the cocking lever. The President looked up and spotted her. She raised a finger to her lips to silence him. The door to the house opened, and she aimed the MP5SD – right at her son.

Nick had his arm around Billy's neck and held her P226 X-Five to his head. They duck-walked out the front door.

"Let the President go, Melissa."

The President started to get up. She tightened her grip on the MP5SD and pointed it straight at Nick. She avoided looking directly into her son's eyes and noticed blood trickle down his arm. He had been shot. She could tell by the dried blood on the shirt that it had been earlier in the day and the wound must have just reopened. She no longer cared about her promise. It just wasn't meant to be.

"Don't get in that helicopter, Mr. President!"

President Sparks stood up. His head darted back and forth between the two who held guns on each other.

He shifted the weight of his human shield. "I'm not stopping you from leaving. She is."

The President started to move towards the Sikorsky.

She never took her eyes off Nick as she spoke. "I will do whatever it takes to keep you off that chopper, Mr. President. Please don't make me do something I might regret later."

"If you aim at him, I will shoot your son."

"Do you have the shot?" she shouted into the air.

"I have the shot," a voice replied from the forest.

"You wouldn't shoot the President," Nick seethed.

"I'll do whatever it takes to keep him alive."

She finally stared at Billy's face. His eyes darted around in fear, and he didn't make eye contact with her. As long as Nick held her son, she couldn't do anything.

"You let the President go," Nick offered, "and I will let your son go."

"Can't do that, Nick." She kept the MP5SD steady on him. Her son blocked most of his body, and if she fired, she would hit her son first.

"Hear that, Billy boy," he mocked. "Your life is worth less than I thought. She's willing to let you die for a complete stranger."

He released his arm slightly and grabbed Billy's head in his hand.

"I want you to look your mother in the eye," he hissed. "And tell her goodbye."

He forced Billy to look at her. Their eyes met. This was her one chance.

Remember what I told you, she thought. Billy's eyes understood. He grabbed Nick's arm and began to struggle and twist. Nick tightened his grip around Billy's neck forcing him to stop. Billy looked back at his mom and raised a finger.

Then another.

When the third finger lifted, she squeezed the trigger and the MP5SD coughed once.

Billy relaxed his legs and dropped down to let his full weight pull on Nick's arm. He was no longer a complete human shield, and the 9mm round caught Nick in the shoulder.

Nick released him when the searing pain hit him, and he fell backwards into the house. He scooted farther into the hallway and kicked the door closed with his foot.

His plan was shot to hell.

Wilkes was instantly by his side. "What happened?"

"The bitch shot me." Nick sat up in the hallway and gripped his shoulder like a bowling ball. He felt around and found two holes. The bullet had exited out the back cleanly.

"How? You were holding her son?"

"We need to get out of here." Nick walked into the back bedroom where Andrew, Rebecca, and Hartford were tied up again. Wilkes had been busy.

"I saw two quads around the back." Wilkes stepped into the room behind him. "And I still have mine."

He removed his blood-soaked jacket. It was time for them to leave. He looked at the three before he grabbed Hartford and yanked him to his feet.

Billy hit the ground and Nick dropped backwards into the house. Melissa stood up to get a better shot just as he kicked the front door closed. She inched towards the house. She expanded her peripheral vision and watched the windows along with the door.

"Are you okay?"

Billy sat up. "I'm okay."

"Get out of here!"

"Dad and Rebecca are still in there."

"Denny," she yelled out.

"Yeah," Denny stepped out of the bushes.

"Get Billy and the rest of them out of here," she commanded.

Denny pulled his mask off and walked up to the President. She pushed Billy in the direction of the President and he jogged over to join them.

"Come with me," Denny said.

"Where are you taking me?" the President asked.

"Wherever you want to go," Denny responded. "We just have to..."

Everyone ducked down when the roar of an ATV started from the back of the house. She ran around and watched as Nick held onto another man as they roared through the trees away from the house. She watched the ATV disappeared into the woods.

Denny darted around the side of the house and saw the ATV disappear deep into the woods.

"Are you going to go after them?"

"No," she replied. "There's nowhere for him to run anymore."

"You got it." he ran back around to the front of the house.

She walked in the back door with the MP5SD raised. She cleared each room as she headed down the hallway to the bedrooms. She heard noises and peeked around the corner. Andrew and Rebecca were tied up on the bed. There was no one else in the room.

She ran in and pulled the gag from Andrew.

"Oh, my god," he sputtered. "He was going to kill us."

She looked around.

"Where's Hartford?"

"They took him."

The roar of an ATV started up and she ran to the window in time to see Billy holding onto the masked driver before they disappeared from view.

She ran out of the house and almost collided with Denny coming in.

"Billy's gone," they both said at the same time.

"What happened?" She demanded.

"When I got back around the front, Billy wasn't there. The President said that another one of us took him away."

"There isn't another one of us. Take the President and get out of here. Don't let anyone near that helicopter."

She ran out the back door and jumped onto the remaining ATV. Nick was making a mistake to take the fight into the rugged wilderness of the Tug Hill Plateau. She trained and fought for four years in the jungles of South America. She was more at home in this environment than anywhere else in the world. It was the one place she was perfectly suited to survive.

The ATV kicked up the muddy ground behind her, and she felt more at peace with herself than she ever did serving greasy food in a motel restaurant.

This was what she was born to do.

This was who she became during her re-birth in the jungle.

She pursued her prey through the forest with a highly tuned animal instinct. She quickly noticed the trail left behind by the quads as they crashed through the jungle. She would never hear their engines over her own, but she didn't need to.

She splashed through a creek, rolled to a stop, and shut off the engine. She turned her head slowly and closed her eyes. She only heard the echo of one ATV in the distance. One of them had stopped somewhere nearby. The muddy tracks in front of her showed that one ATV had traveled more slowly than the other through this area. She glanced in the mirror attached to the handlebars and saw Wilkes peek around a tree.

She was in a trap!

She somersaulted over the front of the ATV as bullets ripped into the chassis. Before the echoes from Wilkes pistol had died, she popped up and fired back with the MP5SD. Wilkes hit the ground and rolled behind the tree. She ran full speed away from the ATV. It didn't provide the cover she needed. Trees threw bark sideways as he fired after her.

She increased the distance between them. The thickness of trees made it impossible for him to hit her at this range. She circled around and found the tracks from his ATV. She located it and hopped on. She didn't have time to deal with this yahoo.

She had to find her son.

Chapter 72

Wilkes heard the roar of his ATV and immediately ran for the ATV Melissa had left behind. He prayed that he hadn't hit anything vital. He turned the key and the ATV sprang to life. He turned the quad around and traveled twenty feet into the trees to collect William Hartford.

He pulled the ATV next to the pile of ropes where he left Hartford. But he wasn't there.

He shut off the engine and listened. He didn't hear anything. Dammit! he thought. Gunshots echoed through the forest and he fired up the ATV. He could still help kill Melissa.

The quad ATV flew off the embankment empty and slammed into a tree. Melissa had bailed out when the first bullet screamed right past her ear. She scrambled for cover as more bullets sought her out. She sat with her back to a tree.

"Give it up, Nick. It's over."

He responded with another hail of bullets that tore into the side of the tree. He must still have her X-Five with its nineteen-round magazine. She hadn't been able to keep track of how many rounds he had already fired. She just had to wait for the telltale sign of the magazine release before she made her move.

"Should we see what your son's life is worth now?" he called out to her.

He talked to cover the sound of the magazine ejecting. She jumped up and swung her MP5SD forward. He held the X-Five pointed right at her. He fired, and the bullet slammed into her body armor. The force of the impact knocked her down. After she hit the ground, she heard the magazine eject and a fresh one get slapped into the SIG-Sauer P226.

She rolled back behind the tree. He had tricked her once. She wouldn't let it happen again.

"It's me you want. Let my son go."

"I will have you. But I think I'll keep little Billy here for a while longer."

"You can't escape. The military is on their way."

"They can't surround the entire mountain range. Your son will die here along with you. And then I will walk out and disappear quietly until the time is right for my triumphant return."

She had to keep him talking. The ground had a depression that went out twenty feet. She could crawl along that and flank him. She needed to keep him from hearing her as she moved.

She called out from behind the tree. "Why did you send someone to kill me in Oregon?"

"What makes you think I had anything to do with that?" he responded.

She didn't have an answer for that. Even if he was behind the presidential assassination, there was no reason to kill her.

She waited. He had stopped talking, and she was lost deep in thought. Too much time had passed. She had to move through the ditch now if she hoped to circle around him. She darted forward. He had already begun to circle and was nearly parallel to her. He fired as she ran.

She dove behind a fallen tree as the remaining bullets tore into it. She heard the X-Five click after its final round. She popped up and aimed at him. He held Billy in front of him. She aimed the MP5SD and he tightened his grip on Billy's neck.

"Drop the gun or I'll break his neck."

Billy cried out as he showed he was serious. She lowered the MP5SD and pulled the strap over her head. She tossed it away from her.

He smiled. "You're weak. You know that?"

"Let him go."

He tightened his grip and Billy cried out. "Why should I?"

"You mentioned that you wanted to walk out of this forest. If you let him go, I'll let you do that. If you don't…"

He opened his mouth to speak when she moved swiftly.

The SOG SEAL Knife sliced through the air and planted itself firmly into Nick's arm. He released Billy and his scream of pain echoed through the forest. She dove for the MP5SD and rolled to a sitting firing position. She swept the barrel back and forth looking for him. Billy lifted his head up and perched on his elbows.

"Stay down!" She stood up and swept the MP5SD in every direction as she looked for a target.

She saw Nick climb over the embankment and fired. He disappeared over the edge. In the distance she heard the throaty roar of an ATV headed her way.

Wilkes revved the ATV and pushed the quad as hard as he could without losing control. Up ahead he saw Nick running right towards him. He slowed down as he reached Nick.

"Turn around and head back to the house." Nick jumped on the back of the ATV.

Wilkes gunned the quad and mud showered the trees around them as he spun it around.

"What are we doing?" he yelled over the roar of the engine.

"The fastest way out of this forest is the Sikorsky," Nick hollered into his ear.

"What about the SAMs?"

"We'll disable the launcher before we take off."

He gunned the motor and increased speed as he weaved in and out of the trees. He didn't think that Nick would mind his recklessness.

Melissa ran to Billy and lifted him up.

"Get up. We have to move now."

"I think I'm gonna throw up."

"That's just your nerves. They'll go away soon."

She trotted over to the ATV. It lay on its side by the tree it had collided with. She hefted it back onto its wheels and turned the key.

The engine sputtered to life and purred happily. She climbed on and motioned for him to join her. He sat down behind her and wrapped his arms around her tightly. She felt nothing. She wanted to enjoy his closeness, but right now she was not a mother.

She was a hunter.

She gunned the motor and turned around to head back for the house. As they got closer, she could hear the familiar thumping sounds.

Someone was taking off in the helicopter.

Chapter 73

Wilkes pulled the ATV to a stop a hundred yards behind the house in the woods. The dense forest muffled the sound of the ATV, but not completely. They couldn't risk being heard returning so they approached the house quietly on foot.

He had a few rounds left in his GLOCK 21 pistol. He circled around to the front of the house and saw that the front door stood open. The USA Couriers delivery van was gone, and he couldn't hear anyone around. Nick rounded the corner of the other side of the house. He motioned towards the front door.

He crouched next to the open door on one side and Nick took position on the other. Nick tossed a rock into the hallway and waited. Nothing happened. He entered the door in a crouch. Each room was empty. The back bedroom still held the towels he had used to tie up the family.

He stood up and walked into the hallway.

"Clear," he said.

He stepped out onto the porch of the house.

Nick inspected the Oldsmobile Cutlass Supreme. It had been riddled by bullets from the Uzi. He pulled open the passenger door and extracted a bag. He pulled the shattered pieces of a compact disc case out of the bag. Nick threw them on the ground and cursed. He slung the bag over the Cutlass and into the woods. He turned and walked up to Wilkes.

"Give me the remote trigger."

Wilkes pulled it out of his pocket and handed it to him.

"We're taking the Sikorsky," Nick said as he de-activated the launcher with the remote. Nick jogged over to the U.S. Marine Corps Sikorsky VH-3D helicopter with the Presidential Seal painted on the side. He looked back at Wilkes.

Wilkes ran to catch up to Nick.

"Get in there and start this bird," Nick said. "I'll secure the door."

Wilkes vaulted the steps into Marine One. He ducked into the pilot's seat and placed the headphones over his ears. He was a trained pilot in the Marines and was pleased to use his skills to help Nick escape. This would make him Nick's number one man. The rotors whined to life and gained speed.

He felt the door close. He pulled back on the flight stick, and the VH-3D lifted off the ground. Below him Melissa roared into the clearing on the ATV. He spotted her and waved as he pulled into the sky.

That's when the alarms sounded.

Melissa skidded to a halt in the clearing. Above her the Sikorsky rose to clear the tree line. She saw Wilkes in the pilot seat. He looked down and saw her. He waved right before he pulled left and lifted higher into the sky.

She raised her MP5SD. At this range she couldn't do any real damage to the heavily armored helicopter. She lowered her machine pistol and watched Nick escape.

Again.

Sssssfft!

The smoke trail slammed into the side of the helicopter with lightning speed, and the VH-3D erupted into a fireball. She pulled Billy down with her as she dropped behind the ATV. She covered her head as debris and fire rained down from the once proud Presidential Executive transport.

The frame of the helicopter stayed intact as it fell, on fire, into the forest. The intense heat and flame licked hungrily at the dry trees all around the wreckage. The sap heated in the trees and soon the fire spread.

She grabbed him and hopped back onto the ATV. She revved the motor to life and gunned for the dirt road. The ATV hit its top speed before she was ready to let up on the accelerator. She shot down the dirt road away from the only oasis she had ever dared to create.

She did not look back.

She knew that behind her the flames would spread and destroy the last remnants of her attempt at a normal life.

Chapter 74

Melissa paced around the waiting room of the Oval Office like a tiger in a cage. She had looked at everything hanging on the walls or sitting in the shelves at least twice. Sitting in a chair closest to the door sat the newly elected Speaker of the House of Representatives, Alexander Baine.

William Hartford resigned as the Speaker the day after they had returned to Washington, DC and moved in with his daughter in Vermont to live the rest of his life out in solitude. His daughter only received minor injuries from her ordeal with Nick's soldier, but she knew from experience that the mental scars would take a long time to heal.

She stood quietly and looked around the waiting room. She ignored the two guards that had been by her side for the past week since Nick's attempt on the President's life. She looked around the room, and her eyes fell on Baine. He was looking right at her. She smiled and quickly looked away.

The phone rang at the secretary's desk, whereupon she answered it quickly. She didn't say a word and hung the phone back up. She looked at Melissa, then at Baine.

"The President will see you now, Mr. Speaker."

Alexander Baine stood up and opened the door into the Oval Office. He disappeared from view as the door closed behind him. President Sparks trusted him implicitly. He had the unique distinction of becoming the first Speaker of the House who was not a member of the House of Representatives. And President Sparks himself pushed for his nomination.

If she were prone to political questions, she would have wondered about the power this Speaker of the House could wield since he was not associated with any political party. Instead, all she could think about was the five thousand acres of scorched earth with her previous retirement home at the center.

Two hikers admitted to improperly extinguishing their campfire and started what was called the Great Tug Hill Blaze.

She immediately recognized the two hikers when she saw their pictures plastered on every news channel. She had last seen them in handcuffs standing next to the U.S. Marine Corps Sikorsky VH-3D helicopter. The Secret Service was willing to do anything to protect the President. But how far was the President willing to go to cover up what really happened?

The phone rang on the desk and the secretary picked it up. She set it back down just as quickly.

"The President will see you now."

She wondered, as the door opened, if this was all the secretary said for eight hours a day. The two guards were suddenly behind her, and she felt their presence now more than ever. They never touched her, but she could feel their energy pushing her through the threshold of the doorway.

A threshold into the unknown.

She walked into the Oval Office to a smiling President. Alan Sparks stood up and came around to the front of the massive mahogany desk. He held his hand out to her.

"I am sorry that it has taken me so long to thank you for coming to my rescue. General Archon told me that, when I had disappeared from radar, no one knew where I was. He said you guessed it right away and risked everything to come to my aid, with minimal support."

She shook the President's hand. She was not expecting this. She didn't know what she expected, but it wasn't this.

"My office has been very busy. We spent the past week replacing everyone who even passed Nick Spanos in the hallway. There have been many changes within every aspect of my administration, but most importantly, the change that didn't happen was my replacement. And I have you to thank for that."

She was stunned. The President looked past her at the two guards.

"You may go now, gentlemen. Your services are no longer required."

President Sparks looked back at her and smiled.

"Please. Have a seat. I wanted to let you know that General Archon has briefed me on all your recent activities. And your history. While I don't agree with your methods, I am glad to see that your loyalty is still with America. I am offering you a complete pardon on all charges."

"What is the price?"

"Only your silence. The country cannot know that an attempt was made on my life. Nor can anyone know how close it came to succeeding. Your silence is of the utmost importance to the security of my position and the comfort of the American people. Maybe even the world."

She looked at the President. She turned her head to look at Alexander Baine. She could tell that he wanted something more from her. She looked back at the President.

"You have it. As long as my family is safe."

"We have already begun the preparations for new identities." Baine took the conversation from the President. "I am erasing their identities from the permanent record. Only the three of us know who they really are, and it will stay that way."

"Then my lips are sealed."

President Alan Sparks smiled.

"Thank you. Do you have any ideas as to what you want to do now?" She had been in a fog since everything she knew had been turned upside down.

"I don't know. I really haven't given it much thought."

The President looked at Baine.

"I will leave you two to talk. It's better that I don't know exactly what's said."

President Alan Sparks disappeared out the east door of the Oval Office and wandered off through the rose garden. She watched him walk away calmly as if he was just out for a stroll. She turned back to look at Alexander Baine. He had waited until he had her full attention before he spoke.

"I would like to offer you a position in a new committee that I have recently formed."

"I am afraid that I'm not one for politics."

"There's very little politics with this committee. It's more of a threat assessment team."

"I thought the Department of Homeland Security had that all sewn up."

"They do, for threats from outside the U.S. What I am talking about are local homegrown groups. I'm talking about the Nick Spanos of the world. There is a new breed of domestic terrorist that is heavily funded and highly organized. They want nothing more than the next revolution of the United States and to force the replacement of the current government. Their only goal is chaos. The President has authorized the formation of the Domestic Crisis Division. The DCD will handle small-scale investigation and interference of domestic terrorist threats before they become a national threat. The United States has spent so much time focusing on the threats outside our borders we almost forgot about the ones who are already inside the gates."

"Are you recruiting me into your secret little organization?"

"You have unique skills that would prove useful."

"How big is this DCD organization?"

"The knowledge of the DCD is limited to the President, General Archon and myself. And now you."

"If it's such a small group, what can I possibly add to it?"

"It is my understanding that you've met Hannah personally."

She couldn't keep the shocked look from crossing her face.

Understanding appeared on his face.

"You can see why I am asking you to help us."

"What makes you think Hannah is still a threat?"

"She spoke with one of the President's aides after the attack on the Vice President with a demand."

"She called someone? Recently?"

"This is why she is considered a very big and real threat."

Her head was spinning. She couldn't believe what she

was hearing.

It couldn't be true.

But if it was true, she finally knew exactly who had sent someone to kill her in Oregon.

More importantly, she knew why.

But first, she had to get out of this office.

"Can I think about it?"

"Please don't think that if you decline something will happen to you. I don't operate that way. If you decide not to become part of this, I will leave you alone. That is, of course, dependent on you forgetting that such a group exists. If you stay quiet, you will not have to look over your shoulder on account of me or the DCD."

"Thank you."

"Melissa, you have a gift. Your survival instincts are stronger that any I have ever seen and I want to give you the opportunity to embrace what you are. Use it for something good. No. Use it for something great."

"I said I will think about it."

"Of course. Let me give you a number where you can reach me should you decide to accept my offer."

He spun a card out to her. Except for the eight-hundred number listed on its face, the card was otherwise blank. No name was listed on the card to identify the number's owner.

"Call that number and I can track your location in less than a millisecond." He held his hand out again. "If I could please have that card back."

She returned his card. How did he know that she would never forget that number after only a single glance? He smiled and gave her a quick wink. He stood up and walked out the east door to join the President who sat on a bench in the rose garden.

She stood up and walked over to the northeast door. Her hand hovered over the door knob that would take her back out to the waiting room.

What would be waiting out there for her?

She gripped the handle and pushed the door open. She looked around and didn't see the two guards that had shadowed her for the past week.

Was she really free? Had they released her to do whatever she wanted? She decided it was best to do what they expected.

At least for a little while.

Alexander Baine caught up to the President in the garden.

"Well?" he stood up from the bench.

"I think she'll take my offer. She will resist at first, but she won't be able to keep herself away."

"I hope you're right," he said and stared at the roses all around him. They swayed peacefully with the light breeze. He wished he felt as much at peace as these flowers.

Melissa walked out of the White House grounds through the Southwest Appointment Gate. She had no idea that this was the gate that had been commonly used by William Hartford. It was the most convenient gate to the hotel that she had lived in for the past week. Her family had been in an adjoining room, and she took full advantage of being able to hold her son and talk with him without the need for internet shorthand.

She had been able to reconnect with the mother inside of her, and it made her both happy and sad at the same time. She knew it wouldn't last forever, so she enjoyed what she could while she had the chance.

She looked at the entrance to the hotel. It beckoned to her with the promise of a different life. All she had to do was enter the gaping mouth and let it swallow her whole. She couldn't cross the street. Her feet wouldn't move. She knew what she had to do before she became lost forever.

But there was still something she had to do before she could resume the peaceful life of a mother.

Chapter 75

Forty minutes later Melissa paid the taxi and stood on the curb. She looked at the main hospital building and was even less sure of what she would say to the General than before she had hailed the taxi. She walked into the bustling entrance and up to the first nurses' station she found.

"Can I help you?" The nurse behind the counter had a pleasant voice.

"I would like to see General Archon. I don't know what room he is in."

"Are you a family member?"

"Yes," she lied. "I'm his daughter."

"One moment, please." The nurse typed a string of letters on her keyboard. She watched the screen as she tapped the enter key.

"Ah," the nurse said at last. "He's in room three twelve. That's on the third floor."

"Thank you." She turned and headed for the elevators.

As she walked, she began to form the questions in her mind that she hoped he could help her sort out. The elevator doors slid open, and she stepped out onto the third floor. She checked the number of the nearest room and walked down the corridor until she found room three twelve.

She knocked lightly.

He must be asleep. She knocked a little louder. Still no answer. She pushed on the handle and the door creaked slowly open.

"He's not there." The voice behind her made her jump.

She spun around and saw an old man pushing his IV unit around on what looked more like a rolling metal coat rack than expensive medical equipment.

"I just asked at the desk..."

"They came for him."

His eyes were full of life in stark contrast to the frail body that stood before her. She looked in the room at the empty bed and back to the nosey patient.

"Who came for him?"

"They always come and move you."

Her panic grew quickly.

"Did you see who took him?"

"They came and moved me, too. The front desk never updated their damn computers and kept trying to put me back in my old room. I tried to tell them. I was moved."

The elevator doors opened and a nurse rushed out. She seemed to be in a hurry as she looked down one direction of the corridor and then another. She spotted them and strode over.

"Mr. Hawkins." The nurse ignored Melissa. "You need to come back down to your room. It's time for your medication."

"I was moved," Hawkins yelled at the nurse.

"You need to come with me." The nurse grabbed his arm and led him away.

Her heart pounded heavily in her chest. She had become overly paranoid. For a brief moment she thought that Nick had somehow survived the helicopter crash and had taken General Archon captive. Her hands still shook as she assured herself that this was impossible. The missile had instantly vaporized everyone in the helicopter. The resulting forest fire burned so hot that the reinforced metal frame of the helicopter had actually melted.

"Excuse me," she called after the nurse. "Where is the patient that is supposed to be in this room?"

The nurse paused and looked back at her.

"I don't know. You'll have to check at the front desk."

The nurse turned back to her complaining patient. She could still hear him even after the elevator doors closed. She ducked into the room and looked around. The bed was still rumpled. Maybe he was in the bathroom. She noticed the other door in the room and peeked in. There was a bathroom in his room, so that wasn't it.

She checked the closet and found his clothes still hanging. He had to be around here somewhere.

She had to visit the nurses' station again to find out where he was right now. She walked out of the room and headed for the elevator. Just after she pushed the button a doctor step out from another patient's room down the hall and walked away from her.

"Excuse me." She abandoned the elevator and walked down the corridor to catch up to him.

The doctor ignored her and kept walking.

"Excuse me, Doctor?" She spoke much louder this time. He had to have heard her.

The doctor instead pushed the door open to the stairwell and disappeared from view. She had just reached the patient's open door and she glanced inside as she passed. It was not another patient's room. It was a uniform closet.

She broke into a full run. She kicked at the release lever on the stairwell door. The door flew open and banged against the wall. She hurled herself down the stairs three steps at a time. She hit the second floor landing and glanced down the stairwell. She didn't see anyone heading down to the first floor. He must be on the second floor.

She reached for the door handle when the light changed in the stairwell above her. She glanced up and saw the door to the roof had been opened. The stairwell darkened as it slowly closed again on its hinges.

She vaulted up the stairs two at a time. She reached the roof access door and paused. She was unarmed.

She kicked the door open and rolled to the side. She rolled two more times before she stopped and crouched on her feet. The roof was completely empty. It took a moment to register there was a rope tied to an exhaust vent and then trailed over the edge of the building.

She ran to the edge and peered over. The doctor was already running across the side lawn. She grabbed the rope and twisted it in her hand to loop it to sit on it like a chair. She pulled her leather jacket sleeves up to cover her hands, took two quick breaths and dropped backwards off the roof.

The heat from the friction on the rope burned her legs through her jeans. She slowed her descent and lost precious time. Her feet finally touched the ground and she released the rope. She cooled her hands on the grass and looked around. The doctor was gone. And so was General Archon.

She ran around to the front of the hospital and spotted the last person she expected. The guard that she had fought with over the bicycle in front of the FBI Digital Storm building in New York.

He walked back out the front lobby doors on his cell phone.

"She's not here."

The man listened for a few moments as he headed to the car waiting on the curb.

"On my way back." The man hung up the phone and opened the car door.

She ran up behind the man and stuck her finger in his back.

"Don't make a sound," she hissed. "Just get in the car."

The man stood there without moving and glanced back at her.

"You really should cut your nails." He pulled away from her. "They're digging into my back."

The man turned around slowly and she lowered her hand. He opened the door to the back seat.

"I am here to take you to see General Archon. Do you still want to do that?"

Chapter 76

Melissa sat silently while they wound their way through Washington, DC. They passed several key monuments more than once. The driver was making sure that he would notice if they were being followed. It made what was originally a ten-minute trip last for almost an hour.

The car pulled to a stop in front of the Washington Hospital Center. The driver hopped out and opened the back door for her like a chauffeur.

"Ask to see a Mr. Hollings. I will wait around the corner. When you are ready to leave, I will be right here."

She stepped out of the car. "That won't be necessary."

"I have my orders."

The driver climbed back in the car and drove away. She walked through the hospital's main entrance and to the front desk. She stood at the reception desk patiently and waited. A nurse finally looked up from whatever had held her attention.

"Can I help you?"

"I would like to see Mr. Hollings, please."

"Of course. Please go to the second floor. Ask for his room number from the visitors' station up there."

She climbed the steps to the second floor. She saw a second station next to the elevator that said "Visitors' Station" in bold lettering across the front of the chest-high semicircular desk. She walked over. The attendant behind the desk looked as if he was already expecting her.

"Please give me the room number for a Mr. Hollings."

"Right this way, please." The attendant stood up.

He walked around the semicircle and proceeded down the hallway. He stopped halfway down and opened a door. She looked inside and saw a long hallway with an armed guard at the other end standing in front of the only door. She looked at the attendant questioningly.

"He's in the room at the end."

She stepped into the hallway, and the attendant closed the door behind her. The guard at the other end didn't move as she walked forward and stopped ten feet from him.

"I am here to see Mr. Hollings."

The guard stepped aside and opened the door. She stepped into the room and saw Archon sitting up in bed watching CNN on the flat-screen television on the far wall.

He hit the mute button on his remote and looked at her with a smile.

"So, what made you go through the trouble of looking me up?"

"I want the truth."

"The truth. That's a broad term. What would you like to know?"

"Let's start with Hannah."

"So he asked you, I'm glad."

"I haven't made up my mind whether to join your little organization or not," she interrupted.

He paused and took a drink of water as if he was considering whether to tell her the truth or not.

"Whether you join us or not, that is entirely up to you. I do, however, still need a favor."

She didn't respond and stood there waiting to hear what

he had to say.

"You and I are the only ones who know about the remote connection that Nick Spanos managed to place into Digital Storm. I would rather this information didn't go beyond the two of us."

"No problem, I won't say anything to anybody."

"I am in no shape to go anywhere, and I need that access point shut down before anyone stumbles across the IP address."

She regarded him for a moment before responding.

"After this, do not contact me."

He nodded his head.

She continued. "Do not contact my family. Do not even acknowledge that you ever once talked with me."

He nodded again. "I understand."

"I'll call you as soon as the connection is severed."

She spun on her heels and left the room.

Chapter 77

Melissa pulled in front of the building that she and Denny had infiltrated just last week.

She looked over at Billy sitting in the passenger seat.

"What I have to do shouldn't take more than 15 minutes, and then you and I can go anywhere we want."

"Be careful, mom."

She smiled as she stroked the side of his cheek.

"I love you, too, sweetheart."

She climbed out of the car and looked over at the ventilation shaft. The screen had been replaced by an iron grate and was locked with, not one, but two hidden shackle padlocks. The shackle completely concealed the lock body, thus eliminating bolt cutters as an option, and making it virtually impossible to pick the six-pin cylinder. She was glad she didn't have to use the ventilation shaft. This time, she had a key to the front door.

She walked into the lobby and climbed the stairs to the second floor. She paused at the security desk and showed her passkey. The guard stood up and fumbled clumsily with his own passkey on the second lock.

"Sorry, ma'am, I'm kinda new at this."

She smiled at him as the elevator doors slid open.

"There we go, ma'am. Have good day."

She walked in and hit the button for the fifth level. As the elevator doors closed, her mind went into overdrive, and she felt goose bumps rise on her skin. Something was wrong. Archon didn't mention anything about a new guard.

She hit every button on the elevator panel. The doors slid open and she darted out onto level three. She looked around. The hallways were deserted. She headed for the vent she and Denny had used to escape. She skidded to a halt. The vent grate had also been replaced by a large iron gate and was bolted to the wall around it.

The elevator dinged and the doors slid closed. She ran to the stairwell and slowly opened the door. She glanced up and down the stairs.

The intercom system squawked to life.

"Hello, Melissa." The voice crackled over every loudspeaker nestled in the ceiling tiles of every level.

She immediately recognized the voice that echoed in the hallway.

And it chilled her to the bone.

She ran into the stairwell and let the door close behind her.

"You shouldn't have come here."

She ran up the stairs and stopped at the second level.

She looked out the door into the second level hallway. The hallway was empty. She crept out of the stairwell.

"I forgive you for disrupting my plan to remove the President from power. If you leave now, you have my solemn promise that I will let you go. You have ten minutes."

The elevator dinged and the doors slid open. She ducked into a doorway that stood open to a small office. The guard exited the elevator and swung a Beretta semi-automatic pistol around in front of him. All remnants of his clumsy demeanor gone. She noted the magazine extended well below the handle. He must have the seventeen-round magazine.

It was not her X-Five, but it would do.

She crouched silently as the guard checked and cleared each room as he slowly progressed down the hallway.

The guard pushed the door open and looked into the room. She crouched just behind the door. The guard entered.

She kicked out and caught the guard in the stomach. The Beretta flew from his grasp, and he doubled over and fell to his hands and knees. She kicked again and sent him sprawling into a corner. She dove for the gun and rolled to a crouch with it trained on the guard. He lay still in the corner.

She ripped the cord off a desk lamp and tied the guard's hands and feet together behind him. She ejected the magazine and checked that it was completely loaded. She slapped the full magazine back into the Beretta and slipped into the hallway.

She stopped at the stairwell and listened. Nobody was coming. She started down the stairs. She had to get to the fifth level and shut down that computer before it was too late.

She hit the fifth-floor landing and paused. She opened the door slowly to the fifth level and peeked out. The hallway was empty.

She stepped out of the stairwell and walked slowly down the hallway. She hugged the wall and held the Beretta ready for action.

Suddenly Nick stepped out into the hallway with his back

to her.

She froze.

He held her SIG-Sauer P226 X-Five tightly in one hand and was looking at his smartphone in the other.

He pocketed the phone and turned to face her as she raised the Beretta.

He spotted her, and his eyes grew dark as she fired.

He ducked, but not quickly enough. The bullet slammed into his arm, the impact throwing him into the wall right before he dropped to the ground, the X-Five skittering across the floor. She stepped closer to where he sat and aimed the Beretta at his head, point blank.

"I watched you die."

He looked directly into the barrel of the Beretta before meeting her fiery gaze.

"You watched Wilkes die, obviously. He was so focused on escape, when he felt the helicopter door slam shut he assumed I was on board. Instead, I ran around the house and reactivated the surface-to-air missiles. There are always casualties in any war. And the world had to believe that I was dead. You had to believe I was dead."

Nick's entire plan unfolded in her mind.

"Just like Hannah was dead?" She jerked the Beretta back to point at his head. "We both watched her die."

He exhaled as if he was tired of explaining the deeper meaning of everything to a child.

"We were the only ones who watched her die."

She grabbed his collar and pressed the Beretta into the side of his face. "That's why you sent someone to kill me. I was the only other person who knew Hannah was dead?"

"Her influence was firmly established all around the world. And the people she helped put into power understood that they ultimately worked for her. I couldn't let that kind of power go to waste."

He licked his lips in anticipation.

"I was starting to make contact with everyone under Hannah's control. I was establishing myself as their savior. I, and I alone, could free them from her."

She laughed. "What a stupid idea."

"I got it from you."

She looked at him quizzically.

"When you gave Hartford our number three years ago and told him when he was ready to get out to call you, I knew that was how I would do it. I would give everyone who felt obligated to Hannah a way out. Those who took it would be removed from power peacefully."

"And those who didn't?"

"They would have to be removed by force."

"Why did you involve me in your little scheme?"

"You called me, remember?"

"You sent a hired assassin to kill me, remember?"

He smiled. "Nobody's perfect."

Her grip tightened on his collar as her anger grew.

"You tried to kill my son."

His smile faded. "It is now something I regret."

He bored into her very soul with his eyes.

Not this time, she thought, and released his collar as she took a step back and tightened her grip on the pistol.

He glanced at the X-Five that lay only a couple of feet away before looking deeply into her eyes.

"You can't kill me."

"Watch me." And with that, she pulled the trigger.

As her finger squeezed the trigger, he slammed his eyes shut.

He took full opportunity of the moment of shock when, at point blank range, she had completely missed him. He launched himself towards the X-Five.

She wasn't going to take the time to figure what happened and bolted for the stairwell as he grabbed up the X-Five.

He fired wildly, and she cried out from the searing pain. He fired several more rounds towards her as she ran.

She kicked open the stairwell door and stumbled down the steps. She gripped her shoulder. The bullet had taken a large chunk of flesh from her upper arm, and the wound on her shoulder started to bleed again. The human body was not designed for this much abuse.

She ejected the magazine and flipped out one cartridge after another. He had fully expected her to get this gun from the guard and had replaced the bullets with blanks. She tossed the useless gun to the floor.

She reached the bottom of the stairwell and stumbled out into the hallway. Her arm bled freely and left a crimson trail all the way to the elevator. She hit the call button and left a smeared print on the lit button. She shed her jacket, wrapped it around her arm, and pulled it tight to slow the bleeding.

Using a little trick he had picked up from his former

assassin, Nick had managed to cheat death yet again.

He followed the trail of blood as it led him all the way down the stairwell. He opened the door to the eighth level and looked down the hallway. At the other end he saw the elevator doors close. He ran into the hallway and dashed to the elevator. He watched the digital display show each level as the elevator traveled upward away from him.

He extracted a key from his pocket and pushed it into the slot next to the call button, the slot reserved for emergency personnel to force the elevator to a specific floor.

He turned it and the elevator stopped. The digital readouts showed that it was returning. He stepped back and raised the P226 X-Five at the elevator doors. He fixed his gaze on the doors and waited.

The elevator dinged and the doors slid open.

To his surprise, and relief, it was empty. Maybe she had actually taken his advice and left.

He pulled his smartphone out of his pocket and looked down at it just as a shadow fell across it.

Melissa brought the fire extinguisher down hard, and Nick buckled under the blow and collapsed at her feet, his smartphone sliding into the corner against the wall.

She retrieved her X-Five. She ejected the magazine and thumbed each round out into her hand. Every round was live ammunition. She loaded each one back into the magazine and slammed it into the handle of the X-Five.

He stirred at her feet. She grabbed his collar, lifted him

with a renewed strength and slammed him into the wall. She shoved the barrel of the X-Five into the side of his face.

It was time to end this. "Any last words before I send you to hell?"

He looked her directly in the eye. No fear showed in his.

"I lied to you when I said this place was just one of the many hubs for Digital Storm. All around us is the only place in the world where every call, every email, every text is stored. Right here. It's ironic, really. This whole system was originally created to catch Hannah. Instead, it captured every private moment shared between people. The government is listening. Nobody has secrets anymore. That is the true seat of power. A power that would have threatened Hannah if she were still alive."

"And you wanted this power for yourself."

He looked at her for a moment.

"I wasn't going to use Digital Storm. I was going to shut it down. People need their secrets."

His smartphone, lying a few feet away, emitted a sharp beep.

She jumped, and he smiled through the pain.

"Relax, it's just my phone."

He ignored the loaded pistol pointed at him and reached across the floor for his phone.

"You should have left when you had the chance."

"What are you talking about?"

"I gave you a ten-minute warning."

He slowly picked up the phone.

"I had asked you to leave. I was trying to leave."

He held the phone out for her to see. "But now you have

sealed both our fates."

She stared at the display. The numbers were quickly counting down, with only seconds left on the clock.

"You will never be free unless you have access to the same information as those already in power."

The timer hit zero and froze.

"Or, you find what gives them their power, and take it away."

The hallway rocked under her feet right before she heard the massive explosion. All around her the ceiling shuddered and collapsed.

Chapter 78

Billy felt the car shake as if from a small earthquake and instinctively looked at the building his mother had entered less than ten minutes before. He watched in horror when the building collapsed inward as smoke and dust quickly enveloped the entire area.

He leaped from the car and rushed towards the building. A stranger on the street reacted quickly and grabbed him as he ran.

"Don't go near there, kid."

"My mom's in there!"

"In where?" The man looked at the rising smoke emanating from the collapsed building. "In there?"

The emotions were too much for him, and the flood of tears erupted from him as he buried his head in the stranger's shoulder.

Chapter 79

This was the second time Billy stood next to a casket that claimed to hold the remains of his mother. Only this time he had to be sure and demanded they open the casket. There had been many assurances that he would not want to see her like this. The damage had been too severe, and he should remember her as she was. If he saw her like this, they told him, it would haunt him for the rest of his life.

It sounded morose, but he couldn't go on without being absolutely sure that his mother was actually dead this time. And that required that he see the body.

When the casket lid was finally lifted, he thought he was going to throw up. He didn't know what to expect, but without correctly shaped bones and a round skull, the human body just doesn't look – well, human. Despite the funeral workers' best efforts, he barely recognized his mother as he looked down on her for the last time. He never looked away as they closed the lid again and screwed the seals shut.

He looked around him at the other people who had shown up to pay their final respects. Other than his dad and step-mom, he didn't know anybody else in that room. The most surprising, although it shouldn't have been since his mother did save the President's life, was the small group of military generals that all looked like they just stepped out of the latest political thriller movie.

Most of the attendees clumped together; with the exception of one man and one woman, who had each arrived alone, and never attempted to talk with anyone else.

The man wandered over and looked at him for a moment before clearing his throat.

"My name is Denny. I knew your mother."

He looked at him and decided to ask his one burning question directly. No sense in beating around the bush. Today was a day for truth and honesty.

"Were you going to marry my mom?"

Denny didn't show any reaction on his face, he only smiled.

"I don't know. Our relationship got a little complicated at the end."

"I think she would have liked marrying you."

Denny raised a single eyebrow. "What makes you say that?"

"We still talked nearly every day. It wasn't much, but she mentioned you a few times. I think she was happy with you."

Denny smiled, and he could see the edges of his eyes misting up slightly. "I was happy with her, too."

Denny placed a hand on his shoulder and gave it a firm squeeze. "You take care of yourself, kid. Your mom has a lot to be proud of in you."

Denny walked away briskly and left the room without looking back.

After a few more relatives and co-workers of his dad had left, the only people left standing around were the military types and the woman who had arrived alone. Billy caught her glancing at him on several occasions during the ceremony and afterwards.

It was definitely a time for honesty.

He walked over to the woman when it appeared she was never going to attempt to approach him.

As he walked over, she smiled a warm smile. He stopped in front of her, but before he could say anything, she spoke.

"Took you long enough to come over and speak to me, Billy."

"I noticed you watching me all afternoon. Did you know my mother?"

The woman looked around the room at the remaining mourners and then back to him. "I would like to think that I knew her better than anyone else here."

He bristled at the comment. The woman seemed to notice it instantly. "Except for you, of course. I see a lot of her in you."

"I don't think my mother ever talked about you."

"I wouldn't think so. She and I met under, shall we say, less than ideal circumstances. I found her half dead in the jungle."

He lowered his head. "She never talked about any of that."

"Those were not her best memories."

"What's your name?"

"I've been called by many names. But when I met your mother, she knew me as Gina."

"Thank you for coming, Gina."

The warm smile faded quickly. "You cannot dismiss me so easily, child. Your mother made a promise to me which she never kept."

His brow furled. The woman had made a sudden shift in

her demeanor that was completely unexpected.

"Well, as you can see," he said as he motioned to the coffin, "she's not going to be keeping her promises to anyone, anymore."

She smiled again, and the sudden storm clouds that had filled her eyes were gone leaving only warmth. "I'm sorry. I'm not used to losing someone close to me, and I'm afraid I'm letting my emotions get the best of me." She wiped at her eyes and laughed slightly. "And I've never known your mother to let a little thing like death stop her before."

She smiled even sweeter than before, and it turned his stomach. The woman was crazy. Must be why his mom never mentioned her.

"Thanks for coming," he mumbled and turned to leave. She grabbed his shoulder and spun him around to face her.

"When your mother came to me, she was broken, and I made her whole again. I can do the same for you."

He looked at her but didn't know how to respond correctly to her. "I'm not broken."

"That's where you're wrong, Billy," her eyes bored into him and her grip tightened. "I can see the strength hiding just below the surface. But there is something holding you back from realizing your true potential."

He groaned. "Now you're sounding like my teachers."

He struggled in her grasp. "Let go."

She gripped him tighter. "Your mother is not gone. She's alive."

His mouth gaped open as she continued.

"But I need you to…"

Before she could continue, something large blocked the

light coming from the side windows and spoke in a deep baritone voice.

"Is everything okay, Billy?"

They both looked up at the massive barrel-chested man who leaned heavily on one crutch.

Gina's grip softened, and Billy replied quickly. "She was just telling me…"

She smiled and released him from her iron grip. "I was just telling little Billy here that as long as he keeps the memory of his mother alive, she will never be dead."

He shot her an angry look. "That's not what you said."

She smiled sweetly at him. "But that's what I meant."

And then she looked up at the highly decorated soldier. "I'm not very good at funerals. I get my words and my meanings all jumbled up."

He stared hard at her. That's not what she was telling him, he was sure of it.

She looked at her hands and then back up. "I really must be going now." She looked at him, gave him a warm smile, and made him even sicker to his stomach than before because the look in her eyes did not match the rest of her face and made her next statement sound more of a threat than the standard American parting.

"See you later, Billy."

And with that, she walked out of the memorial chambers and, hopefully, out of his life forever.

Chapter 80

Nurse Evans felt the presence of God every time she entered Janet Dougherty's room. She had seen pictures of the car accident on the news and knew it was a miracle that anyone had survived, let alone continued to survive the multiple, and necessary, reconstructive surgeries.

She went to church every day for a month and prayed. She prayed that the Lord would spare the life of an innocent girl whose very soul was in danger through an act of senseless tragedy. Never underestimate the power of prayer, she thought. Even from strangers.

And now, her miracle patient was recovering nicely in one of the beds on her route.

And today was an exceptionally good day. It was the first time someone had sent flowers to her recovering patient. She hoped visitors would soon follow. It always broke her heart when someone spent as long as Janet had in isolation at the hospital.

She placed the large bouquet on the table by the window, pulled the curtains aside to let the bright morning sunlight envelop the room and plucked the chart off the end of the bed.

Her patient stirred on the bed and sat up abruptly.

"Good morning, sleepyhead. Today is a very special day for you. The bandages are finally coming off. The doctor will be in shortly to remove them."

Her patient mumbled something as she did every time she came into the room.

"I still can't understand you, dear. As soon as those nasty bandages are off, you can tell me what you have been trying for weeks to say, okay?"

Doctor Nathaniel Willis stepped into the room and pushed a stainless steel tray in front of him with an assortment of shiny tools on it.

"I see our patient is already awake."

"Yes, Dr. Willis, and I think she's just as eager to get those bandages off as I am."

The doctor smiled at the patient.

"Relax, Miss Dougherty. This won't take long."

He cut the edge of the tape that held the bandage in place and slowly spun the rest of the bandage off. Once he was done, he smiled as she handed him a hand mirror.

"Are you ready?"

He held the mirror up to let his patient look at herself for the first time in weeks. She let out a small gasp.

He smiled.

"I know. The reconstruction surgery made you look like your old self more than any of us thought possible."

What the doctor and nurse didn't know, could never know, was that their patent had not gasped from surprise at seeing her face as she remembered it. She gasped because staring back at her from the mirror was not the face of Melissa Stone.

As soon as the doctor and nurse left, she was out of bed.

She opened the closet and found it empty.

What had she expected to find in there? New clothes?

She stared at the chart that said the occupant of the bed, her bed, was named Janet Dougherty.

The last thing she remembered was the deep rumble under her feet right before the world came literally crashing down all around her.

The next thing she knew she was Janet Dougherty, car accident victim lying in the ICU with a fifty/fifty chance of surviving through the night.

She stopped at the mirror and looked at the stranger looking back at her in the reflection.

Behind her on the short table by the window stood the flowers. And from this angle, reflected in the mirror, she could see the tiny note card tucked into the dense flower arrangement.

She slipped the card out of the envelope and read it silently.

'M'

A gift to show my appreciation for everything you have done for me. You know how to contact me when you are ready to come home.

'H'

She glanced once more at the mirror before she slipped out the door and into the hallway of the busy hospital. It wouldn't be long before she found some new clothes to go with her new face and new identity.

She was already home.

Other Books by the Author

A is for Apprentice (Fantasy)

Oliver Twist: Victorian Vampire (Fantasy Horror)

A Tale of Two Cities with Dragons (Fantasy)

Shade Infinity (Science Fiction Thriller)

Peacekeepers X-Alpha Series (Thriller)
    Inherit the Throne
    The Warrior's Code

Steampunk OZ Series (Science Fiction Novellas)
    Forgotten Girl
    The Legacy's World
    Emerald Shadow
    The Future's Destiny
    The Dangerous Captive
    Missing Legacy
    Shadow of History
    The Edge of the Hunter

Fugue: The Cure (Science Fiction Short Story)

Jason and the Chrononauts (Kid's Adventure)

Be the first to know about Steve DeWinter's next book. Follow the URL below to subscribe for free today!

http://bit.ly/BookReleaseBulletin